THE

FOUNDLING

Ann Evans

Ann Evans.

Also by Ann Evans:

The Legacy

When artist Adam and his wife Maggie
move into the big white house on the hill
overlooking the bay they can scarcely
believe their luck.
A drawing of a mystery girl, however,
is about to change their lives forever,
and those of many other people.
Who is she, and what does she want from
them?
The answers have far-reaching
consequences.

An intriguing tale of mystery, romance,
and the supernatural.

For Stan and Purdey.

ONE: MARIANA 20th AUGUST 1976.

Mariana wiped the sweat from her brow and lifted the damp, clinging hair from her neck, twisting it into a shapeless knot and securing it with an elastic band as she hurried homeward. The blistering heat had melted the tar on the road and she carefully skirted around the glistening viscous patches in her new white platform gogo boots. She shouldn't have bought them, and she wondered if she could hide them before Terry got home. She glanced at her watch and quickened her pace – she might just make it. Her stomach began to tie itself in knots and she was now regretting lying to him; with her luck he was bound to find out.

"Come on M," Kate had cajoled her. "It's only once in a blue moon. It's my birthday! I want you there, and you'll easily be home before Terry. Can't you tell him you're working an extra shift?" In the end recklessness had prevailed; she had given in to her friend and hang the consequences. Now, as she headed back to reality with a hangover and the looming prospect of Terry finding out, she wasn't sure it had been worth it. *What if he didn't go to the pub last night? What if he didn't go to work this morning? What if....* there was no point in speculating, she would just have to cross her bridges when she came to them. She crossed the busy main road that led from the station to her home on the outskirts of town. The afternoon traffic was a constant stream now and as the cars slowed for the junction ahead she dodged among them, their horns blaring at her recklessness. She turned the corner into the estate where she lived and strained her eyes along the row of houses. Theirs was the last but one in the row of neat red brick homes.

To her relief there was no car parked on the concrete apron fronting the garage; although she knew that sometimes he would park by the allotments round the back and use the rear door. She debated going round to the back to check, but she didn't have her back door key and it would only delay her further. There was no point in dallying; she would find out the extent of her predicament soon enough. Her heart in her mouth, she turned the key slowly and quietly in the yale lock, holding the rest of the bunch tightly in her palm to keep them from jangling. She pushed the door open slowly at first, then more quickly to avoid the long drawn out creak that would otherwise have ensued. She was feeling sick now; she had no valid excuse for being out until this time when her shift would have finished at six a.m. She had tried desperately to concoct a story in her head, and failing miserably to come up with anything remotely plausible, had decided to trust to luck.

She stood in the hallway and listened to the silence ringing in her ears. Placing her handbag carefully on the table next to the telephone she began to climb the stairs slowly, her legs trembling, her breath constricted, her heart pounding. *Please God, please God,* she breathed to herself through clenched teeth, *please let him be at work.*

She pushed down the handle of the bedroom door, and it opened slowly to reveal the bottom of the bed then

2

the mirror on the dressing table that reflected it's unmade but empty expanse. *Thank you God!* She breathed again, taking in huge gulps of air, her knees weak from the adrenalin rush of relief. She had got away with it; otherwise he would have been there waiting for her.

She eased the boots off and examined her feet ruefully, surveying the scarlet welts of blisters on her heels and toes that were now beginning to bubble alarmingly. In her terror, she hadn't felt the searing pain of them until now. "Bloody hell!" she muttered as she massaged her cramped toes, thinking how a few short years ago she could have worn boots like these day in day out without causing any such damage. She glanced at her watch again. Hell! Terry would be home any minute now; there was no time to lose!

She made the bed, drew back the curtains, and opened the casement window as wide as it would go. Hauling a small suitcase from the bottom of the wardrobe she put the offending boots in it, wrapping them in a red dress that Kate had given her and she had hidden because she knew Terry would say it made her look like a tart. She cushioned them with the various other items of illicit clothing it contained so that they wouldn't rattle around. She replaced the suitcase carefully, making sure it was in exactly the same place as before – not that he would notice she told herself, but it didn't pay to take chances. Downstairs she immediately headed for the kitchen. Her note was still on the worktop by the bread bin where she had left it; the ready meal was untouched in the fridge:

Darling Terry.
They've asked me to do an extra 10-6. Sorry, didn't know how to get out of it. There's food in the fridge. See you tomorrow.
Love, Mariana. X.

She cringed slightly as she read the endearments – *Bloody hypocrite,* she thought, and immediately felt disloyal. Terry wasn't that bad most of the time, and this time she was the one with something to hide. In the living room an empty takeaway box from the late night kebab house in town littered the coffee table, along with a couple of beer cans, an empty coffee cup, a plate with a toast crust and some bacon rind abandoned on its rim, and two cigarette ends in the ashtray. For once the sight of all this made her smile, reassured that Terry had gone straight to the pub from work and then straight to work after breakfast, and her secret was safe. *Christ,* she thought, *hadn't he had enough to drink already without the cans?* She gathered them up and pushed them into the bin in the kitchen. She washed the plate and cup, then dragged the hoover out of the cupboard under the stairs and pushed it round the floor in a perfunctory manner. She opened the windows in the living room, pushing back the net curtains to let the stale smoky air mingle with the sultry scent of roses that wafted in from Dani's memorial garden beneath the window. Finally, she had restored the house to normality for this time of day. She glanced at her watch, frowning slightly. Six forty-five p.m. Terry was late; he would normally have been home by six thirty. Never mind, it suited her purposes; now she would get the tea started and tell him she had overslept. He wouldn't be happy; he liked his tea to be on the table when he got home from work. A can of beer or two however, would mollify him. *Hell, it'll be nothing compared to what might have happened,* she thought.

She put the deep fat fryer on and peeled some potatoes whilst it heated up. Slicing them expertly into evenly sized chips she rinsed them under the tap and, wrapping them in a tea towel, patted them dry. She yanked at the flap that covered the frozen food compartment in the fridge and was constantly sealed with crisp white borders of ice, and withdrew a packet of burgers. Placing three on the grill she glanced at her watch again; it was gone seven. Where could he be? Terry was a creature of habit. Tuesdays and Thursdays were invariably his pub nights; Tuesday being darts night, and Thursday quiz night. He never missed either, but then that was it until Saturday, when he would often go out at nine in the morning and crawl in at three or four on Sunday morning. Doubt began to creep in again, fuelled by her guilt. Perhaps he knew somehow, and this was his way of punishing her; of letting her know that he knew! She began to feel sick again. The chips were crisp and golden brown, the burgers done to a turn. She loaded them onto plates which she placed in the oven to keep warm. Absently, she opened a tin of beans and placed them in a pan on the stove. Her mind wandered.

Mariana and Kate had got off the train at Oxford Road, Manchester, and walked the short distance to Tiffany's Nightclub. Inside, it was cool and dark in sharp contrast to the dazzling sunlight and sultry heat of the summer evening outside. Glittering multifaceted disco balls hung from the ceiling above the dance floor that had tables arranged around it and an artificial palm tree in the middle. Kate led her over to a group of girls sitting at one of the tables.

"This is my mate Mariana I told you about from work," she told them, and they all smiled a greeting. She indicated a small mouse-like girl with a pageboy haircut. "This is Monica; we're staying at her place tonight." Mariana felt awkward. She didn't know any of these women; they looked much younger than her. Their clothes were trendy and their hairstyles had names; unlike hers which was

5

shoulder-length, brown and naturally wavy with no chemical intervention. She smiled at Monica and offered to buy her a drink. She only had five pounds in her purse and hoped she wasn't expected to buy a whole round.

"I'm ok thanks," Monica smiled back, understanding. She could tell that Mariana was a fish out of water, not used to this scene.

"C'mon," said Kate. "You can buy me one if you like, for my birthday."

They pushed their way through the layers of bodies stacked against the bar, Mariana apologizing as she went but noticing that Kate didn't bother. Once or twice she felt something brush her bottom, or a hand grasp her waist; but she thought it was just accidental and paid no notice. They reached the bar, where several young men and women were pulling pints or skimming along the rows of optics drawing off shots and mixing cocktails. Kate ordered two Pina Coladas and Mariana reached for her purse.

"I was only kidding; these are on me," Kate said, pushing the proffered five-pound note aside firmly. "I just want to see you having a good time M, so just try and relax won't you? Oh, and stop being so bloody polite, you sound like a right spaz!"

Mariana was unsure whether to be grateful or offended, but smiled her thanks – it was just Kate's way.

Suddenly she felt an arm around her, and a hand reached for her breast and gave it a squeeze. She whipped round to face the perpetrator. *How dare he!* He was little more than a boy and grinned disarmingly at her; his teeth, his tee shirt, and the whites of his eyes all dazzling in the ultraviolet light. He shrugged and made a gesture that said it was no big deal. He was actually really good-looking, she thought grudgingly, feeling Kate's restraining hand on her arm and thinking better of landing him a sharp right hook.

6

Then he was gone, and Kate was leading her through the throng back to their table. The cocktail was icy cold, sweet and delicious. *I could get used to this,* thought Mariana as she sipped it slowly through a black straw. It was difficult to join in the conversation above the volume of Dr. Hook, The Bee Gees, and Abba, unless you leaned in really close, and Mariana didn't feel she knew the other girls well enough to intrude in such a way. Therefore she sat slightly apart watching the dancers on the floor, mesmerized by their movements and hoping she would be able to keep up when the others decided to join in as inevitably they would. Then her favourite song came on; The Walker Brothers, No Regrets, and the dancers paired off and began to sway closely, intimately, their hands caressing one another unashamedly.

Suddenly the boy from by the bar was standing in front of her, holding out his hand and smiling. He jerked his head in the direction of the dance floor.

"Go on!" mouthed Kate from across the table, and Mariana allowed him to pull her from her chair and onto the dance floor.

He held her closely, his body firm against her; he smelled deliciously of aftershave and washing powder. She closed her eyes and laid her head on his shoulder as a feeling of euphoria drifted over her. His hands caressed her shoulders, her back, her buttocks; his lips brushed her neck.

"What's your name?" He spoke in her ear so that she would hear him.

"Mariana," she replied. "What's yours?"

"Stevie. D'you live round here?"

"No, I'm only here for tonight, it's my friend Kate's birthday."

7

"That's a shame," he said, and squeezed her tighter. "Never mind, let's enjoy tonight." She tilted her face up to look into his soft brown eyes, and suddenly their lips locked in a kiss. The music filled her head, *'There's no regrets',* and she returned his kiss, all thoughts of Terry banished by the moment and the stronger-than-it-looked cocktail. The song drew to an end and he gently released his hold and took a step backwards,

"Thanks, Mariana," he said, and melted away into the crowd.

She stood and stared after him for a moment, her mind whirling. Kate was beckoning to her and the whole group appeared to be buzzing with excitement as she made her way back to them.

"Wow! Mariana," Monica shouted above the strains of *You make me feel like dancing,* "You're honoured; that was Stevie Wanden you were snogging. We call him Stevie Wonder – wouldn't we all like to go there!"

The group of girls was staring at her with obvious respect, and she silently thanked her dance partner for bringing her into the fold. For the rest of the night the girls all danced together, placing their handbags on the floor in a heap and dancing round them. Several of them bought her drinks, and Mariana stopped worrying about her moves but just watched the others and copied. They had accepted her now; she knew nobody would criticize. She felt happy and relaxed. Once or twice she caught sight of Stevie dancing with other girls, although never the same one twice, and never close. She didn't mind; it was a one-off, she was well aware of that. In spite of the cocktails she had consumed, she could still taste his kiss and smell his aftershave, so she knew she hadn't dreamed it.

As two a.m. approached and the night drew to a close, another slow dance came on; Dr. Hook, A Little Bit More.

He appeared out of nowhere, and the girls all clapped their hands and cheered as he pulled her onto the dance floor again. He kissed her neck, her eyelids, her nose, and then her lips; a searing kiss that lasted almost as long as the song. She surrendered herself to the moment, forgetting everything else, especially that she had to return the next day to reality and Terry. At the end of the dance he released her and stood holding her hand.

"Goodnight, Mariana," he said softly. "You're pretty special; thanks for tonight." He released her hand and turned to go. "Have a nice life," he added as he joined a group of young men who all turned and waved at her on their way out. He gave her one last backward glance as the doors swung shut behind him.

Monica's house was on an estate half a mile from town. They caught the late bus that left from just outside the club and deposited them at the end of Monica's road. Her mum was still up, watching a horror movie and smoking a cigarette.

"Did you have a good night girls?" she asked. "There's some chips on the go; I thought you might be hungry." She smiled at Mariana and wished Kate a happy birthday.

They ate their chips, then said goodnight to Monica's mum and went upstairs to bed. Monica had a double bed that she and Kate shared, and there was a folding zed-bed for Mariana.

"Thanks for tonight you two," said Mariana. "I had a fab time!"

"We noticed," laughed Monika, "I can't believe you snogged Stevie Wonder – twice! He seemed to like you a lot."

"He was nice; shame I didn't meet him a few years ago," replied Mariana ruefully.

"Good job you didn't. You'd have got arrested for cradle-snatching; he's only nineteen," laughed Kate. "Goodnight"

The doorbell shook her from her reverie. The beans were bubbling furiously in the pan, sticking to the bottom. She stirred them hastily but they were beyond redemption. She scraped them into the bin and put the pan in the sink, running cold water into it as the doorbell shrilled again. She wondered who it could be.

She peered through the kitchen window. There was a police car parked on the concrete apron. Her stomach lurched sickeningly – what had Terry done now?

She opened the door and pasted on a smile to the policeman and policewoman who stood there. They removed their headgear; the policeman spoke.

"Are you Mariana Harding, wife of Terence Harding?"

"Yes," replied Mariana, searching their faces. "Is he in some kind of trouble?"

"May we come inside for a minute Mrs. Harding?" the policewoman said, and Mariana held the door open as they passed through before leading them into the living room.

"Please sit down," said Mariana. They remained standing.

The policeman cleared his throat uncomfortably. "I'm afraid there's been an accident," he announced, twisting his cap in his hands uneasily and looking to his colleague for support.

10

"What sort of accident?" Mariana asked, overwhelmed by a sudden feeling of dread. "To Terry? At work? Is he ok?" *Stupid question*, she thought, *they wouldn't be here if he was!* "No Ma'am, not at work. He was involved in a collision on the bypass, and I'm sorry to say he died from his injuries at the scene." It sounded blunt and brutal but Mariana supposed there was really no easy way to tell it.

She sank onto the sofa. The policewoman sat down beside her and put a sympathetic hand on her arm,

"Can we make you a cup of tea?" she asked.

Mariana nodded dumbly, and the policeman made his escape to the kitchen with almost indecent haste. Through a haze of jumbled thoughts and emotions, she heard him rattling around in there. Guilt and remorse overcame her. *How many times had she wished her husband dead? How often had she imagined her life without him, and found it immeasurably improved?* Even now she felt no real sadness at his loss, only a sadness that there was none. She shivered; suddenly the room felt cold even though the temperature outside was in the high twenties.

"It's the shock Ma'am," said the policewoman, patting her hand in a kindly gesture.

"Mariana; my name's Mariana," she said. *Christ, the woman made her sound like the Queen Mother!*

"Yes of course, sorry Dear." Mariana gritted her teeth. She wished they would go; she needed to be alone to absorb this, the implications of it all. She didn't want patronising platitudes from strangers; they had no idea what was in her mind. The policeman brought her tea and she noticed thankfully just the one, none for him and his colleague.

"Thank you, I'll be alright now," she said dismissively.

The policewoman stood, and then asked, "Is there anyone you would like us to call?"

11

Mariana felt herself losing control. *She had had a shock, but it hadn't rendered her incapable.* She took a deep breath.

"No thank you, I can manage. I'd like to be left alone now." She rose to see them out.

"Thank you Ma...er, Mariana, we'll see ourselves out if you're sure there's nothing else we can do." The policewoman smiled again sympathetically and made to leave, then added, "I'm afraid you will be required to make a formal identification, and there will be an inquest, but it certainly appears that your husband was completely blameless for the accident. His b... he's in the police morgue; perhaps you could get a friend or relative to accompany you down within the next day or so to make the identification." She took Mariana's hand. "I'm so sorry for your loss my dear," she said and followed her colleague out of the door, closing it softly behind her.

The silence was deafening; it was as though the world had stood still. Mariana sipped at her tea; it was tepid, milky, and far too sweet. She carried it through to the kitchen and poured it down the sink, noticing the burned saucepan but not remembering how it got there. The oven hummed, keeping warm two plates of burgers and chips; she turned it off. *What now? Why did she feel nothing?* Last night seemed a million miles away now and the thought of it brought the guilt flooding in once more. *When did he die?* she wondered. She cast her mind back to the scene when she arrived home. It must have been either this morning on the way to work, or just an hour or so ago on his way home. *Why hadn't she asked them more about it?* She had just wanted them to go, and now she was left without the answers she sought. She must ring Kate; she would know what to do.

12

She picked up the phone in the hallway. Her legs felt suddenly weak, and she sank to the floor beside the table and leaned against the wall; it felt pleasantly cool against her back. She closed her eyes and tried to calm her thoughts. Her heart was racing and a sharp pain stabbed at her temples. Her dry eyes felt like sandpaper against her closed lids. *They shouldn't be dry, should they?* She tried to force tears, squeezing her eyes tight until her eyeballs ached with the effort, but none came. The phone fell from her hand, the dialing tone changing to a strident, continuous buzz. Slowly, she pulled herself up to stand and absently placed it back on its cradle. Kate would be catching up on her sleep now, and besides, Mariana was well aware of how she would react to the news, and she wasn't sure if she was ready for that just yet. Her legs shook alarmingly, and she shivered again with cold although outside the pavements still shimmered with heat and barely a breath of air filtered into the house through the open windows. She made herself a cup of coffee and took it into the living room where she sat and examined her feelings honestly and objectively. She glanced around the room; everything looked different. She picked up the ashtray off the coffee table and took it into the kitchen. Terry maintained he had a right to smoke in his own home, and although not a heavy smoker he liked to smoke last thing at night and first thing in the morning; Mariana could always smell it as she descended the stairs. He would light up after meals too, although she had managed to dissuade him from smoking in bed for safety reasons. She opened the bin and dropped the ashtray into it; she was surprised how cathartic it felt. She ran her hands through her hair, pushing it back from her forehead. What should she do with her life now that Terry was gone? She had never lived alone before. For some reason the idea was daunting, even though his very presence had frequently placed her in danger. She would face new challenges now she realised, and probably new dangers, but Terry was gone and although it was tinged with sadness, her overwhelming feeling was one of relief.

Immediately the thought entered her mind she felt a moment of panic. *What if it was a mistake, and Terry wasn't dead at all? What if, even now, he was lurking somewhere in the house listening, hoping to catch her pouring out her grievances to Kate on the phone or even to the walls or her dead mother and sister as she frequently would when alone in the house.* She closed the living room window, locked the back door and put the chain on the front door, then went from room to room checking that they were empty. She looked in cupboards and under beds, and after checking each room went back and checked again in random order just to be certain. When she had finished, she sank back onto the sofa and breathed again. She chided herself for her paranoia – how many times had she gone through this ritual when she had had a private rant whilst he was out? There was no need any more, she told herself firmly, and tomorrow she would go and identify his body to remove any shred of doubt.

She fetched a tumbler and a bottle of wine from the kitchen and poured herself a glass. She held the tumbler aloft and stared at the ruby liquid for a moment before lowering it to her lips as she thought, *this is the first day of the rest of my life.* Then guilt and fear flooded over her again. *She had wished him dead, and now he was. Maybe she was all the things he said she was!*

"I'm sorry Terry," she whispered, and began to weep.

TWO: TWO WEEKS EARLIER.

Mariana cowered back against the sideboard feeling the sharp corner digging into her side. Terry moved closer, thrusting his face into hers, his mouth contorted, his lips drawn back from his teeth, flecks of foam flying as he spat the words out in harsh, vitriolic tones.

"I said, where's my fuckin' tea?" his eyes glittered menacingly and he braced his arms against the cupboard, with Mariana trapped between them.

"And I said I didn't make any!" Mariana's tone was defiant even though her knees were weak with terror. "You didn't come home last night, and I didn't know where you were. Why should I make tea for you when I don't even know if you're going to be here to eat it?"

He jabbed at her viciously with a forefinger, first on her breastbone, then on her face; she flinched.

"Don't touch me again or I'll call the police," she warned him, and watched the fury intensify. His eyes were hard like glass between the narrowed lids, full of hatred and contempt.

"Oh, you will, will you; and what will you tell them eh? That your husband wanted some tea and you're such a lazy cow you didn't make him any after he's been working hard all day. I don't think they'd have much sympathy for you, you mad bitch." The finger jabbed again, systematically punctuating his words, because he knew she couldn't reach the phone anyway.

He's the one who's mad, she thought, *stark, staring mad!*

"I hate you!" she said, staring him directly in the eye, "and I wish you were dead!"

He stopped jabbing and stared at her now in horror and disbelief.

"Oh you do, do you? You mad twisted bitch! The truth's coming out now isn't it? You pretend to love me and all the time you want me dead! No wonder everyone hates you, because they do you know; everyone, even your own sister; she couldn't wait to get rid of you. No wonder you don't have any friends – who could put up with you? Look at you, you ugly bitch. You think you can treat me like this? Well, I'm not putting up with it any more, now get out of my sight!"

He grabbed a handful of her sweater and flung her across the room. She stumbled and clawed frantically at a chair to save herself from falling and hitting her head. Recovering her balance she turned and fled up the stairs to the bathroom, since it had the only door with a lock on it. She heard him bounding up the stairs after her and sank to the floor sobbing uncontrollably. *She wanted to die,* she thought, *but not at his hands.*

He was banging on the door. "Why have you locked this door!" he yelled. "What are you doing in there? Come out, I haven't finished talking to you!"

"I'm on the toilet," she lied. "I've got an upset stomach." There was a moment's silence, then to her immense relief she heard his footsteps retreating down the stairs and the front door slamming behind him. She listened intently and heard the car start up and drive off at speed. With a sigh of relief, she unlocked the door and stepped out onto the landing, the tears cascading down her face.

She stood before the mirror in the bedroom and surveyed the ravages of her face, bruised from his jabbing finger, runnels of mascara streaking down her cheeks, her eyes wild and red-rimmed from crying. She began to cry again at the sight. *He's right*, she thought. *I am ugly, but it's because of him.* He was right too, about her having no friends. *How could she have friends when she couldn't invite them home?* Terry liked his privacy and didn't welcome visitors, especially her friends of whom he always disapproved and was constantly putting them down. They were all bitches or stupid brainless tarts, and Terry hated them even though he had never even met them. In referring to them he always prefixed their names with 'that' – 'that Kate', he would say scathingly. No, she couldn't have any friends – except Kate, who knew all about him and also knew how to handle him. Kate, who had been through a similar relationship a couple of years ago but had the sense to get out. In fact, Terry would throw Mariana out on a regular basis, but he didn't mean it, and she also knew that as long as he had breath in his body he would never leave her alone. She was his, he often told her so. She belonged to him; they were husband and wife and in his book that was irrefutable. Kate's ex had moved on; she had returned to live with her parents, and he was married to someone else now. She didn't have to spend her life looking over her shoulder; it had been easy for her, Mariana thought bitterly. No, even Kate didn't fully understand her predicament.

She returned to the bathroom where she soaked a flannel in warm water and held it to her face; it felt soothing and comforting, cocooning her flaming cheeks in its warm damp softness. She pushed the wet hair back from her brow and stared into her own eyes in the mirror.

"You're not ugly, and you're not a bitch," she told herself firmly, "and lots of people would like you if they knew you; certainly nobody would like him if they could see him in action." They never did, however, and no one would have believed it of him. They knew another Terry; the one she fell in love with all those years ago; the Terry who had a dazzling smile, who was good fun and easy going; the one who was still there sometimes, but perhaps decreasingly so. Goodness knows, they might even think she was to blame; so she told no one except Kate. She didn't always tell Kate, she didn't want to become a burden and she was aware that Kate thought she should be more assertive and not give in all the time just for a quiet life; but look what happened when she tried to assert herself! No, she would bide her time; something would happen one day to free her from this life of hell. When Dani died they were drawn together, and even his nights out stopped for some time, but gradually things returned to normal and her temporary peace was shattered once more. Since then things had gone from bad to worse.

It was after ten before he returned. Mariana had gone to bed. She didn't ring Kate; it wasn't fair to involve her when she knew she wouldn't take her advice. She hoped he would have calmed down by the time he came home, as was often the case.

"I'm sorry," he would say, and she would answer,

"I'm sorry too," even though she had done nothing wrong. Things would then return to normal, and they would both act as though nothing had happened. Sometimes it would take longer, and instead the next phase would begin – the silent treatment that could last for days punctuated only by her pathetic attempts to smooth things over. At such times she was grateful for her job; it might be

18

boring and low-paid, but its mind-numbing monotony helped when the turmoil in her brain was as much as she could cope with, and she would join in the banter with the other women so that by the end of her shift things didn't seem so desperate. She mostly worked the six a.m. til two p.m. shift, with an occasional ten p.m. til six a.m. The factory bus passed the bottom of their road at five thirty-five, and she would slip out of bed at five and dress in the spare bedroom to avoid waking Terry. Then she would creep downstairs to grab the sandwiches she had prepared the night before, closing the door softly behind her. Putting her shoes on outside the door she would run for the bus. She would eat the sandwiches on the bus, saving one for her break time at ten.

Today had been different. Last night was quiz night at the pub, and Terry was in good spirits at teatime in anticipation of his night out. He complimented her on the casserole she had made and held her close when he left, kissing her on the lips and telling her that he loved her and not to wait up.

"Have a nice glass of wine why don't you?" he said indulgently.

"Maybe; I'm off tomorrow, so I suppose I could."

"There you go then; have two if you want."

She watched him go; he turned to wave and smile at her as he climbed into the car. He looked handsome, and she thought, *If only he could be this nice all the time.*

She drank the whole bottle. It was a merlot; mellow and fruity. She used her favourite glass, one of the few left from her mother and father's collection that, sadly, had diminished over the years through inevitable breakages.

"Nice things should be used and not hidden away," her mother used to say, and Mariana had always taken her at her word. She turned the flame effect of the electric fire on, and the tall standard lamp in the corner behind the sofa. The light reflected in the crystal glass as she turned it in her hand. Mariana liked nice things – fine china, crystal glasses, soft fluffy towels and pure cotton bedlinen. She liked scented, soothing face creams such as Nivea, and Oil of Ulay, and her favourite perfume was Revlon's Charlie. She had taken Terry into Boots at Christmas, and in a fit of generosity he had bought her the matching set of perfume and body lotion.

She wondered how he was getting on in his quiz. She would have liked to go to quiz night but past experience had taught her that it would only end in tears. At some point she was certain to say the wrong thing or happen inadvertently to glance unseeing at some other man, or even to encourage in some way unbeknownst to her an admiring glance or two in return, and the curtain would come down on Terry's face. The evening would end abruptly and all hell would let loose when they got home. No, it just wasn't worth the risk; let him have his nights out; she would simply sit back and enjoy the peace and freedom.

The wine made her hungry. She found a packet of crisps in the kitchen and crushed them between two slices of heavily buttered bread. She put her favourite record on the stereo; *A Night at the Opera* by Queen. She turned the volume up and Freddie Mercury's voice soared through the room sending a tingle down her spine. No, she didn't need to go out with Terry; she was happy to be home alone.

It was after midnight when she went to bed having dozed off for an hour or so on the sofa. She rinsed her glass and replaced it on the shelf in the kitchen with her other treasures, frowning slightly as she caught sight of the time on the cooker clock; *where was Terry?* The pub would have closed at eleven; he should have been home by now. She climbed wearily to the bathroom and quickly cleaned her teeth. Day off tomorrow, so she would change the sheets on the bed, and hoover all through. She climbed into bed and turned on the clock radio, keeping the volume low. She stretched her legs out reveling in the extra space her husband's absence allowed her, and within minutes was sound asleep.

When she awoke it was after seven and she was still sprawled across the bed with no restriction. *Where on earth was Terry?* He couldn't have gone to work; it was too early. She rose quickly, putting on her dressing gown and padding silently down the stairs. Perhaps he had come in late and fallen asleep on the sofa, in which case he would not be a happy bunny this morning when he woke. The living room was empty, however, as was the kitchen. She crept silently back upstairs – he must be in the spare room; perhaps he hadn't wanted to disturb her. But no, the spare room too was deserted; evidently Terry had stayed out all night.

As the day wore on she kept expecting the phone to ring. Surely he would ring and explain where he was. She toyed with the idea of ringing the garage where he worked, but she knew what the consequences of that might be and decided against it.

Teatime was approaching. She stood in the kitchen, a brace of pork chops wrapped in greaseproof paper in her hand; she had been down to the butcher's that morning to get them. *Why hadn't Terry phoned? He must know she would worry.* He hadn't stayed out all night since the night Dani died. She was angry now; *how could he treat her this way!* She opened the fridge door and threw the chops in. She made herself a Spam sandwich and took it through to the living room, which is where Terry found her when he came home from work; sitting in front of the television with her feet up, apparently without a care in the world whilst he was starving.

The clock radio showed that it was ten thirty-seven when Mariana heard the front door closing and footsteps on the stairs.

"Please God," she prayed. *"Let him be calm!"*

She heard him go into the bathroom and minutes later the toilet flushed. She turned on her side, drew her knees up into her chest, and pretended to be asleep. The bedroom door opened and light flooded in from the landing – he left it open; that was a bad sign, and she cringed, trying to breathe deeply and evenly as though she were asleep.

Suddenly the covers were wrenched off her and she sensed him standing by the side of the bed looking down at her. She kept perfectly still, holding her breath, trying not to screw her eyes up. Perhaps he would let it drop if she did nothing more to provoke him. Several seconds passed; she could feel his eyes roaming her body and resisted the overwhelming urge to grasp the covers and pull them back over herself. She felt small and vulnerable exposed to his critical gaze.

"Still here Bitch?" he said at last, leaning down towards her. He spoke quietly, calmly; there was no smell of alcohol – so he hadn't been at the pub then. She lay still, inwardly praying he would go away; he didn't.

"I thought I told you to get out of my sight," he said menacingly. "What are you still doing in my bed you filthy slut?"

He grasped her arm and hauled her out of bed. She stumbled against him as he manhandled her towards the wardrobe.

22

"Now pack your bags and get the fuck out of here." He began to snatch her clothes from the rail, throwing them on the bed in a tangled heap. He dragged a large suitcase from on top of the wardrobe and began stuffing everything into it. He snatched her makeup and her Nivea cream from the dressing table, and her underwear from the drawers. He crammed them all in, then dragged the case down the stairs. Mariana pulled her dressing gown around her and stood on the landing watching him silently, her mind searching desperately for something to say to calm him down, the tears flowing again.

"Terry what are you doing?" she cried. "It's late! Come to bed; you must be tired." She was beseeching now, the words catching in her throat, her stomach churning, her hands shaking. He was in the kitchen; she heard the tinkle of breaking glass, and ran down the stairs.

"You can take this crap with you too," he yelled, stuffing what was left of her mother's crystal glass into the suitcase.

She sank to the floor, wailing and wringing her hands, her grief and fear overwhelming her. "Terry stop, please stop!" she cried. "Can't we talk about this? I was just worried out of my mind wondering where you were. You only said you were going to quiz night. Why didn't you phone?"

He paused for a moment, "Shut up Bitch, stop your whining. Take this and get out!" He hurled the suitcase in her direction, its contents spilling out onto the hall floor. She tried to retrieve them, noticing that all her treasures were scattered amongst the clothes, broken and sad; the pathetic remains of her childhood and her life before Terry. The scalding tears flowed down her face as she dragged the heavy suitcase to the door.

23

"Where do you expect me to go?" she asked in a small voice.

"You should have thought of that," he answered sneeringly, "before you decided not to make your husband a decent meal. Why don't you go to one of your friends, those dirty scrubbers at the factory? I know all about what you tell them!"

"I don't tell them about you, if that's what you mean. I'd be ashamed to admit what a bully I married," she retorted, and flinched as his hand lashed across the side of her head. She dragged the suitcase out of the door and into the porch. It was after midnight now, and the street was deserted. He slammed the door, and she heard the key turn in the lock.

She shivered; after the heat of the day, it was a cold night. The stars were twinkling brightly, myriads of them above the orange street lamps. She closed the zip on the suitcase and sat on it, hugging herself against the cold. The covered porch was quite big and if she stayed around the corner by the dustbin no one would see her from the road. She would just have to stick it out until the morning and hope he calmed down. She unzipped the case again and dragged out a jumper. *Shame he never threw in a coat,* she thought wryly as she donned the jumper and replaced her dressing gown over the top. She found a pair of socks and pulled them over her bare feet, massaging her toes to warm them.

She saw the light go out on the landing. He would be tucked up in the warm bed now between the clean, ironed sheets she had put on it earlier, without a thought for her. *Where the hell did he think she would go?* He knew she had nowhere, and no one to turn to. Even if she wanted to go to Kate's there was no way she could get there at this time of night. She huddled in the corner of the porch; she

24

was exhausted and in spite of the cold and the extreme discomfort she felt her eyes closing and her head nodding as she drifted into sleep.

She woke with a start, not knowing where she was; but then she remembered. She glanced at her watch; it was five thirty. Soon the factory bus would stop at the end of the road; it would wait a few minutes, and then continue on its way without her. There was no way she was going to be able to go to work today; she would have to invent some excuse. Her neck was stiff and aching; she felt the cold had penetrated her very bones. She huddled into her dressing gown and tried to sleep again. Terry would be up at six thirty and would hopefully leave for work by seven, but would he let her in?

An hour later she heard the key turn in the lock, and she knew it was over. He didn't come out to her or say a single word. He stayed in the kitchen as she dragged the heavy suitcase inside and up the stairs. She left it by the end of the bed and crawled under the covers to warm up, hugging her knees tightly and shivering violently as she heard the front door slam then the car start up as Terry left for work.

After a couple of hours' sleep she phoned work. "I'm sorry, I can't come in today, I've been throwing up all morning," she lied. Actually, she thought, it wasn't that much of a lie; she had a sick feeling in the pit of her stomach, her head was pounding, and her ear was throbbing; it was turning purple too, and she plaited her hair to one side so that it covered it. She took some paracetamol, tipping them into her hand from the glass bottle in the medicine cabinet. She stood for a moment, surveying the contents of the cabinet, wondering if there were sufficient drugs in there efficiently to end her life. She decided it wasn't worth the risk, it might not work, and it

25

certainly wouldn't be as easy as they made it look in the movies She tidied the kitchen and replaced what was left of her treasures on the shelf. The wine glass was gone, as were the two little glass elephants that her sister Mae had given her for her birthday once because they were supposed to be lucky. *As good luck charms go,* she thought bitterly, *they weren't so hot.* With a heavy heart she wrapped the fragments in kitchen roll and placed them in the bin.

It's only things, she told herself, but she remained unconvinced.

Later she cooked the pork chops for tea, with mashed potato, carrots, cabbage, and gravy. Terry could rarely resist a nice bit of home cooking.

At precisely six-thirty she heard the car pull up outside. She stood in the kitchen anxiously wondering what mood he would be in. He came in and saw the chops in the pan on the stove. He made no comment but went upstairs to the bathroom. She could hear him whistling as he had a wash and knew that the storm was over. She set the little round table in the kitchen with two place mats, knives and forks. He came downstairs and took his place at the table. She placed the steaming plates of food on the table and slid into place opposite him. They ate without speaking – she didn't want to risk saying the wrong thing and starting it all off again. She picked at her potatoes; she really wasn't hungry, and she still had a sick feeling in the pit of her stomach.

"Don't you want that chop?" Terry asked, spearing it with his fork and placing it on his plate before she had time to answer. She rose wearily from the table so she wouldn't have to watch him eating. He ate noisily, his mouth open as he chewed. Whenever they argued the sight of him eating always repulsed her, although normally she barely noticed. She deposited her plate on the draining board and left the room.

THREE: LORNA.

Why do I stay with him? Mariana asked herself later that night as she lay beside him in bed hoping he wouldn't want sex. She couldn't remember the last time she had actually enjoyed it – probably not since Dani died; it was as though a part of her had died with her. Terry had always been a selfish lover and never made much effort to please her, it was all about her pleasing him. In the early days it hadn't mattered, she was young and madly in love with him and he made no demands that she wasn't happy to meet; but all that changed after they married, and worsened over the years until there was nothing romantic any more in their sexual activities. They used to make love, but now they just had sex. She would lie beside him afterwards feeling used and worthless.

Tonight she lay rigid waiting for the snoring that would signal a reprieve. When it began at last, she realised she was wide awake now. Very carefully she slid out of bed and tiptoed from the room. She crept downstairs, stopping to listen halfway. The snoring continued; her absence had gone un-noticed. She moved quietly about the kitchen making herself a cup of tea and then settled at the little round table to drink it and reflect on her life.

She knew the answer to her rhetorical question. She couldn't leave him because, simply, she had nowhere to go.

Mariana's parents and her younger sister Mae had died in a car crash when she was fifteen. She would probably have died with them, except that a bout of flu meant that she had been left out of the family outing that day and had stayed at her elder sister Lorna's house instead. Lorna was Mariana's senior by eight years. She was small and dark like Mariana, but lacked her vitality and rarely smiled, her mouth thin and dragged down at the corners and her features pinched. Her hair was dull black compared to Mariana's rich brown locks, and thinner, already beginning to fade to grey. At twenty-three, she was on her second marriage. George was a far cry from Lenny, the childhood sweetheart she had married when she was eighteen against her parents' wishes. Lenny owned a petrol station outside Horsham and once they were married he sacked his full time assistant and gave Lorna the job of serving petrol, checking oil, wiping windscreens, and selling cigarettes, sweets and pop from the kiosk. Lenny, she soon found to her cost, was violent and controlling as well as lazy and feckless. Quite content to let her run the business single-handedly, he spent most of his time in the betting shop squandering her hard-earned profits. Lorna though, was no fool, nor willing to be any man's meal ticket, and less than two years later she left him. She returned to the family home where she found she was obliged to share a room with twelve-year-old Mariana, since Mae was now in possession of her old room. Lorna resented her fall in status and vowed to escape again as soon as ever she was able.

George was a sales rep in his forties and a regular customer at Lenny's garage, where he would often linger and chat to Lorna over the counter in the kiosk. When she left he tracked her down and asked her out. Lorna saw an opportunity and seized it with both hands. George was steady, reliable, and kind, and although life with him would never be exciting, it would certainly be safe. Lorna had no illusions; it was the best she could hope for. George owned a pretty cottage in Wisborough Green, just a few miles from where her parents lived.

On the day of the accident Mariana's parents and her younger sister had gone for a day out in London because it was Mae's thirteenth birthday. They planned to do some sight-seeing and some shopping, and catch a show in the evening. They were to have gone on the train, but at the last minute a friend offered them a lift. All four of them died in an accident on their way there.

Reluctantly, Mariana moved in with Lorna and George. They were an extraordinarily close couple and clearly didn't welcome the intrusion. Lorna laid down strict house rules and George, although kindly enough, largely ignored Mariana. She felt like a cuckoo in the nest and spent most evenings in her room pining for her parents and sister, and her old life. At the time she had often found fault with both, but now she would have given anything to have them back. Life goes on however. At weekends she would catch the bus to Billingshurst and meet up with her friend Sue; then on to Horsham where they would get some chips for lunch, spend the afternoon trying on clothes they couldn't afford, then sit in the Wimpey bar making a single Coca Cola last until they got thrown out.

One Saturday in July Lorna's car broke down, and she called the garage in Billingshurst to come and pick it up so that it could be mended. The breakdown truck arrived, and the driver was Terry.

Mariana was just leaving to catch the bus into Billingshurst. She glanced at the tall, handsome mechanic in passing, noticing his long dark hair, his lazy blue eyes with their heavy eyelashes, and the tattoos on his forearms. He caught her looking and rewarded her with a dazzling smile and a wink. She lingered for a minute or two and watched him hitching the car to the truck, winching it effortlessly into position with its front wheels suspended, then she continued on her way to the bus stop.

The bus was late as usual. A light drizzle was falling, and she wished she'd thought to bring an umbrella – but there again, she would probably only lose it. Suddenly the tow truck pulled up alongside her with Lorna's car on the back.

"Want a lift to Billingshurst?" He leaned out through the window, at the same time releasing the catch on the passenger door. *Why not,* thought Mariana.

"Thanks," she said, clambering up into the truck. It smelt of engine oil and cigarettes, and he had to push a pile of rubbish off the seat to make room for her.

"Sorry," he said with a sideways grin. "I don't normally carry passengers. What's your name?"

"Mariana," she answered.

"I'm Terry. Where are you off to then this early in the morning?"

"Anywhere away from my sister! She likes me out of the way at weekends."

"D'you live there then? How come?"

"My parents died in a car crash a couple of months ago, so now I live with my sister. She's eight years older than me."

"Hey, I'm sorry! That must've been hard on you. Your sister seems a bit of a dragon if you don't mind my saying so."

31

Mariana laughed. "I don't mind at all; I couldn't have put it better myself. She's not that bad really; she hasn't had it easy and I don't suppose she ever dreamed she'd get stuck with bringing me up either."

"What d'you do for entertainment around here? It's like the back of beyond. I haven't even found a decent pub yet; they're all full of farmers and pensioners."

"Most people go to Guildford or Crawley on a Saturday night, but Lorna's only let me go once. Much as she hates looking after me, she feels responsible for me and after what happened to the others she doesn't like me getting lifts. If they'd gone to London on the train you see, they'd still be here now."

"You don't know that," Terry answered. "It might just have been their destiny, and the train would've crashed instead. You can't go through your whole life being scared of cars you know. Tell you what; let me take you to the flicks in Crawley tonight. I promise to get you home safely." He turned and flashed her that smile again. She felt herself weaken; he was dead good looking, and Sue would be so jealous.

"Well, what d'you think. Is it a date?"

"I'll have to ask Lorna," she answered, with butterflies in her stomach. *A date! She'd never really been on a proper date.*

"I'll pick you up at six," he said confidently. "Oh, and in case you're wondering, we won't be going in this!" Mariana laughed, her tension gone.

"Thank goodness for that," she said. "Why didn't you say so in the first place."

He dropped her off outside the garage where he worked, and she walked round to Sue's house. Sue was busy dolling herself up ready for their afternoon out.

"I need to be home by five," said Mariana. "I've got a date."

32

"Wow!" Sue was suitably impressed. "Who with?"

"His name's Terry; he's a mechanic at Car Jacks," she answered smugly. "We're going to the flicks in Crawley."

"Wowee! I've seen him around; the one with the tattoos. He's dead good-looking. How did you manage that?"

"He's fixing my sister's car and he gave me a lift here in the tow truck."

"Blimey, you're not going out in that are you?" her friend fell about giggling.

"No Silly, he has a car. He's picking me up at six and I haven't asked Lorna yet."

"Why don't I put your hair up for you?" Sue's dyed blonde hair curled around her ears in a short bob and she was secretly envious of Mariana's luxuriant burnished locks. "Go on, it'll make you look about eighteen, honest. I'll come back to yours with you this afternoon and you can drop me off back here when you go out."

Mariana hesitated; she wasn't sure what Lorna would say about that; she had never brought a friend home before, and she baulked at the thought of having to ask Terry to give Sue a lift home on their first date. However, she had never been very good at being assertive.

"Ok," she said. "Thanks."

"What are you wearing?" Sue asked next. "D'you want to borrow my black and white dress?" She hunted in her wardrobe and pulled out the dress. It was very short; mostly black, with a wide v-shaped section in white at the front, and cut-away sleeves."

"This'll look fab on you. Come on, try it on."

The dress was much more trendy than anything Mariana owned, and she loved it. Sue folded it and put it in a bag along with some hair curlers and a large bulging make-up bag. They got their chips in Billingshurst and ate them on the bus on the way back to Lorna's house. Mariana was relieved to find no one in.

Sue wandered around the house, with Mariana following nervously keeping watch for George's car. Sue looked in every room, opening drawers and picking up ornaments to inspect them whilst Mariana fussed and clucked around her, worrying that she might drop something or leave something out of place. She even insisted on going into Lorna and George's bedroom in spite of Mariana's protestations – she herself had never set foot in there. She watched from the doorway as her friend inspected everything.

"Please Sue," she pleaded. "What if they know we've been in here? I'll never hear the last of it; Lorna's very private."

"Oh alright Worrydoll! There's not much to see anyway." She was standing in front of the dressing table holding one of Lorna's necklaces up against her. "This'd look great with that dress Mariana. Why don't you borrow it?"

"Put it back! For goodness sake Sue, let's get out of here." Mariana was shocked at her friend's behaviour; clearly she didn't know her as well as she thought she did. Just then a car pulled up on the gravel drive. Mariana grabbed Sue's arm and physically dragged her out of the room and across the landing into the relative safety of her own bedroom.

"Stay there!" she whispered fiercely, shoving her down onto the bed. "I'll be back in a minute."

Closing the door behind her, she tiptoed carefully into her sister's room and replaced the necklace in the jewellery box on the dressing table. She hoped everything looked normal; although not being familiar with the room it was difficult to be sure. She closed the door silently as

34

George and Lorna entered the kitchen below. The floorboards on the landing creaked loudly, however.

"Mariana, is that you?" Her sister came to the bottom of the stairs. "What are you doing home already?" Mariana heard the irritation in her voice and her heart sank. She made her way down the stairs hesitantly.

"We didn't go to Horsham. I brought Sue here because she's doing my hair for me. I'm going out tonight if that's ok."

"Well you might have asked me first before bringing strangers into my home," grumbled Lorna. "Where are you going, and who with?" Mariana took a deep breath, her stomach churning alarmingly.

"Sorry, I didn't think you'd mind; we'll stay in my room til it's time to go. I'm going to the pictures with Sue and her boyfriend. He's picking us up here at six." She thought, *why am I lying when she's bound to find out?*

"Well, don't be too late back. You know how I feel about you gadding about in cars." With that Lorna disappeared back into the kitchen and the matter appeared to be closed. Mariana heaved a sigh of relief – clearly her sister was just thankful to be rid of her for the evening. She ran back up the stairs.

"Mariana! What about your tea?" Her sister had returned to the hallway.

"Don't worry, we'll get some chips or something." Mariana didn't wait for an answer but dived into her room closing the door firmly behind her.

Sue was busy going through her underwear drawer.

By the time they emerged from Mariana's room at five to six Sue had executed quite a transformation on her friend. Her hair had been divided with one section back-combed and piled up on top of her head, held in place with

35

a white comb, the remainder cascading in curls (courtesy of Sue's heated rollers) down to her shoulders. Her finger and toe nails were painted fuschia pink to match her lips, and she had copious amounts of makeup on her eyes (although Mariana had drawn the line at false eyelashes). Certainly, she looked much older than her fifteen years. They listened on the landing for a minute and could hear the television on in the lounge. They crept down the stairs, and when they reached the back door Mariana called out,

"I'm off now Lorna, I'll see you later." They hurried outside without waiting for an answer, running down the path to the gate giggling uncontrollably.

"Phew!" said Mariana when they were out of sight of the house. "Lorna would have had a fit if she'd seen my makeup. Listen, you'd better get in the front to start with, in case she's watching from the bedroom window. I told her Terry was your boyfriend.

It was nearly twenty past six when Terry drew up in a slightly battered red mini, and Mariana was beginning to wonder if she was about to be stood up. He leaned over and opened the passenger door. He looked somewhat puzzled as Mariana started to clamber into the back.

"This is my friend Sue," she said, by way of explanation. "Can we drop her off in Billingshurst? I didn't think you'd mind." She didn't want to have to explain why Sue was sitting in the front seat; it would only make her appear childish. Terry looked a little put out but said nothing. Sue chattered away like a sparrow all the way to Billingshurst with Terry answering her barrage of questions in monosyllables, glancing every now and then at Mariana in the rear view mirror. She felt uncomfortable; his gaze was inscrutable and she wondered if she had blown it before it started. By the time they dropped Sue off Mariana knew that Terry had come from up North a few months ago; he was twenty-two; his parents had split up when he was twelve, and he had left home at eighteen after his mother shacked up with a man whose dislike of Terry was entirely reciprocated. Although the questions had come from Sue, she couldn't help feeling that his answers were directed at her, sitting silently in the back seat as she was, reading his eyes in the rear view mirror.

"Phew!" he said as she clambered from the back and settled herself on the front seat giving Sue a cheery wave goodbye. "She'd talk the hind legs off a donkey that one! Now, are you going to tell me what that was all about?"

Mariana felt herself colour and decided she would have to own up.

"I told Lorna you were Sue's boyfriend so she wouldn't have a fit on me. She thinks I'm going to the flicks with the two of you." Terry threw back his head and laughed out loud.

"I've a good mind to go after your friend and invite her along," he chuckled. "Don't you want to be alone with me then?" With that, he leaned forward suddenly and kissed her. She was completely taken by surprise, but soon found herself kissing him back. His lips were firm and although his breath smelt faintly of tobacco she thought it was very manly, mingling as it was with the scent of his aftershave. A tingle spread through her, and in that moment Mariana fell head-over-heels in love.

They dated regularly after that, although he never came to the house again but would pick Mariana up from the bus stop instead, or sometimes from Sue's house when he worked a half day on a Saturday. When school broke up for the summer, Mariana would go into Billingshurst and hang around the workshop whilst he worked. She would make him cups of coffee or fetch him some chips for his lunch. Sue complained that she never saw her, but Mariana could think of only one thing. Lorna didn't suspect anything and was just relieved that she hadn't brought any more friends home with her.

They had sex on their third date. Afterwards Mariana felt very grown up and wondered if people could tell she had 'done it'.

"Is he good at it?" asked Sue when she told her. She had confided in her because she wanted to know that it was ok, and that it didn't make her some kind of slut because she was having sex at fifteen. Sue laughed,

"Don't be s'daft. You love him, don't you? And he loves you, so that's ok."

Mariana didn't know if he was 'good at it', having had no previous experience for comparison, but she certainly enjoyed it and was always eager for more. All through the long summer holidays they would meet up, and he would take her places in the mini. They would walk in the Sussex countryside or along Brighton beach, and would make love in secluded but perhaps not entirely private places, as well as in the back of the mini.

He took her to his flat only once. She was disappointed to find that it was untidy and smelt of stale cigarettes and beer, and the sheets on his bed looked like they could do with a good wash. Whilst he went out to get some more cigarettes she started to tidy up. She washed the dishes and threw all the empty cans and takeaway cartons in the bin, and tidied the rather grubby throws and the cushions on the sofa. She found the airing cupboard and hunted in there for clean sheets. She had never seen bedlinen so tired and stained, and all were in need of an iron. Her mother used to keep her linen cupboard piled with crisp, ironed sheets and pillowcases, all arranged according to size and

"Because I say so. Don't you trust me?" *Not really,* thought Mariana.

"I do – but.........."

"Aw! Don't be daft. Look, I'll ring you soon as I get there, and every night. I've got connections up there; I can get a job easy, and I'll soon find us a little place, you'll see."

"Will we be married Terry?" she asked. She knew Lorna would expect that, and doubted if she would let her go otherwise.

"Of course we will Angel. We'll go down the registry office in Horsham on Monday and get the ball rolling, and we can get married in about a month, by which time I should have found us somewhere to live. Will that put your mind at rest, if we do that?"

They were married on Valentine's Day. *How romantic, said Sue,* with Lorna and George as their witnesses and Sue as the only guest. Terry was true to his word and less than a week after the wedding they set off for their new home on the Cheshire border. Mariana said a tearful goodbye to Sue, and a slightly less tearful one to her sister.

"Take care of her," Lorna said to Terry, and a look passed between them that Mariana was to remember later.

"I'll come and stay with you when you're settled in," said Sue. "Help you with the sprog an' all." She stood and waved them out of sight.

It began as soon as they were married.

The first time Mariana saw their new home she was delighted. It was a modern terraced house on a small housing estate on the edge of town, with a line of allotments at the back, and only a fifteen minute walk from the park. There were two bedrooms, a lounge and small kitchen-diner, an open plan front garden next to the garage, and a small enclosed back garden. All her efforts to persuade Terry to reveal details of it in advance had failed and she spent the long journey from Sussex worrying that it would be another grotty flat. The previous week, immediately after their wedding, Terry, with the help of George, had loaded the furniture from his flat into a hired van and driven it up there to establish their new home. Mariana, Lorna and Sue had been left with the task of cleaning the flat before handing over the keys to the letting agents.

"Good Lord, Mariana, didn't he ever do any housework?" exclaimed Lorna, surveying the state of the flat; the grubby, scuffed walls and stained carpets, and the curtains that were missing half their plastic hooks leaving them dangling crookedly, with big gaps at the top. The enameled kitchen sink was now an indeterminate colour, as was the formerly avocado coloured bathroom suite.

"I doubt it," replied Mariana, searching under the kitchen sink for some cleaning products and finding nothing. "I tried once but he wasn't exactly pleased; I think he just liked living like a pig in muck."

"Well, I hope he's going to buck his ideas up now you're married. You're going to need a bit of help when this baby's born. You two start by taking those curtains down so I can wash them, and then you can give the floor a good brush since there doesn't appear to be a hoover. I'll go and fetch some cleaning stuff and I'll be back in half an hour."

"Shall we go and get some chips?" said Sue after Lorna had gone. "We're going to need a bit of energy to tackle this lot."

44

It took them almost three whole days of hard work, but they transformed the flat and managed to get Terry's deposit back.

"You keep that," Lorna told Mariana firmly. "You've earned it. Open a post office savings account with it, you never know when you might need a bit of money of your own."

"Oh, I don't know – what will Terry say?"

"Mariana, for once in your life, listen to me! Don't tell Terry. He can't have been expecting to get his deposit back and doesn't deserve to. From now on you are going to be dependent on him, and I'd feel happier if I knew you had something of your own. The post office will give you a savings book. Hide it, guard it, and if ever you need to, use it."

Reluctantly, Mariana agreed. *Poor Lorna*, she thought to herself, *she's still bitter about Lenny and thinks all men are not to be trusted. Well, it's going to be different with me and Terry. He loves me, and I know he'll look after me.*

Terry unlocked the door of their new home and swept her up in his arms.

"Blimey, you're turning into quite a lump!" he said jokingly. She wrapped her arms around his neck, smiling happily. He pushed the door open and stepped over the threshold.

"Welcome to your new home, Mrs. Harding," he said, and putting her down, kissed her soundly. The kiss lingered and she felt his excitement mounting.

"Let's go and christen the bedroom," he said, his voice gruff with desire.

"Later; I want to look around first," replied Mariana, gently extricating herself from his grasp. He gripped her arm viciously, preventing her from moving.

"Ouch! That hurts; don't be so rough. You don't know your own strength!" she cried, half jokingly. Surely he hadn't meant to be so rough with her.

"Get upstairs Bitch, you're in my house now and you'll do as I say. You'll have plenty of time to look around when I'm slaving my ass off to keep you. Right now you can show me how grateful you are for all this." He pushed her towards the bottom of the stairs. Mariana bit back the tears. What had got into him? She was tired, and she didn't feel like having sex. Besides, she was aware of the baby growing inside her and had thought she felt it move the day before. Surely they shouldn't be doing this now.

"Terry, I'm worried we'll harm the baby. Do we have to do this?" she pleaded as he steered her up the stairs. The bedroom overlooked the allotments but there were no curtains at the window yet. The bed was unmade, strewn with the same dirty sheets that were on it in the flat. Mariana glanced around. There were bin bags piled up between the bed and the window so that you couldn't get in from that side. Evidently Terry had done little to prepare for her homecoming.

"You've got bloody weeks to go yet," he sneered, pushing her down to sit on the bed. "You can't seriously expect a man to go that long without it." He undid his jeans, and stood over her. "Here Bitch, there's another way you can please me that won't harm your precious baby."

Dani Mae was born on 3rd July, two weeks early. Mariana was pegging out the washing when she felt the first contractions. She'd had a few painful cramps lately, but this was the real thing; somehow she just knew it. It was Wednesday morning, a warm and sunny July day. They had no phone in the house; Terry said they couldn't afford one. Mariana secretly thought that if he drank less, they

46

might be able to, and since she knew nobody and her only support was over two hundred miles away, it would hardly have been a luxury. Now, she hobbled down to the phonebox to phone Terry at work. The pains were regular now, every ten to fifteen minutes. "I'll be there as fast as I can Angel," he said, sounding concerned. "Just hang in there, and I'll get you to the hospital in plenty of time."

She returned to the house and took the small suitcase Lorna had given her out of the wardrobe. She had packed it a week ago. "Best to be prepared early," Lorna had said. Once a week, she would go down to the phone box to call her sister. It was comforting to hear her voice. A month after she left for her new life, Lorna had told her that she too was now expecting a baby. She and George were over the moon. When she told her Mariana was overcome with emotion and broke down in tears on the phone.

"Whatever's the matter, aren't you pleased for me?" Lorna asked anxiously.

"Oh of course I am, but I wish I wasn't so far away," replied Mariana and found herself blurting out everything she had vowed to keep to herself; Terry's drinking habit, his unpredictable moods and his violence, and also the fact that, most of the time, he didn't seem particularly interested in their baby. There was silence at the other end, then Lorna said,

"Look Mariana, you have to take him in hand. Is there no one you can talk to there; no one who could have a word with him? I can't do anything from here, and I can't be spending my time worrying about you. You must stand up to him, and then he'll realise he can't get away with it. Look, you should have thought about all this before you went and got yourself pregnant. I'm sorry Mariana, but

47

you've made your bed, and I'm afraid you're just going to have to lie in it. I have my own family to think about now. He'll be fine once the baby's here; some men get funny about these things. I have to go, I'll speak to you soon."

Mariana had said nothing further about her predicament but in future tried to find positive things to tell her sister. She thought about stopping the phone calls, but she felt so isolated and perhaps her sister would be more sympathetic when her own child was born.

She checked the contents of her suitcase once more, fingering the little outfit she had prepared for the baby to come home in. Lorna was busy knitting for her own baby, and had sent her a little white matinee jacket with a matching bonnet and bootees. She gazed at the tiny garments – goodness, how small they were; like doll's clothes. Sometimes, she was terrified when she contemplated the huge responsibility she was about to take on. In Terry's more tender moments she was reassured; once the baby was here, he'd be a great dad.

"Fancy us having a sprog," he would say. "A real little person we made." He took her shopping every payday and one day he came home from work with a folding pram and a pile of baby clothes that one of his workmates had given him. Mariana was delighted, but worried about the pram.

"It's bad luck to have a pram in the house before the baby's born," she told him. "Can't your mate hang onto it for a while?"

"For fuck's sake, you ungrateful bitch, don't be so bloody ridiculous! Bloody women!" He stormed out of the house and that was their weekend ruined. He returned late that night and barely spoke to her until Monday morning when suddenly all appeared to have been forgotten. She had put the pram in the garage out of sight in the hope that would dispel the bad luck, and he never questioned its absence.

Where was he? The pains were increasing in their frequency and ferocity, and Mariana was beginning to feel very scared. She had never been to any ante-natal classes, but had had a visit from a midwife when she was six months pregnant to discuss the birth and prepare her for what was to come. She had left some leaflets with her, and now she frantically rummaged in the kitchen drawer to find them. She started to breathe with the contractions, counting the time in between them – still eight minutes; there was time.

Almost an hour after she had phoned him, Terry arrived. He was carrying a bunch of flowers and was very excited.

"I got you these Angel. I stopped off at the flower shop specially. The traffic's bad today, there's a midweek friendly football match on; took me ages to get through town."

What could she say? He meant well, but if he'd only come home along the bypass instead of going through town to get the damn flowers he'd have been here over half an hour ago.

"They're lovely," she said. "Thanks," and hugged him.

Terry drove to the hospital like a man possessed. The road leading up to it from the bypass was littered with potholes, and Mariana winced, as her contractions seemed to coincide with each sickening jolt.

"Terry slow down!" she cried anxiously.

"For fuck's sake! I thought you wanted to get there quickly. Stop whining will you? You'd think they'd do something about this bloody road." He slowed down a bit, however, swerving to avoid the worst of the ruts.

Half an hour after they arrived at the hospital, Dani Mae was born. Terry had already chosen a name for his son, since he was convinced that was what they were having. He was to be named after his childhood hero, the footballer Danny Blanchflower. His disappointment when Mariana produced a little girl was only thinly disguised.

"Never mind," said Mariana, "we'll call her Danielle; it's a nice name, and she'll be Dani for short." She had wanted to call her Eleanor Mae after her mother and sister, but three names seemed a bit excessive, and Mae went best with Dani. Secretly, she was relieved that she wouldn't have to decorate the baby's room with Tottenham Hotspur regalia as Terry had planned.

After Dani was born Terry seemed to lose all interest in them both and began to spend more and more time at the pub. When he was home he would sit in front of the TV with a can of beer and a cigarette, in spite of Mariana's protestations.

"Terry, I do wish you wouldn't smoke when Dani's around, it can't be good for her."

"This is my house, and I'll bloody well smoke when and where I want to." He replied caustically. "She doesn't have to be in here all the time, you should put her upstairs to sleep."

It all came to a head when Dani was five months old. It was the week before Christmas, and Mariana asked Terry for some money to buy their daughter a Christmas present.

"What the hell for? She's five months old for fuck's sake!"

"I've seen a lovely teddy in that shop by the arcade I wanted to get her. It's soft and gorgeous, but it's a bit expensive."

"A teddy bear? She's got dozens of the bloody things!"

"I know, but this one's special, it's looks so real, and she won't grow out of it like some of her others."

"I never heard such ridiculous nonsense in my life! No Mariana. If you must buy her a present, make it something useful because she's not going to know anything about it anyway. Here," he fished in his pocket and withdrew a five pound note, "get her something with that, I dunno, a bloody coat or something." With that, the matter was closed.

Mariana thought about her post office account, which as yet she hadn't dared to touch; but he knew about the teddy now, and knew that it was expensive, so she couldn't lie about it and get away with it. She did, however, decide to dip into it to buy him his present. She had nearly ten pounds saved up from the money he gave her and she could add to that. After much deliberation she had decided to buy him a watch. He had one already, but it was quite old and he had replaced the strap a few times. She had seen a nice Seiko watch in H Samuel's, with one of those expanding bracelets. It was twenty-two pounds, but he needn't know that.

The next day was bright, cold and sunny, and she pushed Dani in her pram down to town to withdraw some money from her post office account. H Samuel's was in the arcade by the bus stop and she had to pass the shop with the teddy in it to get there. He was still there in the window – dark brown, with long silky fur, large amber realistic-looking glass eyes and an authentic-looking black rubber nose. Mariana sighed, but it was no use, she'd never get away with it now. She walked on by, and leaving the pram by the window where she could keep an eye on it, went

51

into H Samuel's, emerging shortly afterwards with the watch. To her surprise and delight, there was ten percent off it, and she had over two pounds worth of change left over. She was cold, and she decided to treat herself to a hot chocolate in the café by the bus station.

She settled herself by the window, and sipped at the delicious hot, sweet concoction with little marshmallows floating on the top. She pushed them down with her spoon, melting them in the steaming liquid, then sipped again ecstatically. Dani sat in her pram by her side, gazing at her with quizzical blue eyes. She pushed a molten marshmallow into her daughter's mouth and watched her suck at it eagerly, laughing as Dani pursed her lips into little rosebuds as the gooey mixture dribbled out again. Mariana retrieved the excess with her finger as Dani pushed her little fists into her mouth and sucked loudly on them, making gurgling sounds of pleasure.

"Was that nice Dani? Did you like Mummy's marshmallow then? Maybe Mummy will buy some to take home with us, would you like that?"

Dani spread her lips in a toothless grin, and Mariana bent down and kissed her baby-soft cheek. As she did so, a shadow fell across their table. She looked up, and Terry was standing there. She froze when she saw the look on his face.

"What the hell are you doing in here?" he asked, his voice quiet but menacing.

"Got money to burn have we?" he added, glancing significantly at the large mug, half empty now, of hot chocolate. "You know what? I just happened to be out on a job, picking up a repair from over by the park. I thought I'd have a look at that damned teddy bear you've been whining on about. Then I saw you sitting in the caff like some bloody teenager. Haven't you got anything better to do?"

I am a bloody teenager, thought Mariana, then replied,
"I just needed a sit down and a warm before going home. I've just been doing some window shopping, that's all."

"It bloody better be all," Terry muttered. "I'll see you later, but don't wait up, I'm going to the pub after work." He turned on his heel and marched off.

My God, thought Mariana, *There's one rule for me, and another for him. He can go and sit in the pub til God knows what time, but I'm not allowed a hot chocolate in the middle of the afternoon!* She drank down the rest of her now lukewarm chocolate, and walked home. The sky had clouded over and rain threatened. It was as though Terry had stolen the sunshine from her day.

That night he didn't come home until after two. She had just got Dani down after her night feed when she heard him coming up the stairs. She hoped he wasn't still angry at her. She had hidden the watch in the drawer of her bedside cabinet at first, but in the darkness, she could hear it ticking loudly, so she put it in Dani's room instead, hidden away in the drawer with her nappies – Terry would never find it in there!

She heard him in the bathroom, and then the door opened and light flooded across the bed. He came round to her side of the bed and sat down.

"Get up," he said roughly, yanking the covers off her. "You and me need to talk." She slowly raised herself to a sitting position.

"What about?" she asked.

"I don't want you here," he said. "You can pack your bags and get out." He said it quite calmly, regarding her steadily, waiting for a reaction. She couldn't smell beer on him. *Strange,* she thought.

"Terry, it's two o'clock in the morning. What about Dani?"

"You can take her with you, I don't want either of you here. You can pack your bags, and in the morning I'll run you to the station. You can go and stay with your ugly sister or your slut of a friend Sue."

"Terry, stop it. It's nearly Christmas, I'm not going anywhere. I can't just land on Lorna like that, and don't call my friend a slut, she isn't. Why are you being so mean? What am I supposed to have done?" The tears began to flow, in spite of her efforts to prevent it because she knew it would only add fuel to his fire."

"Stop sniveling Bitch. As for Sue, why don't you ask her what she was doing with me every Friday night before we were married? Ha! You really had no idea did you? She had a bit more go about her too, if you know what I mean," he said pointedly.

"I don't believe you; Sue wouldn't do that, she's my friend."

"Well, you can ask her tomorrow when you see her can't you. Now pack your bags, there's a train to London at seven and you can get another one to Billingshurst from there."

"And how am I supposed to pay for my ticket?" she asked. He began to laugh, a hollow, mirthless laugh that made her blood curdle.

"I'll give you some money, and you can pay me back out of this," he said, throwing her post office book on the bed. "Thought you could keep your little nest-egg from me did you? I saw you in there this afternoon, getting some money out. I suppose you were going to buy that fucking teddy bear, only I caught up with you and spoiled your little plan.

"You *followed* me?" she asked incredulously.

"I went to the post office to tax the car, and there you were. I knew where you were going, so I moved the truck and came after you. Didn't expect to find you in the caff though. Perhaps you shouldn't leave your handbag in the hall if that's where you hide your money. Where did you get all that money from anyway? Did the ugly sister pay you off too, same as she did me?"

"What are you talking about? What d'you mean, paid you off?"

"Ha! You didn't honestly think I married you for love did you? Oh no! Your sister gave me the money for the deposit on this house out of your inheritance. She was supposed to keep it for you until you were twenty-one, but she couldn't wait to get rid of you, so she gave it to me on condition that I married you."

He left the room. Mariana sat in stunned silence. There was a rushing sound in her ears. She felt dizzy and thought she was going to faint. Her sister had betrayed her, and had given her inheritance to Terry. The house was in his name; that's how he always referred to it – his house, bought with her money! She remembered the look that had passed between her sister and Terry when they were leaving, warning him presumably to keep his side of the bargain. Well he hadn't, and there was nothing she could do about it now. She rose from the bed and dressed slowly feeling dazed and numb. She packed a suitcase and took it down the stairs, carefully manoeuvering it from stair to stair so as not to wake Dani. Terry was sitting with his feet on the kitchen table, leaning back, his arms folded across his chest, watching her. Mariana eyed him dispassionately; how could she ever have thought she loved him? He had robbed her of her dignity and her inheritance, and she didn't want to stay in *his* house a day longer. She would take Dani and go to Lorna as he wanted; not for him, but for herself. She sat in the living room, looking around her, wondering whether she would miss it. Lorna would have to take her in; she owed her that much after what she had done; but she knew it wouldn't be easy in such a tiny cottage with two small babies.

Dani woke just after six as always. Mariana fed her, dressed her, and packed a small bag with essentials for her. As she piled nappies into the bag, she saw the watch sitting at the bottom of the drawer. She wanted to hurl it at the wall, smash it to smithereens; but instead she slipped it into the bag with the nappies – she would sell it; try and get some of her money back.

They drove to the station in silence. Terry bought her ticket, and gave her a further twenty pounds.

"That'll get you to your sister's and you'll have some to spare," he said, handing her the money.

"That's big of you," she muttered sullenly. There was nearly two hundred pounds in the post office account. "You won't be able to draw that money out you know," she said.

"Oh don't worry; I'll find a way," he replied with a smirk. He stashed her bags and the pram on the luggage rack. "Goodbye Mariana," he said. "Have a nice life." He glanced at his daughter, and Mariana wondered if he had at least some regret regarding her. "Probably not even mine," he sneered, and walked away as the train began to roll.

Mariana stared at her ticket – *one way,* it said. She cradled Dani in her arms and wept silently. For hours, the train rattled past fields and houses, towns and villages, stopping at major stations, but speeding through the smaller ones. Mariana made a nest of blankets on the seat

56

next to her for Dani to sleep in. She was weary; she had had no sleep, and soon she felt her eyelids drooping and nodded off to the click-clack rhythm of the train.

Mariana and Dani both slept most of the way. As the train chugged slowly through the London suburbs, Mariana awoke, and for a moment wondered where she was. Then she remembered, and misery engulfed her. She must now go cap in hand to the sister who had betrayed her, and the friend who had possibly betrayed her even more, and she wished with all her heart that she hadn't decided to buy her husband a watch, otherwise she might have remained in blissful ignorance. She knew, however, that eventually she would have had to face up to the mess her life had become. She began to weep again for her old carefree teenage life; for her parents and her younger sister, and for her romantic dream that had become a nightmare. She looked at Dani, tucked up now in her pram that the man sitting in the next seat had kindly helped her off the train with, and knew that she was the one thing she would never regret. She studied the train timetables; there was one to Billingshurst in half an hour. She found a café and looking at her meagre twenty pounds, she settled for a tea. Dani was hungry now, and she gave her the bottle she had prepared before leaving home. She asked for some hot water to warm it in, and the somewhat sour-faced waitress banged a bowl of it down on the table; the contents spilling out across the table when Mariana stood the bottle in it. The café was dark and depressing, or perhaps it was just the way she was feeling. Dani drank her bottle eagerly – *she's such a good little girl,* thought Mariana, *she doesn't deserve this, and neither do I.* Suddenly angry, she took strength from it. She wasn't going to let this ruin her life. Somehow, she would rise above it!

Her new determination carried her on the last part of her journey, which seemed to take nearly as long as the previous one, the train stopping at every station with a groan and a hiss of brakes, and a slamming of doors that made Dani jump. However, once again a kind person helped her off the train and she warmed to the goodness of human nature and set off for Sue's house carrying her suitcase with Dani's bag stashed underneath the pram. It seemed a long way and her arms ached as she swapped the suitcase from one hand to the other.

Sue's house looked much the same as she remembered. She rang the doorbell, staring at the concrete step and remembering the day she sat there after Terry threw her out of the flat. If only she had refused to get into his car that day. If only she had had more sense then none of this would have happened! Then she looked at her daughter; sleeping now, her arms above her head, her cheeks flushed and her mouth and eyelids making little fluttering movements. No, she could never wish to be without Dani, whatever happened.

The door opened and Sue stood in the doorway taking in the scene before her; Mariana, a suitcase, and a baby in a pram.

"Mariana, oh my God! What on earth are you doing here? Why didn't you call me?" Mariana watched her friend closely. Was there a note of dismay in her voice? She certainly didn't seem overwhelmed with joy to see her.

"I thought I'd surprise you," she said. "This is Dani Mae." She indicated the pram. Sue stepped down and peeped inside.

"Oh, she's lovely – but where's Terry?"

"I've left him," said Mariana decisively. She preferred the sound of that to '*he threw me out*'. Her friend looked at her sharply.

58

"That was quick," she remarked. "I saw Lorna a few weeks ago and she said you were fine."

"She would, but then again what does she care! Do you know she paid Terry off so that he would marry me and take me up North?" Mariana watched Sue's face and in an instant knew the answer to her question.

"Oh my God! You did know! Before or after I got married? I can't believe she told you and you never told me. How could you? I made the biggest mistake of my life and you could've stopped me. I would still have had Dani and Lorna would've had to let me stay." Sue said nothing, but fidgeted uncomfortably, avoiding eye contact. Then the penny dropped.

"Or was it Terry who told you on one of your Friday nights?" Mariana said, her voice breaking with emotion.

"I'm sorry Mariana…." *So that was it! Terry had been telling the truth!*

Grabbing the pram, Mariana turned tail and headed off down the path without a backward glance. She felt numb, sick, and very, very angry. She pictured them together on a Friday night; laughing at her for being so naïve and stupid. When she got married, Sue had known it was a farce, and she had known that Terry didn't really love her. Lorna was less blameworthy – she had really thought she was helping – but Sue? Sue had been guilty of the ultimate betrayal of her so-called best friend. If she had an ounce of decency in her she would have told Mariana at least about Lorna's plan, even if she had failed to confess to her own misdoings. She could have stopped the wedding and stopped Terry getting Mariana's inheritance.

She sat on her suitcase at the bus stop. Lorna had some questions to answer, but she was pretty sure she had acted out of good intentions, and she couldn't possibly have known the extent of Terry's worthlessness.

The cottage looked the same; reassuringly so. She could see her bedroom window as she turned up the drive dragging the pram awkwardly through the gravel with one hand because of the suitcase. It was such a relief to put the heavy case down at the door. She hesitated – should she just walk in; or should she ring the doorbell? She decided on the latter, and heard the shrill sound echo through the house.

"Can you get that please George? I'm just changing Eleanor."

The door opened and there stood her brother-in-law.

"Good Lord!" he exclaimed. "Mariana!"

"Hello George," she smiled at him a little wearily. She longed to sit down on a comfy chair with a nice cup of tea. George was staring at her in disbelief, and something else – annoyance. His gaze took in the pram and the suitcase and her disheveled appearance.

"Who is it?" Lorna's voice called from upstairs.

"It's your sister," he replied, and to Mariana, "I suppose you'd better come in." He stood back and she manouevered the pram into the hallway, leaving the suitcase by the door. He left it there, shutting the door behind her.

Lorna was coming slowly down the stairs carrying her baby daughter whom she had named after their mother. *She was lucky,* thought Mariana, *she had a free choice!*

"Mariana, what the hell are you doing here?" she asked. "Where's Terry?"

You too, thought Mariana. *Is that all any of you can say?*

"He's thrown me out," she replied, "and Dani."

60

"He's *what?* He can't!" her sister cried.

"No; it wasn't part of the deal, was it," replied Mariana pointedly. "Well, he's welched on your little arrangement, so here we are!"

"He told you," said Lorna in a small whisper. "After everything I gave him, he told you. I can't believe it."

"Well, you'd better believe it! How the hell do you think I felt when I found out? He's taken my post office book too, and I have less than twenty pounds to my name." Mariana's anger gathered momentum. "How could you? How could you give my inheritance away without even asking me? What sort of man did you think would agree to a deal like that? What sort of man do you think would need to be bought in order to marry the mother of his child? You must've known he didn't really love me. You knew, and Sue bloody well knew too, because she was sleeping with him behind my back! Well, I'll show you what sort of man he is shall I?" She lifted up her sweater and revealed the bruises on her body – always on her body so that no one would see. Once he had given her a black eye, and on seeing it, became even more angry, confining her to the house until it had healed.

"This is what he does to me. This, and other things you really don't want to know about. If you hadn't done what you did, I wouldn't be in this mess."

"You were pregnant; you were already in a mess." Her sister spoke quietly, but vehemently. "I did what I thought was best. You said you loved him."

"I did; I was a child; but I've bloody well grown up since then I can tell you."

Dani woke, and began to whimper. Mariana lifted her out of the pram. She looked around at the strangers before her and began to wail, and Eleanor immediately joined in.

"She's tired," said Mariana. "I need to get her down for a proper sleep; she's been pushed from pillar to post since six o'clock this morning. She started to mount the stairs.

"Eleanor has your room now Mariana, you can't put her in there. I'm afraid she'll just have to sleep in her pram, and you can have the sofa for tonight. Tomorrow, George will run you in to Billingshurst to catch the train back home. You're just going to have to go home and sort it out with your husband. I can't have you bringing your troubles to my door; I've my family to think of now."

Mariana stared in stunned disbelief. This nightmare couldn't be happening to her. Surely any minute now she would wake up – but wake up when? How far had the nightmare taken her? Where would she go back to if she could? There was no clear answer, only a black void of despair.

After an uncomfortable evening in which the three adults sat in stony silence, no one knowing what to say, and a sleepless night on Lorna's sofa with Dani cradled at her side for comfort; Mariana said goodbye to her sister, knowing it was unlikely she would ever see her again.

"I'm sorry Mariana, but it's the only way. You must sort your life out as best you can. Terry will come round, especially when he reads the letter I shall be writing to him."

"Oh, you're so good at fixing things aren't you Lorna. Well, good luck; and I hope you don't ever need a port in a storm."

She climbed into George's car, and began the long journey home.

FOUR: RACHEL.

Rachel sat on the bench and watched the world go by; the dog walkers, the joggers, and the young mothers with prams. She glanced at her watch. Dan was late, but then he often was. She placed her hand on her stomach, feeling for the swelling that was barely perceptible yet, but in a few months time would be a living, breathing little person. This should be a happy time – isn't that what they called it, the Happy Event? She wondered how he would react when she told him, and she wished she felt more confident about it. He had always been moody and unpredictable; unreliable too. Sometimes she wondered what she saw in him, and then he would smile in that special way, and his handsome face would light up as he drew her into his arms.

"You're my little angel," he would whisper, "and don't you ever forget it."

Rachel was eighteen, and had just finished a secretarial course at the nearby technical college. Her parents kept nagging her to find a job but she knew it was pointless; it wouldn't exactly go down very well when she asked for maternity leave almost immediately. She knew Dan earned good money, and she'd get some benefits when the baby was born. They would manage fine, and they'd move in together and be a proper family.

She pushed back a lock of lifeless bleached-blonde hair. She must get her roots done, she thought; perhaps Dan would give her a few quid if she asked him nicely. She patted the tiny bump again; she wasn't even showing yet at four months for which she was grateful; but once she'd told Dan and had it out with her parents she couldn't wait to show it off to the world.

It was gone eleven now and clearly he wasn't coming. Perhaps she had got mixed up and wasn't supposed to meet him till this evening, or perhaps he'd had to work an extra shift. He drove delivery vans for a living. She had asked him which firm he worked for, but he just said, "I'll show you one day, it's not far," and silenced her with a kiss. He never did show her and she sensed that the subject was closed.

She stood, and made her way home with a heavy heart. She had been all fired up to tell him today, and now it would have to wait at least until tonight. The longer she left it now, the worse it would sound. *Why did you leave it so long to tell me?* she could imagine him saying, and he would be justified; after all, a man has a right to know he's about to become a father.

Her mother was sitting at the kitchen table with a mug of tea in front of her and a cigarette in her hand. The smoke curled in a blue spiral towards the ceiling, which should have been white but was stained yellow from the smoke and the chip fat.

"Back already Rach? I thought you were going to the job centre. Now you're here you can go down to the Co-op and get me a loaf and some milk to save my legs."

Rachel shrugged assent and poured herself a glass of milk, draining the bottle since she was going for more.

"Did you forget to order it then?" she asked her mother.

"Forgot to put the bottles out, that bloody milkman won't leave it unless you do these days. What's got into you anyway, drinking milk?"

"Dunno, just fancied something cold. Shall I get some squash aswell then?" Rachel looked at her mother objectively; she wished she wouldn't smoke, she'd read somewhere it was bad for babies, and her mother was right, she couldn't stand milk, but the same article said to drink it when you're pregnant so she was making the effort. She wanted her baby to be healthy; it would be enough of a problem as it was.

"If you must," her mother replied, stubbing the cigarette out in her saucer. "Run along then, we'll have our lunch in the park today, there might not be many more days as nice as this."

Rachel dropped a kiss on her mother's upturned face; her skin felt surprisingly soft against her lips. She would be forty next year and most of the time looked older; but that was because her hair was always drawn back in a shapeless knot on her neck and she wore those dreadful full-length pinnies that cross over in front and tie round the back. She couldn't remember when she last saw her dressed up, not even at Christmas.

I'm going to be different, she thought, *I won't let myself go just because I have kids.*

They sat on the same bench she had occupied earlier. Her mother handed her a corned beef sandwich.

"Are you sure they didn't have any white Rach?" She eyed the granary bread with distaste. "It's a bit chewy don't you think? Not to mention expensive."

"Only a few pennies more Mum, and it's good for us. I like it better than the white stuff." She munched on her sandwich, secretly agreeing that there was really nothing nicer than soft white sliced bread. She felt a little guilty for lying but it was, after all, in a good cause. "Go yourself next time if you don't like it!"

"Cheeky mare!" retorted her mother amiably. She was still wearing the pinny, with her raincoat over the top although the day was hot and sultry.

Rachel had known Dan for nearly five months now. They met in the Flying Horse one Saturday night in April. She was out with some of the girls from college, and had noticed him propping up the bar alone. He was tall and good-looking, with blonde hair that Rachel immediately realised was dyed like her own He looked considerably older than Rachel and had a self-assured air about him. She brushed by him as she went to the bar for some more drinks and saw a flicker of interest in his lazy blue eyes. Rachel leaned on the bar next to him as she ordered the drinks. She felt his eyes on her, taking in her flared jeans that clung low on her hips and her peasant top that showed off her slender midriff and ample cleavage. As she took the tray of drinks off the bar she turned and smiled at him, lowering her eyes and snaking her hips as she sidled past his stool. She felt his eyes burning into her back as she rejoined her companions.

He was waiting outside as she knew he would be, leaning against a maroon Ford Cortina in the pub car park, smoking a cigarette.

"Catch you up," she told the other girls, and they clattered away down the road in their high heels without question, chattering like sparrows. She walked over to the man; he threw his cigarette down and held out his hand to

66

her. She took it, and he drew her towards him wordlessly, encircling her waist with his arm and kissing her on the lips, his tongue exploring her mouth. She surrendered herself to the kiss; he smelt of beer, tobacco, and aftershave. His body was lean and firm, and as he pressed her to him she felt his erection and pressed her body up against it hungrily.

"What's your name babe?" he asked, his voice hoarse and low.

"Rachel; what's yours?"

"Dan, my name's Dan," he said. "Can I give you a lift?"

Rachel climbed into the passenger seat next to him and they drove a short way in silence, his hand resting lightly on her inner thigh. She watched his profile as he drove one-handed down the narrow winding streets and out of town towards the wood-fringed park near her home. He stopped the car in a secluded spot on the far side of the park and took her in his arms. They made love on the front seat, not bothering to move to the back of the car; Rachel barely felt the handbrake grazing her backbone or the metal window-winder pressing against her head. He was practised and slick, he knew how to press all the right buttons and they climaxed together with a searing intensity that left her sated and breathless.

"Wow!" he said, as they scrambled back into their clothes, "You're quite something!" He kissed her tenderly now, his lips soft, his eyes shining in the light of the street lamp across the road that filtered through the steamed-up windows of the car. He sat back, his arm across her shoulder.

"Smoke?" he asked, taking out a cigarette and then offering the packet to her – Benson and Hedges, she noticed – expensive; *he must have a decent job,* she thought.

He opened a window and they smoked their cigarettes silently for a minute or two.

"Where d'you live?" he asked. "I haven't forgotten about the lift." He flashed her a cheeky grin.

"Just over there," she indicated the street of terraced houses on the opposite side of the park. "I often walk in here, I like watching the people."

"People watching eh? I like doing that too!" he exclaimed. "Well, Rachel whatever-your-name-is, I could meet you there if you like one day next week, and we'll watch them together."

"I'd like that," she replied, smiling at him. The thought had crossed her mind that this might be a one night stand, but she really wanted to see him again, and was relieved that he felt the same.

"How about Tuesday evening? I'll meet you on the bench by the pond at seven."

"Ok, I'll be there," Rachel smiled at him. "Seven it is."

He turned on the engine and drove around to the other side of the park to her street, where he dropped her off, waiting until she had put her key in the door before driving away.

On Tuesday Rachel was already sitting on the bench by half past six. She watched an elderly man with a small boy feed the ducks that had gathered pushing and squabbling, at the water's edge. The little boy squealed with delight as they devoured chunks of soggy bread, and the pigeons swooped down to glean the crumbs that had fallen onto the path. His granddad showed him how to throw the bread so that it landed in the water and not on the grassy bank,

"We don't want them choking now do we," he said, and the little boy hurled his bread with renewed vigour until the bag was empty. Then Grandad heaved him up onto his shoulders and they set off along the path towards the gate. Rachel remembered doing the same thing with her father many years ago, before he lost interest in everything but the Racing Post and a can of McEwans Export.

Dan had said seven, but it was nearly half past before he came loping across the park, and Rachel was just about to give up and go home. There was a chill in the air as darkness approached, and she shivered in her thin v-necked sweater and wished she had brought a coat.

"I thought you weren't coming," she said reproachfully.

"Don't be daft, I just finished work late, that's all," he said, and silenced her with a kiss. "C'mon, lets go for a walk." He put his arm around her as they strolled along the path that led past the pond.

"Where is it you work?" she asked him.

"I drive delivery vans for a firm the other side of town. I never know what hours I'll be doing; depends how far I have to go and if there's any hold ups on the road. Sometimes I do overnighters. How about you my Angel?" She smiled to herself at the endearment. She was no angel, and no one had ever called her one before!

"I'm at college doing a secretarial course; I'll be finished this summer then I can try for some jobs." She looked up at him, "Doesn't sound very exciting does it?" she said.

"Oh, it might be; you never know what job you might get. You might end up working for some rich tycoon who'll fall madly in love with you and buy you a big house in the country or something." He flashed her a grin. "If you worked for me though, nothing would ever get done!" He pulled her to him and kissed her long and hard. She responded eagerly and they moved behind some bushes where he threw his jacket on the ground and laid her on it.

"What if someone comes?" she asked nervously; she felt very exposed as he removed her jeans and unzipped his.

"No-one's going to come except you and me," he laughed. "And if they do, well, who cares. Don't you want me Angel?" he lowered his body onto her and pushed his warm erection against her thigh, straddling her with his arms. She had little choice but to go along with it, straining her ears anxiously for the sound of footsteps and faking a climax. He didn't seem to notice, to her relief.

After that, they met two, sometimes three times a week, always at the same place, mainly in the evening, but also occasionally on a Saturday morning. He would take her for a drink, or a walk, and they would have sex in his car or in some semi-secluded place, but he never took her home to his place, no matter how many hints she dropped. He didn't refuse outright, he merely dodged the issue with vague promises.

"I'm having some work done there," he said, "it's a mess, and not good enough for you, my angel. When it's finished you can come and stay if you like." That satisfied her for a while, but after weeks went by and he didn't offer to take her there, she asked again when they were in the back of the car.

"Is it nearly finished? It would be lovely to sleep with you and spend all night in your arms instead of having to go home," she said eagerly, "I don't care if it's not perfect – go on Dan, please!" she cajoled, kissing his face and brushing her bare breasts against his chest persuasively.

He narrowed his eyes and looked at her coldly. "Don't keep fuckin' asking you silly bitch, I'll tell you when it's done," he said through clenched teeth, and she recoiled in shock, watching him struggle to control his anger.

"I'm sorry," she heard herself say, "I didn't mean to push you, I just can't wait till we can be together properly."

"Well, don't ask again, we go there when I say, ok?" his eyes softened again but he pushed her head down roughly "Now, show me how sorry you are Angel," he said.

That night, alone in her bed at home she remembered the look on his face, the tone of his voice, and the half hour or so she spent afterward placating him, feeling used and worthless as he lay there not touching her. She buried her face in her pillow and cried herself to sleep.

She sat on the bench now with nothing to do but remember the good times and the bad. With a shock, she realised that the former was fast being over-run by the latter. She glanced at her watch; he was almost an hour late – even Dan normally kept better time than this. She would give him another five minutes until eight o'clock then give up. It was a beautiful sunny evening, with a slight breeze that was welcome after the intense heat of the day. The park thronged with happy people and Rachel suddenly felt alone and scared. How would he take the news of the baby? Somehow she thought he would be less than chuffed. What if he didn't want to know; what if he dumped her? Panic welled up through her and settled like a lump of lead in her throat. What had she done? She had believed he loved her, but now she wasn't so sure.

Dan was her ticket out of the claustrophobic terraced house where you couldn't break wind without everyone knowing. The house where her father sat in front of the telly every night wordlessly with a can or two of beer, and her mother sat in the kitchen in her pinny with a cigarette and a cup of tea, having tucked her two youngest children up in their beds – Johnny and Jimmy, the twins who had come along unexpectedly when Rachel was already a teenager. They were nearly six now; loud and boisterous, constantly demanding attention, constantly going AWOL so that Rachel would be sent to search for them. She would sometimes search for an hour or more before returning home to find that they had been there all along, hiding somewhere just so that she would have to waste her time looking for them. She supposed she loved them; but they were a constant thorn in her side, and she couldn't wait to escape and have her own place. Dan was the key, but she was beginning to wonder if he was tired of her, and the thought terrified her. If only he would give her the chance to show what a good homemaker she could be.

Since realizing she was pregnant she had begun to assemble a bottom drawer with pretty things she had found in the sale at Woolworths; some porcelain candlesticks, two mugs with heart-shaped handles that bore the words *His* and *Hers*, a soft ivory coloured waffle blanket bound with satin ribbon, and other little luxuries, including her pride and joy, a large poster of The Kiss by Gustave Klimt, that she had bought from Athena on an outing to Chester one day. When she felt low, she would take everything out of the drawer and arrange them on her bed, dreaming of how they would look in Dan's splendid house that must surely now be almost finished.

It was now eight-fifteen and with a heavy heart she rose and made her way home. She would return on Tuesday and hope he kept their regular rendezvous. She tried not to think about the alternative, because she knew that if he chose to avoid her, she had no way of finding him.

She couldn't face going home just yet. Perhaps she had got the place wrong, as well as the time. Perhaps she was supposed to meet him at the pub. She wandered across town to the Flying Horse and sat in a corner for half an hour nursing half a lager, but there was no sign of him and she felt uncomfortable sitting there alone. A man approached her, leering at her lecherously.

"Hello Darlin'," he said, leaning towards her with beery breath. "You waitin' for somethin'? I got somethin' here for a pretty little thing like you." He made an obscene gesture.

"I'm waiting for my boyfriend," she said, feeling the colour rush to her face. "I must've got the wrong pub." She rose from her seat and pushed past him, hurrying out of the door to the sound of derisory laughter behind her. Choking back the tears and the panic that threatened to overwhelm her, she made her way home, constantly scanning the streets for a glimpse of the maroon Cortina. At home she lay on her bed and the full implications of her predicament flooded her mind. She was pregnant and she had been dumped, end of story. The house was quiet; Saturday night was her mother's bingo night, and the twins were spending the night with their grandmother as always. Her father would have gone from the betting shop to the pub, and before she met Dan she would have been out with her friends. Once or twice she and Dan had come back to the house and made use of her little single bed, so if he wanted to find her he knew where and when to come. She began to invent reasons for his standing her up. He might be ill, or his car might have broken down – she didn't really know how far away he lived, but as he was always in the car she assumed it was some distance. If only she had pressed him for more information instead of believing that he would reveal all in good time. By the time her mother came home from bingo she had convinced herself that there was nothing amiss. Dan had been unavoidably detained (she had read that somewhere) and he would be there as usual at their meeting place on Tuesday evening.

"You're home early Rach," her mother observed, hanging her coat up behind the kitchen door. She sat down at the kitchen table and lit a cigarette. "Have you fallen out with your new friend?" Her mother always referred to her boyfriends as her friends; Rachel found it endearing. She had mentioned Dan, but not that he was so much older. She had reported on their evenings at the cinema and their meals at the Indian restaurant or nights playing darts at the pub – all fictitious, of course – they would have a drink, then find somewhere to have sex, and that was it.

"No Mum; he's not well, so he couldn't come out tonight."

"Oh, that's a shame! Still, best he doesn't pass his germs on. When are we going to meet him then? You've been seeing him for a while now haven't you?"

"I told you Mum, he's really shy, but I'm sure you'll get to meet him soon." Rachel gave her mother a hug, smiling to herself at the image of a shy and retiring Dan turning up at the door with flowers for her mother and sitting down to supper with her father who would have to keep his shirt on for once. Then she had a brainwave,

"I'll invite him over at Christmas," she said, "if you'll promise to take that pinny off, Mum!"

Her mother laughed, "I'll think about it, you minx, but that's four months away, he'll probably be long gone by then!"

"Thanks Mum, that's charming! Nice to see you have confidence in me!" she made a moue, feigning offence, and they laughed together; but deep down, she had a sneaking suspicion that her mother was probably right.

FIVE: DANI.

Dani was just four years old and Mariana only twenty when tragedy struck. Gemma, one of Dani's little friends from playgroup, was having a birthday party. It was Dani's first party, and Mariana had bought her a new dress for the occasion.

Terry wasn't happy. "I can't believe you wasted my money on a bloody stupid frock!" he berated Mariana. "She's got perfectly good clothes she could have worn."

Mariana wasn't budging, "They're all wearing party dresses," she insisted. "Anyway, she'll probably go to lots more parties, so she can wear it again, and I can let the hem down when it gets too small. Look how sweet she looks Daddy."

Terry glanced at his daughter disinterestedly and said, "Well, if you're going to a bloody party, I'm going to the pub; don't wait up!" and left the house, slamming the door behind him. Mariana felt the tears pricking at her eyes and blinked them back; she mustn't let Dani see she was upset.

"Why is Daddy grumpy?" asked the little girl, looking anxiously at her mother with her big blue eyes.

"He's not grumpy sweetheart, he's just a bit tired. He'll be fine tomorrow and you can tell him all about the party then." Dani cheered up, but later, as the party got under way, Mariana thought she was a little quiet, not eating very much party food or joining in with the games after they had finished the birthday tea.

"I feel sick Mummy," she said, the tears welling in her eyes.

"I'm sorry Sarah, I think I'd better take her home," said Mariana, feeling her daughter's head and finding it a little too warm for her liking.

"Oh, that's a shame! I hope she's not coming down with something," said Gemma's mum anxiously.

"Nothing a good night's sleep won't put right I'm sure," said Mariana. "She's been so excited and I think it's all been a bit much for her." They walked the short distance home, and within half an hour Mariana had tucked her daughter up in bed, the party frock hung where she could see it.

"I'm hot Mummy," she complained, shivering nevertheless, "and my head hurts."

Mariana held her hand comfortingly. "Your hands are awfully cold," she said, tucking them under the covers gently. "Try and go to sleep; you'll be better in the morning."

Dani got worse however, crying and being sick. *Where was Terry?* Mariana wondered. It was now after eleven and he still wasn't home. The pub would be shut now, and he'd been in there since it opened up. He must have gone on somewhere afterwards she supposed. Should she risk leaving Dani alone and run down to the phone box on the corner to ring the doctor? She would wait a little longer, surely he'd be home soon, and she couldn't leave her daughter in her distressed state, even for a few minutes.

At last Dani drifted off to sleep, her breathing shallow and fast. Mariana looked down at her pale face and the dark curls clinging to her forehead. *Poor little thing,* she thought. *Fancy being unwell at your first ever party. I'll have to try and make it up to her when she's feeling better.* Wearily, she made her way downstairs and put the kettle on. Tomorrow was Sunday so perhaps they could all go out somewhere together for once, even if it was only down to the park to feed the ducks. She sat down on the sofa with her cup of tea and before she knew it she had drifted off to sleep.

She was woken by the sound of Dani crying again; a long, mournful wail that galvanised her into action, taking the stairs two at a time.

Dani was burning up with fever, and she had been sick on her bedclothes and all down her favourite pink nightie, the one with little yellow ducklings on.

"Mummy, it hurts," she wailed.

"What hurts my darling?" Mariana asked anxiously. She had never seen her daughter like this; in spite of the fever she looked deathly pale.

"My legs hurt, and my head; Mummy make it stop," Dani pleaded, and Mariana's heart ached because she didn't know how.

"Come on," she said gently. "Let's get this yucky old nightie off and I'll find you a nice clean one; and then you can sleep in Mummy's bed."

"Where's Daddy?" Dani sobbed as she raised her arms so that Mariana could slip the soiled nightie over her head.

"Oh, don't worry; he'll be home soon – Dani, what's that?" she said, frowning as she pulled the nightie off and noticed purply red spots all over Dani's body. "Lean forward Sweetheart; let Mummy see your back." Her back, too, was covered in the same rash.

"No wonder you don't feel well; you must have measles or something. Mummy will get the doctor in the morning. She transferred Dani to her bed. "Daddy will have to sleep in your room when he comes home." *If he comes home, she thought.*

She lay down beside her daughter and stared into the darkness. Dani was sleeping soundly again now and Mariana felt sure the worst was over, and in the morning she would be her bright, happy self again.

When Mariana woke again it was morning. She glanced at the alarm clock by the bed; eight-thirty – she and Dani had slept all night. She slipped quietly out of bed so as not to disturb her and padded to the bathroom. She glanced in the mirror, grimacing at the sight of her face that was ravaged by anxiety and lack of sleep. Downstairs, she made herself a coffee and took it through to the living room. *Where the hell was Terry?* He had never stayed out all night before and she was beginning to feel worried rather than angry. *What if something had happened to him?* When Dani started school she would get a job; and then they would be able to afford to get a phone in.

She heard his key turn in the lock and he came through the front door, banging it shut behind him.

"Ssssssh! You'll wake Dani!" Mariana told him angrily. "Where the hell have you been?"

"Nowhere; just out," he replied curtly and began to climb the stairs.

"Dani's asleep in our room," said Mariana, coming to the bottom of the stairs. "I had a terrible night with her; she wasn't well at the party, but she's sleeping now."

"Huh!" retorted Terry. "Told you it was a waste of money didn't I? So she didn't even enjoy the bloody party then; after all that fuss!"

"She couldn't help being ill, could she? She was worried about you Terry, slamming out of the house like that. I think that's what made it worse. Go and give her a kiss so she knows you're back; but try not to wake her up properly, she's hardly slept."

Terry went quietly into the bedroom and Mariana returned to the living room. She would question him again later; right now Dani was her main concern.

"Mariana!" Terry yelled from the bedroom. "Oh, my God! Mariana!" She leaped up – whatever was the matter? She stood at the bottom of the stairs looking up. He was standing on the landing now with Dani cradled in his arms. She looked strange, her head flopping backwards, her arms dangling limply – lifelessly!

"Oh, God no! No, no, no!" Mariana heard herself scream, the sound echoing in her head as though it came from somewhere else; and then she fainted.

Dani died of meningitis; the findings of the post mortem were conclusive. On a grey day in October and a week before her own birthday, Mariana laid her daughter to rest in the vast cemetery at the far end of the park; watching silent and numb as the little coffin disappeared from sight into the cold and lonely ground. For a while afterwards, she and Terry became united in their grief, and she refused Lorna's offer of a short break down in Sussex after the funeral. After more than three years of no contact she had telephoned her to tell her of Dani's death, and her sister had been full of remorse for abandoning her and turned up on the morning of the funeral to pay her respects.

"Mariana," she said. "I'm so sorry for turning you away that day. I just couldn't face anything destroying my life again, and since you had a child, I thought it was better for you to have a bad husband than none at all. It's different now that you only have yourself to think of; he has no hold on you any more. Come and stay for a few days, just while you think things through. I'll take Ellie in with George and

I, and you can have her room until you get sorted. You have options now Mariana, and you need to look after yourself."

"I'll be ok," Mariana insisted. "Terry and I need to be together right now. They've offered him time off work, but he won't take it.

"I can't tell you what to do, but this would be a good time to leave, Mariana. You'd be fine on your own, and if you divorce him, you'll at least get half the house. Think about it."

"I will, but I can't leave him right now; she was his daughter too remember. I can't add to his grief, it wouldn't be fair. Maybe this is the wake-up call he needs; I have to give him a chance."

Lorna sighed. "I'm sorry you see it that way, I was hoping at least some good could come of this. You must love him, I suppose, but I'll never for the life of me understand why. Goodbye Mariana; but if you ever need me, you know where I am."

Mariana hugged her sister, and watched her leave, biting back the tears. She knew she would never ask her for help again. In spite of the apology, she would never feel able to trust her.

SIX: THE BIRTH.

The weeks passed and there was no sign of Dan. Luckily Rachel carried her pregnancy well, and by six months was barely showing. She decided to take a job on the local industrial estate in an electronic components factory where she could work shifts thus avoiding her parents, and also where she would be obliged to wear a shapeless overall that conveniently hid her burgeoning waistline. She had made up her mind to tell her parents at Christmas, when everyone was full of festive spirit and kindness, and hopefully she might be forgiven.

The factory bus, which served the entire industrial estate, would drop her off by the entrance to the park, and she would take the shortcut home past the duck pond and the funny green folly where she and Dan had spent many a passion-filled hour.

One morning in late October as she made her way home from a night shift, she saw flashing blue lights on the other side of the park. They appeared to be in her street, and as she rounded the corner she realised with a jolt that an ambulance was parked outside her house. She broke into a run, and as she neared the ambulance she saw two men carrying a stretcher out of her front door, followed by her white-faced and anxious mother.

"Mum, what's happened?" Rachel put an arm around her mother's shoulders. Her father lay on the stretcher, his face deathly pale, a tube attached to his arm and an oxygen mask covering his face.

"It's your Dad, Rach. He's had a heart attack," and her mother began to weep. "It's a bad one. They had to put those paddle things on him; I thought he was a goner."

The stretcher had been loaded into the ambulance.

"Go with him, Mum; I'll see to the twins, " said Rachel, and watched as the men helped her up the steps into the ambulance which then drove off at speed, blue lights flashing and siren blaring, ripping apart the early morning air.

Her father was in hospital for two weeks. They said there was little they could do for him except ensure that he had complete rest with no worry or undue excitement, either of which could trigger another, probably fatal, attack. Rachel knew she must keep her pregnancy a secret now at all costs, for it would certainly be upsetting enough to cause her father's death. If only she could find Dan; but it was an impossible task. She spent hours combing the streets searching for his car. Every now and then, she would see a maroon car and her heart would somersault and her knees go weak, but it was never his. She checked the pubs where they used to drink; the Flying Horse and the White Lion, but he was never there, and nobody seemed to know him which wasn't really that surprising, since he had been alone when she first met him. She pored over the Yellow Pages, searching for local delivery firms. There were several, but when she phoned them, only one had someone named Dan working for them, and after sending her pulse into overdrive, he turned out to be a man in his fifties.

It wasn't too difficult to keep her expanding girth hidden. No one questioned it when she ditched her tight jeans and skimpy tops for flowing kaftans and maxi dresses, no one cared. The money she earned at the factory enabled her to buy some new things; it might have been different had she needed to ask for the money. She bought a maxi coat too, that covered a multitude of sins – or at least it covered her sins!

She formulated a plan. She knew she wouldn't be able to keep this baby. She searched around for somewhere she could safely give birth when the time came without being seen, and bought a book on childbirth so that she would be prepared. She also bought a large hold-all bag that she could leave the baby in somewhere he or she would be found quickly. She bought some baby clothes, and hid them in her bottom drawer together with a small pack of disposable nappies, some baby milk powder, and two bottles. She knew she must think of everything and have it all ready, because it was going to be traumatic enough giving birth alone and she might lose her nerve if everything wasn't organized and planned. She prayed every night that nothing would go wrong, and that she could do this thing all alone. She prayed, too, that someone kind and sensible would find her baby and take it to the hospital. She prayed that that it would be looked after, and most of all loved. In the side pocket of the bag, she put a pack of floral patterned notelets and a pen – she would know what to write when the time came.

By Christmas she had everything ready, and the bag was packed and hidden away in the bottom of her wardrobe. Christmas was a somewhat frugal affair; but Rachel chipped in for bicycles for the twins, and enveloped in her factory overall, helped her mother cook the dinner. Her father was still unable to work, and her mother now had a cleaning job at an office complex in town, working five afternoons a week. Her parents had become closer since the heart attack and now sat together in the evenings watching television, although her mother still wore the pinny, and still went to bingo every Saturday night. Rachel worked extra shifts when she could; preferring earlies so that she could rest in the afternoons and resume her search for Dan in the evenings. If only she could find him, she thought, there was still time for them to become a family and she wouldn't have to give her baby away. Often she cried herself to sleep at the thought of parting with it; but she had no choice, not without Dan.

It began on the last Saturday in January. Rachel had worked an early shift that morning and had spent the afternoon sleeping. Her mother called up to her as she left for her bingo session,

"I've left you some tea Rach. Check on your Dad before you go out will you?"

"Ok," she answered. "See you later." She heard the front door close and peered through the net curtain to watch her mother hurrying down the street with the twins in tow. She padded to the bathroom; she had a pain in her back, but then she had had a few lately and it had come to nothing, so she wasn't unduly worried. She splashed her face with cold water and wondered whether to go down town again to look for Dan. Suddenly she felt something trickling, and then gushing, down her legs onto the bathroom floor. Panic flooded over her, and she felt sick as she realised that her waters had broken. This was it! Whatever happened now was up to her; there was nobody to help her, and she must stick to her plan and pray that there were no complications. She mopped at the lino with a towel and stuffed it in the bottom of the wash-basket – she would have to deal with it before her mother saw it on Monday morning. She took a clean towel from the airing

84

cupboard on the landing to replace it with, then quickly dressed in warm clothes.

The bag felt heavy and cumbersome as she lugged it down the stairs trying not to make any noise. She deposited it by the back door. Another pain assaulted her, doubling her over with its intensity. She was scared now; sick with fear in fact. She longed to tell her father what was happening and beg for his help and his forgiveness, but she knew she had to face this alone, and thanked her lucky stars that it had at least begun at probably the most convenient time, rather than at work, or when everyone was at home. She waited for the wave of pain to subside before popping her head around the living room door. Her father was sitting there in his dressing gown watching the sports results, his Pools coupon in his hand. He no longer went to the betting office, but allowed himself a couple of lines on the football pools each week.

"I'll see you Dad," she said, forcing herself to sound cheerful. "Tell Mum not to wait up for me; I'm going to a party with the girls from work, and I'll probably stay over."

"Oh, ok, have a nice time then," her father answered. "Don't you want your tea then?"

"No, we're having food there; you can eat mine if you like."

"I might do that, better not to waste it eh. Bye love."

Rachel blew him a kiss from the doorway and then closed the door as another pain gripped her. *I must start timing them,* she thought. She waited for the pain to subside again; then picking up the heavy bag and a torch from the hallstand, she left through the back door and down the ginnel at the back of the house so that her father wouldn't see her from the front room window. It was a dry, cold evening; the moon and stars were already out even though it wasn't yet dark. She shivered with cold and fear, and

85

drew her coat around her. She must reach the folly before the pain got too bad. Her heart pounding, she hurried across the road and into the park. Another pain hit her and she sank onto a bench near the entrance, taking deep breaths as her book had instructed her to do and riding out the contraction. An elderly man walked by with a small white dog on a lead. He eyed her with consternation,

"Are you alright, Miss?" he asked tentatively. Rachel looked at his kindly face; at the little dog that was laughing up at her and wagging its tail; and wished with all her heart that she could tell them what was happening to her. They would help her she knew, and she would have her baby in a warm hospital with doctors and midwives; not in the cold folly with only a book and her own wits to guide her through whatever lay ahead.

"It's just a stitch thank you," she replied politely but firmly. "I'll be ok when I've sat for a minute."

The man and dog went on their way and as she watched them disappear around a bend in the path, the tears began to course down her face. *Oh, Dan! Where are you? Why have you left me to do this alone?* She searched the sky with its twinkling stars for answers, and found none. It was almost dark now and her breath formed white clouds on the icy air. She grasped the handles of the bag and made her way towards the folly at the far end of the park.

Two more stops later she reached the folly and was relieved to find it empty. She put the heavy bag on the bench and rummaged in it for the things she needed. The pains were becoming more frequent now and gradually intensifying. Each time she thought she could bear no worse, the next wave proved her wrong. She told herself that, right now, there would be hundreds, no thousands, of women all over the world going through the very same process as she was. She reminded herself of a documentary she had seen recently where young girls in an African tribe gave birth in some secluded part of the bush soundlessly and without any help. *If they can do it, I can do it,* she told herself adamantly. She carefully laid the soft ivory blanket on a section of the bench together with the baby clothes and a nappy. From a plastic carrier bag she took two small towels, a face cloth, and a bottle of the water that she had boiled the previous day. Every two or three days for the past two weeks she had replaced the water in the bottle with a fresh supply. A small pair of scissors, a ribbon, and two plastic clothes pegs completed her makeshift obstetric kit. Finally, as a fresh wave of pain washed over her and she knew instinctively her time was near, she took a plaid travel rug from the bottom of the bag and laid it on the concrete floor of the folly as far away from the draught of the doorway as she could. She took off her tights and knickers and lay down on the rug. The pains now were coming so fast there was barely any time between them. The pain was excruciating; Rachel bit down on a towel to stop herself from crying out. At this time of night there was unlikely to be anyone down this end of the park, but you never know, and she couldn't risk being discovered now. Suddenly a tide of pain overwhelmed her and she almost fainted. She felt an urgent need to bear down. She tried to remember what it said in the book. She pushed herself up to sit against the wall of the folly, and felt between her legs. There was something there; it must be the baby's head. She grasped it gently in her hands and as the next wave of pain washed over her she bore down with all her strength and felt the head move into her outstretched hands. One more push and she was holding her baby. She began to sob with relief as she lifted the baby and laid it down on her stomach. She wrapped the towel around and rubbed the baby gently until it began to cry. She shone the torch under the towel – a little boy! She began to laugh and cry simultaneously – he was perfect!

"Hello you," she whispered. "I'm going to call you Daniel after your daddy." A teardrop fell onto his face and he grimaced comically. She counted his little fingers and toes, gently drying them with the soft towel. She cuddled her son and he grasped her finger with his tiny hand. She took the clothes pegs and clipped one to the cord near to where it was attached to the baby. The other one she clipped on further down. Summoning all her courage, she took the scissors and cut through the cord between the two clothes pegs. Kneeling on the blanket, she dampened the face cloth with water and carefully washed the baby and dried him and tied the ribbon around the cord by the clothes peg, just to be sure. Then she put on his nappy and the little outfit. He was so tiny; he felt so fragile as she maneouvred his little arms into the sleeves of the babygro, pulling it down over his nappy and tucking his toes into the feet. It looked enormous on him and she wondered what he weighed. She put the warm cardigan over the top and with trembling fingers fastened the tiny buttons. Then she wrapped him snugly in the ivory blanket and placed him in the hold-all bag. Another painful cramp washed over her, and she felt the afterbirth slide out between her legs. She put it into a plastic bag and, wetting the flannel again, washed herself down and dried herself with the other towel. She put the flannel and the towels into the plastic bag, then folded the tartan travel rug so that the clean side faced outwards and placed it on the bench. She felt completely drained and exhausted, but elated too – she had done it! Everything appeared to be alright, and little Daniel no worse for his somewhat ignominious birth. Her planning had paid off and now she must wait until morning. She couldn't see her watch; the moon was high in

88

the sky and she thought it must be after midnight. She sat on the blanket on the bench and drew her coat around her, feeling the cold acutely again now that the adrenalin rush was over. She reached into the bag, lifted her son in his blanket and cradled him in her arms. He was sleeping peacefully. She wondered if she should try to feed him. Her breasts felt full of milk, but he looked content, and the thought of taking her jumper off when the grass outside was turning white before her eyes made her decide to wait and see if he was hungry.

She didn't want to put Daniel down; this was the only time she was going to spend with him; the only time she would hold him and cuddle him and breathe in his delicious warm baby smell. Her eyes felt heavy, and she realised that however hard she tried, she could no longer keep awake. Reluctantly, she tucked him up in his bag again; she couldn't risk falling asleep and dropping him. She curled up on the blanket on the narrow bench, tucked her knees up and pulled her coat around her ice-cold legs. Before she knew it, she was sound asleep.

When she woke, dawn had tinted the frozen grass with gold. For a fleeting moment she didn't know where she was; then it all came flooding back and she knew that nothing would ever be the same again. Daniel was waking up too, and he began to whimper, the sound muffled by the half-zipped bag. Now would be the time to feed him, she thought, so that she could leave him knowing he wasn't hungry. The thought of leaving him filled her with dread. How was she going to be able to walk away, not knowing what would become of him? It would be all over the papers, how a newborn baby was abandoned in the park by some heartless cow of a mother. She would have to listen to everyone asking how anyone could do such a thing. She would have to live with the guilt for the rest of her life.

She eased the little bundle out of the bag, and unbuttoning her coat and lifting her jumper, she put him to her breast. He began to suck immediately; it was the strangest sensation, it made her feel warm and happy. She had read that some mothers have trouble breastfeeding their babies, but ironically, she seemed to have no such problem. Daniel sucked greedily making funny little noises, grasping fistfuls of her breast, and pausing every now and then to gaze at her, trying to focus his eyes. She would never have believed it possible to love anything so much. If only she could take him home; if only her father hadn't had a heart attack, if only....

It was seven-thirty, and she knew she had to go before the dog walkers began to arrive. She would hide behind the bushes a short distance away and make sure that someone found him. She took a notelet and wrote a brief note, placing it in the envelope. She had wanted to put a photograph in, just so he would know what she looked like; but that would have meant she would be identified as his mother, and all this would have been in vain. She must summon all her courage, and do what was best; for her dad, and for Daniel, who would surely be given to some desperate childless couple who would care for him far better than she could although they couldn't possibly love him more than she did. She kissed his cheek one more time and closed the zip on the bag halfway to keep out the cold. Weeping silent, bitter tears, she retreated behind the bushes a dozen yards or so away where she could see the entrance to the folly and anyone who went in there.

She crouched down behind the rhododendron bushes, anxiously searching the park for signs of life. Somewhere not far away she heard a dog barking. She was sore and she could feel a slow trickle of blood running down her legs. Her head ached and she felt nauseous and exhausted. All that paled into insignificance however, when she saw a black dog run across from the direction of the duck pond and enter the folly, where he began barking loudly. Rachel heard Daniel begin to cry; the dog must have frightened him. She leapt up, and was about to intervene when a woman came into sight, also running. The woman shouted to the dog, and as she entered the folly the barking stopped. There was silence for a few minutes, and then the woman came out and looked around her. She called out and Rachel had to steel herself to remain in her hiding place – the woman was offering to help "You don't have to do this!" she was calling, her voice echoing on the frosty air.

Oh, but I do, Rachel cried inwardly, wishing she could respond. *You have no idea!* Her stomach was churning with nervousness; it was all she could do to remain in her hiding place. The woman went back inside and reappeared shortly carrying the hold-all. After casting a furtive look around she set off across the grass towards the far entrance of the park with the dog trotting at her heels; passing within inches of Rachel as she crouched behind the bush. With a shock Rachel recognized her as someone she had sometimes seen on the factory bus, although she had never spoken to her. She prayed that the dog wouldn't notice her; but fortunately it had spotted another dog in the distance and ran towards it, barking again, until the woman called it back. Rachel stood and watched them go; the woman was hurrying now, half running, the bag bumping against her legs as she went. Rachel wondered where she was taking Daniel and debated whether to follow her, but decided it was too risky. She was sure she would take him to a hospital, or perhaps the police station – she would know where when the news got out. She was stiff and aching, and very cold. Picking up the travel rug and carrier bag she began to make her slow, painful way home. She deposited them in one of the large waste bins that stood outside the Chinese takeaway at the bottom of her street, pushing them well down beneath the layers of garbage, fighting back the waves of nausea that washed over her. She fumbled with her key in the lock, her mind and her fingers numb now, and silently let herself in. It was just after eight; it was Sunday morning, and her parents would sleep for at least another hour. She longed for a hot bath but it would have woken them, so instead she crawled into bed and pulling the covers over her head, sobbed into her pillow, unimaginable grief tearing at every fibre of her being.

SEVEN: THE RETURN OF TERRY.

Somewhere in the darkness of the house, something was moving. Mariana lay rigid, listening intently, but the elusive sound had stopped. Slowly she began to relax and drift back into sleep.

"Wake up Bitch, I'm back!" Suddenly Terry was standing by the bed staring down at her. "You didn't really think I'd leave you did you?" he sneered, bending down to peer into her face, making her flinch involuntarily. "What the fuck is this?" he indicated the new duvet cover she had bought, then moved to the bottom of the bed, grasping it between his hands and tearing the seam open. "Thought you'd make a few changes did you? Treat yourself. Couldn't wait to be rid of me could you?" His blue eyes glittered in the semi-darkness; there were flecks of foam on his lips and she knew it was going to get worse.

"Been spending the life insurance have you? I knew you would, that's why I cancelled it. That was meant for Dani, not for you. What gave you the right to reinstate it you cold calculating little bitch?"

"I'm sorry Terry, but it's a good job I did, or I'd never manage. You know I don't earn much at the factory." *Why am I apologising? I need to stand up to the bastard, I've done nothing wrong!*

"You might, if you ever went to work. Oh, yes, I know all about your games you evil scheming cow; you and that little tart Kate; lying to me, telling me you're working when you're out whoring in Manchester. Don't think I don't know what goes on; don't think I don't know what you say about me behind my back to that scum you work with, you evil, twisted bitch!"

"I didn't. I don't. You're wrong Terry; I tried to love you; I did love you once, so much; but you made it awfully hard sometimes you know." *I'm doing it again!*

"I made it hard eh? You pathetic little bitch! Love me? Why would you love me? Don't I make your life a bloody misery? Isn't that what you tell everybody? Maybe I've been too soft on you all these years. Yes, that's it; I've been good to you, given you everything, and you throw it all back in my face every chance you get. You're nothing but a fucking spoilt little princess; always whining about not having any friends. Why the fuck would anyone want to be your friend – except that airhead scrubber Kate. She only sticks with you because she feels sorry for you for being such a pathetic, whining little scrote. I mean, look at her; divorced at twenty-two; just goes to show how fucking worthless she is; she's nothing more then scum. You're two of a kind, you and her – worthless scum!"

"Terry please; lets not fight and argue any more. I thought I'd lost you forever. What happened? Where have you been?" *Why don't I just tell him to fuck off?*

"Somewhere you'll never know." He was laughing now; a hollow, mirthless laugh that cut through her and made her shiver involuntarily; leaning towards her, his face close to hers, he smelt of stale sweat and aftershave. "Did you really think I would make do with a pathetic little scrote like you? You're past it Mariana; you don't have what it takes any more. I've been seeing someone else for months, and it's not the first time – where d'you think I was the night you let Dani die? You couldn't even look after our daughter properly you useless bitch."

"Terry, stop it! Where the hell were you then? She kept on asking for you, and you didn't come home until it was too late. Perhaps if you had been there we would have taken her to the hospital, and she'd still be alive!" *That's a little better,* she thought, her anger at his sheer callousness making her bold.

"Where did you think I was? All you thought about was yourself, and spending money on pathetic pink party dresses. You weren't interested in pleasing me any more, so I found someone who was. I've never had any trouble finding women to please me, even before we were married – remember your so-called best friend Sue?" *As if she could forget!* "You were like a kid playing with dolls; you didn't care about me any more. Well, it's easy to make babies; I've done it loads of times. Dani was nothing special – look around you, you'll see me looking back at yo everywhere you go." He leaned over her and regarded her with cold, expressionless eyes.

"One day you'll wake up and realise what you had. Nobody will ever love you like I did Mariana. If only you'd behaved yourself and loved me back as I deserved instead of plotting against me. I'm going now, but I'll be back, just when you least expect it."

"Good. Go; but don't come back Terry. Please just leave me alone." She began to sob now, heavy choking sobs that constricted her throat and stopped her breathing.

She woke up, gasping for air. The room was dark. Her nightdress was clinging to her and a cold sweat stood on her brow and trickled slowly down between her breasts. She turned on the light and sat up, flinging the duvet off, looking for the tear down one side, but there was none. She swung her legs over the side of the bed and sat trembling and chilled in her damp nightdress. The room was empty; she was alone, and it must have been a dream. It was so vivid that it stayed in her mind even with the light on.

She made her way downstairs, but not before checking in the wardrobe, under the bed, and in the bathroom and the spare bedroom. She switched the lights on as she went until the whole house blazed with light and nothing could hide in the shadows. In the living room, she turned on the stereo and put a record on the turntable, then changed her mind and went into the kitchen to put the kettle on. The clock on the kitchen wall said four-thirty, but there was no glimmer of light yet in the sky, only the amber street lights outside the window.

She checked the front and back doors, even though she knew that she never went to bed without locking them securely. Turning on the outside light, she peered through the hammered glass on the front door but nothing moved in the shallow porch. She did the same in the kitchen, peering through the window at the back garden and checking that the gate was shut and tied with rope as it had been ever since Terry died. She scrutinized the shrubs and bushes that lined the path and clambered over the shiplap fencing, but there was no sign of movement. She pulled down the roller blind to shut out the night again and made herself a cup of coffee, strong and sweet.

She sat on the sofa, her legs curled beneath her, sipping at the soothing liquid and reliving the dream. Where did all that come from? Was Terry really unfaithful to her throughout their marriage? She must have thought so somewhere deep in her subconscious. Perhaps her mind had conjured it up to compensate for her own guilt over the night out in Manchester. She would never know if he knew about it, or at least suspected, so her mind had invented a counter-claim against him of infidelity, just to ease her conscience. Ever since they first married, he had had his nights out without her, and sometimes he would stay out all night. He never offered an explanation, and after the first time she questioned him about it and his violent reaction she had learned to ignore it and live with her vague suspicions.

Terry had been gone for two months now but sometimes it still felt like a dream from which she would wake to find everything as it was before. Yes, she had made changes; made the house hers instead of theirs, getting rid of anything he had chosen and she had gone along with for a quiet life, the things that had always given their home a somewhat masculine look. Now it was lighter and more feminine. She had been busy with paint; and the bedroom was now a warm shade of lilac, with a flamboyant feature wall of birds of paradise wallpaper in shades of deep purple and green. She had bought the wallpaper and the rather extravagant matching duvet set in John Lewis in Manchester on an impulse one day, *Just because I can,* she had thought, with a delicious sense of power and freedom. Terry thought anything fancy was a waste of money, and she still remembered with bitterness the row over Dani's party dress that had blighted the little girl's last day on earth.

All these things must have combined in her mind to form the nightmare that she was still having trouble dispelling. Perhaps she had begun somewhere in the recesses of her mind to forgive Terry, or even to think that she may have been somehow to blame. The dream must have been sent to remind her how things were – not all the time it's true, but often enough for her to live her life in constant fear of the next outburst whilst never really knowing what might trigger it. No; even the short periods of hiatus were blighted by insecurity; she would be walking on eggshells, then one day would forget and relax, and would say or do the wrong thing. She had never been a particularly confident girl; after losing her parents and sister so young she was all too conscious that life could be a total bitch, but since marrying Terry her self-worth had taken a massive nose-dive, and now she must gradually find the remnants of it and make it bloom again. Yes, that must be it. The dream had come from her own subconscious to make her fully appreciate what she now had.

Her coffee finished, she made her way back up to bed, determinedly turning off the lights as she went. The bedroom looked serene and welcoming; she had rearranged the furniture so that now the bed was no longer reflected in the dressing table mirror as you opened the door, but placed instead to take advantage of the uninterrupted view over the allotments to the fields beyond. She had painted the dark mahogany headboard, the bedside cabinets, and the dressing table in pale cream, and cream linen curtains now hung at the window in place of the dark brown ones that Terry had favoured because they shut out the light. It was a total transformation and a deliberate move to obliterate the memory of the abuse she had suffered in that room. Now, it was her sanctuary; it had been her first priority, and the rest of the house would soon follow suit.

She climbed into bed and lay back on the soft pillows with a sigh. She wasn't going to let him back into this room; not even in her dreams. She turned out the light; the soft tones of the autumn dawn were filtering through the curtains and casting gentle shadows in the corners of the room. Somewhere on the allotments a cock was crowing, and gentle rain began to beat a rhythm on the windowpane. She snuggled down under the duvet contentedly and fell asleep.

The next day she visited the local animal re-homing centre, and came back with Alfie.

EIGHT: THE FOUNDLING.

It was a bright, cold January morning. Mariana woke to the sound of Alfie being sick.

"Great!" she muttered, leaping out of bed. He was lying on the sheepskin rug by the bed, a pool of green vomit between his paws. *At least,* she thought, *he has the grace to look guilty.*

"Oh, Alfie! You've been eating grass again!" She shooed him out and took the rug into the bathroom, where she managed to rinse out the stain without getting the backing too wet. She hung it over the bath to dry and made her way downstairs to sit in the kitchen with a cup of coffee. Alfie lay stretched out by the back door looking up at her questioningly through beetling brows. She drained the last of her coffee. "Come on you, let's go for a walk."

Alfie leapt up, his tail whizzing round in circles, and pulling his lead down from behind the door he danced across the kitchen whimpering excitedly. Mariana smiled; it was impossible to be down for long with him around. Outside the winter sun was low in the sky and so bright that even the blades of grass threw shadows, and every pebble and tussock took on mountainous dimensions on the face of the lumpy landscape. The grass was encrusted with pearlescent frosting, the trees stiff and sparkling white

100

and completely bare, their intricate skeletons stark against the pale turquoise winter-sun sky, the bark on their boles deeply scored with light and shadow and crows arranged in their branches like Christmas tree decorations. She tucked Alfie's ball into her pocket, drew on her gloves and pulled her scarf up around her ears, walking briskly past the allotments at the back of the house towards the park some half a mile away with Alfie trotting eagerly at her heels, his eyes constantly on the bulge in her pocket that was his ball.

The park was deserted; it was just after seven forty-five, and even the most diehard dog walkers were having a bit of a lie in on this chilly, albeit sunny Sunday morning. She unclipped Alfie's lead and let him run free, his pawprints punctuating the frosty grass as he ran on long spindly shadow-legs, Throwing the ball as hard as she could, she watched him run in circles, disappearing behind the bushes before reappearing and depositing the ball at her feet. With each throw it became increasingly slimy and Mariana was glad she was wearing gloves.

They worked their way across the park, past the partially frozen pond where the ducks huddled together in a corner or wandered dejectedly along the path, transformed by the low sunlight into long-necked shadowy swans. Later, they would throng to the Sunday visitors for food. Mariana thought sadly how she would have been one of those visitors four years ago, when she would bring Dani down three or four times a week, the little girl clutching her bag of bread and biscuit crumbs and giggling delightedly as the feathery mêlée squabbled and pecked about her feet.

"Sorry ducks," said Mariana. "I'll bring you some next time." Alfie made a dash for the ducks, barking excitedly, scattering them in a flurry of raucous quacking. Mariana laughed; she knew he wouldn't hurt them. She smiled inwardly at the sound of her own laughter, a sound that she had heard seldom over the past four years.

At the far side of the park was the Folly; a small round green building with wooden sides, a conical tiled roof, and no door but just a narrow opening at the front. The entire structure lay huddled behind tall rhododendron bushes and inside a bench ran around its circumference. It was a favourite haunt of courting couples in summer, but in the wintertime was normally deserted. As she approached it Alfie ran on ahead and disappeared inside, barking again. *What was the matter with him?* Perhaps some ducks had wandered inside, or even a stray cat seeking shelter from the cold.

"Alfie shut up!" she yelled. His barking reached a crescendo, piercing the frosty air and ringing in her ears. She thought she heard another sound; the thin wail of an animal in distress. Running now, she reached the Folly, gasping for breath, her heart pounding wildly. He must have some poor creature cornered in there.

"Alfie leave!' she yelled as she entered the narrow doorway and stopped dead.

Quiet now, Alfie was standing by the bench, sniffing at a large hold-all that had been left there. The wailing sound was emanating from within the hold-all, and with a chill that had nothing to do with the temperature Mariana realised what it was – the sound of a baby crying. She pushed Alfie aside and opened the partially zipped-up bag. There, wrapped in an ivory blanket, was a tiny baby.

"Oh, my God!" whispered Mariana, and reaching into the bag she gathered the bundle up in her arms and lifted it out. The baby stopped crying instantly and gazed at her with unfocused eyes. It was dressed neatly and cleanly in an all-in-one babygro and a little yellow knitted jacket. In the pocket of the bag she discovered two baby's bottles and a plastic rattle in the shape of a rabbit. At the bottom of the bag she found a tin of SMA milk, a small pack of nappies, and a tiny white teddy. Everything was brand new. Pinned to the blanket was a small envelope; she opened it with trembling hands and read:

'My name is Daniel. I was born last night. My Mummy loves me very much but she can't keep me. Please look after me and love me.'

Mariana stared at the note in astonishment and read it again. Neatly written in a well-formed hand on floral notepaper, it had clearly been part of a plan. Whoever had done this had thought it all through carefully and placed the baby where he was sure to be found. Mariana tucked the little boy back into the bag and ran outside. Perhaps the mother was somewhere about, waiting to see who found him.

She called out. "Hello, are you there? Please come out. I can help you; you don't have to do this." There was no answer, however, and the deserted park held on tightly to its secret. Alfie was lying down in front of the hold-all, clearly on guard. He looked up at Mariana questioningly, his tail thudding slowly on the concrete floor.

Daniel. The baby's name was Daniel! This was too weird! Mariana sat down on the bench, her heart pounding louder than ever. The baby was sleeping again now; sucking greedily at his little fist stuffed into his mouth, his cheeks flushed, wisps of dark hair ruffled against the soft ivory woolen blanket that was edged in shiny satin ribbon. Daniel – Danielle; the names were the same. This was a sign; she was certain of it now. Something had made her walk this way on this morning; it was her destiny to find this baby, and it was her duty to keep it.

She picked up the bag; it was heavy and cumbersome, but she knew she must hurry before people began to arrive to walk their dogs, feed the ducks, and let their children run free. She must get him home before he became hungry and started crying. The bag in itself didn't look particularly suspicious; but if the baby were to cry it would, to say the least, be awkward. She half walked, half ran back along the way she had come, except that she took a direct line across the grass instead of going along the path past the duck pond. A small terrier appeared from behind the bushes, and Alfie ran to play with it, his barking echoing on the icy air.

"Alfie no!" she shouted. He recognized the urgency in her voice and for once came back to heel, where he stayed all the way home. She ran along the path past the allotments, struggling to prevent the bag from bumping against her legs. She noticed with relief that all the neighbouring windows were shrouded in closed curtains; nobody was yet up and about. With shaking hands she unlocked the back door and thrust the bag through into the kitchen, the warmth hitting her in a delicious wave as she opened the door. She closed the door and leaned against it momentarily, her heart pounding, her chest aching and a stabbing pain in her side from running with the heavy bag. Then she knelt and unzipped the bag, reaching in and gently lifting the tiny bundle that she cradled to her chest, feeling an overwhelming avalanche of love. "Dani; oh! Dani!" she whispered. "You came back."

She sat on the sofa with Daniel relaxed in her arms, her mind whirling. It was a miracle. Everything that had occurred in the past few months had led to this, she was sure. If Terry hadn't died; if she hadn't bought Alfie on an impulse visit to the rescue centre; if he hadn't been sick this morning at such an ungodly hour – no, this had happened to her for a reason, and she must act accordingly. She knew that she should call the police, or social services.

Somewhere out there was a woman who had just abandoned her baby, and maybe needed medical attention. She read the note again; it was pretty specific: *'Please look after me and love me,'* it said, not, *'please take me to social services.'* Clearly whoever had left him there was hoping that just such a person as she would come along. Also the fact that everything was so carefully planned and executed, the baby washed and dressed, the basic essentials included, and she had even given him a name, told Mariana that here was a woman who knew her own mind; strong and capable, and clearly able to look after herself. There must have been some overwhelming reason why she decided to give her baby away. A gift; that's what he was, and she would be letting both he and his mother down should she hand him over to strangers. No, her mind was made up; she would keep this gift that was certainly intended for her alone. She gazed at the tiny sleeping baby; he stirred and made little baby noises. He looked just like Dani when she was a baby, the same dark wispy hair, the same little nose and big ears – but then she supposed all babies look pretty much the same. She immediately chided herself for the thought. No, in her heart of hearts she knew without a doubt that this was Dani; that she had come back; that the woman who gave birth to this little boy was aware who he was, and had acted accordingly. She hadn't abandoned her child at all; she had merely returned him to his rightful mother.

The baby stirred and sucked at his fist again, regarded her with his baby blue eyes, then screwed them up and began to make snuffling little cries. Mariana placed him down on the sofa, wedged him safely with some cushions, and went to make up a bottle. As she put boiling water into the bottle and stood it in a bowl of iced water to cool, she reflected on the predicament she was in. Danny would need an awful lot more equipment than he came with, and

105

with no pram or buggy she had no way of going out shopping. She could order things from her catalogue, but they wouldn't come for a couple of days even if she paid extra. No, she was going to need help; and there was only one person she could trust – Kate. She was thankful now that she had shunned the neighbours all the years she and Terry had lived there. He didn't like the idea that she might be discussing their private life with other people, so she had never made any friends except at work, and even there her only close friend was Kate. When Terry died she vowed that things would change, but somehow she never got round to it because the neighbours steadfastly avoided her in the way that people often do when someone is bereaved; even someone they know well, let alone a relative stranger; so she decided that socialising could wait. She doubted if any of them really noticed her at all, which would now work in her favour when she suddenly appeared with a baby seemingly out of the blue. She knew some people went through their entire pregnancy without really showing, and she remembered the scandal of a girl at school who had a baby during the summer holidays when nobody, not even the other girls in her class, suspected she was pregnant. She returned after the holidays as though nothing had happened, having had her baby adopted, but she didn't stay long, hounded out with taunts and name-calling from the girls, and an avalanche of unwanted attention from the boys who thought their luck would be in. Mariana remembered that sometimes she had joined in with the taunting, and looking back now, felt deeply ashamed.

Danny was in full voice now and she hurried to finish making up his bottle. He sucked greedily at it, gazing up at her, his little fingers gripping one of hers tightly. When there were but a few drops remaining, his eyes closed and he stopped sucking, his lips and eyelids making little fluttering motions, his hand flopping down and resting on her knee. It was a shame to disturb him, but she knew she must wind him and gently raised him to a sitting position, where he immediately let out an enormous burp, opened his eyes momentarily, and went back to sleep. *That was easy,* thought Mariana, and chuckled to herself. *This baby was just perfect in every way.* Laying him back down in his cushion nest, she went to phone Kate.

It was less then half an hour later that Kate's brand new Fiesta drew up on the concrete apron by the garage. Mariana still didn't have a car, although Kate never tired of trying to persuade her.

"It's not like you can't afford one M," her friend had insisted, somewhat peevishly. "Whatever the bastard did to you, at least he left you well provided for."

"No, he bloody didn't!" retorted Mariana, when Kate first presented this argument. "After Dani went, (even after all these years, she still could never quite bring herself to use the word 'died' when referring to Dani's departure) he stopped the direct debit for the life insurance. It was just lucky I found the bank statement and managed to persuade the insurers that it was a mistake on the part of the bank. They re-instated the policy and I paid for it from my account from then on. Terry didn't even know he was still insured, and he certainly wouldn't have liked it. That, my dear friend, is the only reason he left me well provided for!"

"What's the panic?" Kate was asking now, using her key to enter. Mariana had simply said to her, "I need you to get over here, pronto," and had rung off with no further explanation. Kate entered the living room, where Mariana sat on the sofa with Danny in her arms.

"Oh, my bloody God! Where did that come from?" Kate stopped in her tracks, staring incredulously at her friend. "Christ M, you haven't nicked a baby have you?"

"Don't be silly, of course I haven't. Someone gave him to me, his name's Danny," replied Mariana, calmly and logically, as though babies got bandied about between mothers all the time.

Kate sat on the arm of the chair opposite. "What d'you mean, gave him to you?" Had her friend completely lost the plot? She was aware that grieving people do strange things sometimes, but this was crazy, and besides, Mariana wasn't grieving *that* much surely.

"Sit down properly, and I'll explain," said Mariana. Kate slithered down onto the seat of the armchair and sat, leaning forward attentively. *This had better be good,* she thought.

Mariana related the morning's events to her friend as accurately as she could, although she may have embroidered slightly the part where she called out to the mother, and added that she searched the bushes in the vicinity to no avail – *well, it wasn't really a lie, more of an exaggeration.* Kate's eyes widened as the tale progressed, and she began to understand exactly what effect this finding must have had on her friend. Mariana handed her the note – the note that proved she wasn't making it all up, and that the child really was named after her lost daughter.

"So you see," she concluded. "This was meant to be; I was meant to find him and I was meant to keep him – it says *'look after him and love him'* and that is exactly what I intend to do." Her eyes challenged Kate to disagree, and Kate knew she couldn't.

"Ok, I understand, but I don't think it's strictly legal to just take on a foundling baby without some sort of red tape to be negotiated," she said gently. "Don't you think people will wonder where he came from?"

"Huh!" snorted Mariana scornfully. "Nobody round here even knows I exist. Why would any of them wonder about anything I did? I could have been pregnant and nobody noticed, especially through the winter months. The only one I worry about is Lorna, and you're going to have to help me out with some ideas there. At the very least she's going to be hurt that I didn't tell her. She'll think I still resent her for what she did all those years ago."

"Well," Kate said thoughtfully. "When I saw you sitting there with him, I honestly thought you'd lost the plot; I mean, grieving people don't always act rationally do they? She will assume your forgetting to mention that you were pregnant was a reaction to losing Terry.

"You're a genius! I won't say anything to her; I'll just pretend I'm scared to admit to having Danny because everyone I love gets taken from me. How does that sound?"

"Pretty plausible I guess, and by the time she finds out about him you'll be used to having him around and it will seem more like he's actually yours anyway. Ok, I'm with you; I don't see I have any choice. What do you want me to do?"

"In a word, take me shopping!" answered Mariana.

"That's three words actually, and I told you you should have got a car. You're going to have to now. Have you any idea what it's like lugging prams and baby stuff on buses? I know lots of people do, but not when they've got gazillions languishing in their bank accounts!"

Mariana laughed, "I haven't got gazillions! I paid off the mortgage remember. In fact, it doesn't seem so much now I'm going to have a baby to bring up. We'll go for lots of walks, me and Danny and Alfie, and you can take us out at

109

weekends in your car. What I will buy is a super duper pram that he'll be safe and comfy in."

"Ok, you win; we'll go shopping tomorrow; I'll ring in sick. What would you do without me eh?"

The next morning they went to Mothercare, with Danny wrapped in his blanket to hide his now less-than clean only outfit. Mariana bought a beautiful Marmet coach built pram; sleek and gleaming, with a cream coloured body and a navy hood and apron. The body could be lifted off the chassis and the chassis then folded so that it fitted in Kate's car. Next, they chose a Moses basket that would fit nicely beside Mariana's bed. It was made of soft woven rush with a broderie anglaise lining and covers to match. They bought clothes and bottles, bedding and nappies, baby toiletries, pram beads and toys, and a sterilising kit. Kate's little car was packed to the gills as they set off back home with all their spoils.

"I've spent an absolute fortune," said Mariana happily, having just written a cheque for what amounted to more than two week's wages. "Thanks Kate, I'd never have managed that lot on the bus!" They placed the pram in the living room and settled little Danny in it, resplendent in a new blue babygro. Mariana made up a bottle for him and Kate fed him, whilst Mariana cleared out one of her drawers for Danny's clothes, and set up the Moses basket on its wooden stand beside her bed. She went into the spare room, and planned how she would turn it into a nursery, with pretty wallpaper and pale carpet, and later on a proper cot and some nursery furniture. Tomorrow, she would tuck Danny up in his pram and walk down to the town for some paint and wallpaper from Woolworths.

110

"Coffee," said Kate, appearing in the doorway with two steaming cups in her hands. "I suppose you'll be wanting my services as a master decorator next."

"I didn't know you were, but if you're offering…."

"Are you going to go all traditional with blue and white, or shall we think of something way out and original?" asked Kate, setting the cups down on the windowsill. "We seem to have a blank canvas, at any rate." The room was painted white, with plain beige carpet and curtains and contained only a single pine bed and a chest of drawers.

"It used to be all pink and pretty, but after Dani had been gone for a year I gutted it and I couldn't really be bothered to do anything with it. Way out and original sounds good to me."

"We'll go and check out that wallpaper shop the other side of town, they'll have more choice than Woolies. I can't take any more time off this week, so it'll have to be the weekend. Talking of work, what are you going to do about it M?"

Mariana shrugged; truth to tell, she couldn't care less. She had only continued at the factory for something to take her mind off things, and she was quite happy to give it up.

"D'you want me to tell them? I'll just say you've had a family crisis or something and you're having to give up work for a few months. You never know, you might want to come back one day."

"Can't see that I will – you're right, I don't really need the money; but I suppose I of all people should know that you never know what life will throw at you, so if you can pass on my apologies…."

"I'll tell them you've had to go to Sussex suddenly; leave it to Auntie Kate."

"Auntie Kate – it suits you!" laughed Mariana.

NINE: LIFE'S A BITCH.

When she awoke Rachel was alone. Seemingly every bone and muscle in her body ached but her baby was gone; she felt a great void where he used to occupy her body and her mind. She glanced at the clock beside her bed. It was after eleven, and her parents would shortly be leaving for her grandmother's house where they and the twins would have Sunday dinner. Thankfully, they had left her to sleep and certainly wouldn't disturb her now. She waited until she heard the front door shut and peeped out through the net curtains to see them walking down the road arm in arm, the twins running to and fro across the street with their football. They looked, she thought, like a Lowry painting as they faded in the distance. She smiled to herself; they spent so much more time together since her father's illness; he spent less time at the betting office and more time with his sons. *It's an ill wind*, she thought. If he hadn't had his heart attack – but there again, if he hadn't, he would have had a grandson too.

She was still wearing her clothes from the night before, and her skirt was sticking to her legs uncomfortably because of the congealed blood that had soaked through her clothes. She put on her dressing gown, and made her way painfully downstairs. A fire blazed merrily in the hearth so there

113

would be plenty of hot water. Her mouth was parched and dry; she made herself a cup of tea and found some Anadin tablets in the kitchen cabinet. She sipped at her tea gratefully, gazing into the dancing flames and wishing that the last twelve hours had been a bad dream. In her mind's eye she saw again the woman hurrying across the frozen park with Daniel in his holdall, the black dog running at her heels. She wondered what she had done with him – was he even now being looked over in the infirmary, or had she called social services and left him in their hands? How would Rachel find out where he had gone? Even when the news broke she would have no way of knowing where he might end up, but at least, she supposed, she would know that he was none the worse for being born in such an unsuitable place.

Panic washed over her – *what had she done?* She had abandoned her child and she would never see him again. She began to cry; tears of regret that stung her already sore eyes and coursed down her cheeks into her mouth mingling with the hot tea and making it taste bitter. She made her way back upstairs and ran a hot bath, pouring in a copious amount of bubble bath. The water was soothing and she lay back savouring the comfort as it seeped into her tired body and washed away the dried blood and mucus. She immersed herself completely, lying under the water and blotting out the world for as long as she could hold her breath. Afterwards she dried herself and sprinkled on talcum powder. There was blood on the towel and on her sheets so she stripped the bed, and dragging the twin-tub out from its home underneath the kitchen units she put a wash on, not forgetting the towel that she had mopped the bathroom floor with what seemed like an eternity ago. Just for good measure she emptied the linen basket – her mother would merely assume she was being helpful. Once

114

she had dried her hair and dressed in clean clothes she felt almost normal, and curled up in front of the fire to wait for the washing machine to obliterate the evidence of her activities the previous night.

By the time her parents returned that afternoon she had restored everything to normal, with fresh sheets on her bed and the wash load drying on the wooden kitchen maid hoisted high above the range. She had thought that her body would return immediately to its former shape, and was surprised to see that she still looked pregnant, her breasts swollen and tender. Never mind, it would give her the opportunity to appear to go on a diet and lose the weight she had put on over the past few months gradually.

"Nice party?" asked her mother, sitting down at the kitchen table and lighting a cigarette. "We didn't hear you come in."

"Oh, you were asleep; I stayed over but I didn't get much sleep."

"What it is to be young," said her mother. "Thanks for doing the washing – I would've changed your bed on Thursday."

"Oh, I took a cuppa up and spilled it all over my sheets, so I thought I'd better run them through the wash," replied Rachel. "I've done all the stuff in the linen basket."

"Oh Rach, you're as bad as the twins! You know I don't like food and drink in the bedrooms; it's a good job it was only the sheets! Are you ok? You look a bit pale. Too much to drink I suppose."

"Oh, I'm just a bit tired still, I think I'll go back to bed for a bit." Rachel dropped a kiss on her mother's upturned face and went back to her room. As she climbed the stairs, she heard her mother talking to her dad in the living room.

"She's got a hangover John; she looks like death warmed up."

She didn't hear her father's reply.

The next morning Rachel woke early after sleeping soundly all night. *I must have been tired,* she thought, with a twinge of guilt because she hadn't lain awake all night thinking of Daniel. She wondered what he was doing now. Would he still be at the hospital, or would he already have been given to foster parents? He was so tiny, but he had seemed to be perfectly healthy, and she was glad that she had been so careful to eat and drink properly during her pregnancy; her son would have enough to deal with without health problems. The letterbox clattered as the morning paper fell through. Would an abandoned baby on the Welsh borders make the national news? Rachel went downstairs and retrieved the paper from the hallway. She quickly leafed through it, but there was nothing. The local paper came out on a Thursday; she may have to be patient until then. She would watch the local news on TV tonight; surely he would get a mention there. She was down for an early shift, but it was already seven o'clock. She'd have to phone them later with some excuse, she didn't want to lose her job, although now perhaps she really could look for something better. She decided to take a few days off; she would say she had the flu or something. In fact, she felt a lot better than she thought she would, except for the pain in her breasts, which were gorged with milk. She retrieved her Pregnancy and Childbirth book from its hiding place on top of her wardrobe and leafing through it, found the section on To Breastfeed or Not to Breastfeed. It stated that she may have considerable pain for a few days and she should wear a good bra day and night which might help, but other than that there was nothing else she could do

116

except take painkillers, so she supposed she would just have to put up with it.

"Rachel!" her mother called up the stairs. "Aren't you going to work today?"

"No Mum; I'm having a couple of days off. I thought I'd go down the job centre later."

"I'm glad to hear it. I knew you'd get fed up with that factory job; you need to use your brains and your qualifications instead of wasting all that time you spent in college. Will you take the twins to school for me?"

"Ok Mum, I'll be ready in a minute." She returned the book to its hiding place, combed her hair and put on her shoes.

Half an hour later she was standing outside the school gates, watching the twins run across the playground towards the door. There were several other mothers standing there too; some with babies in prams. She didn't know any of them since she rarely brought the twins to school, but some of them didn't look much older than her, even though they had two children. She wondered what it would have been like if she and Dan were still together; what it would have been like to have a little family of her own. She also wondered what these women would have thought of her if they knew what she had done, and she didn't somehow think they would understand. She waved to the twins who had turned to check that she was still there before disappearing through the big double doors. She had a terrible secret now that she would carry with her for life; a secret that would forever come between her and anyone she wanted to become friends with, and that would certainly blight any relationship she might have. She hadn't seen her friends much since she started seeing Dan, and she hadn't really got to know any of the girls at the factory

117

because she didn't want them to guess that she was pregnant. Now that she found herself alone with her terrible secret and with no-one to share it with, its burden felt all the greater. *I've ruined my life,* she thought; *Dan has ruined my life.*

Later that day she went down to the job centre, but there was nothing available except shop work or the same sort of shift work she was doing now, and she returned home disheartened. Her mother had always prided herself on her daughter's 'brains'. Rachel enjoyed reading books, not just trashy magazines, and had a passing interest in art and history, gaining good grades in both at school. Art and history don't get you a decent job though, and she had settled for secretarial college instead.

"You get them from my side of the family," her mother would say in reference to her brains.

She returned home through the park and as she approached the folly she felt compelled to go inside. She sat on the bench and relived the birth of her son, remembering every detail in sharp relief. The tears welled up in her eyes again as she recalled each moment of the brief time she had spent with him.

"Oh Daniel," she sobbed out loud to no one, "I'm so sorry. I love you; I'll always love you, and one day I'll get you back." That was it! She would somehow find him and get him back. If it took her the rest of her life; one day she would tell her son how much he meant to her.

She walked home with a heavy heart, but also with a new purpose. As she rounded the corner at the end of her street she saw the ambulance once more parked outside her house, echoing the scene of three months ago. Her mother was standing in the doorway as before and two ambulance men were carrying a stretcher towards the waiting vehicle. She hurried over. The person on the stretcher lay motionless, completely covered with a red blanket. Her mother stumbled to meet her, arms outstretched, tears flowing down her face.

"It's your father Rach. I came home from work and found him. He's gone Rach; he must have had another heart attack; he was just sitting there in front of the fire and his cup of tea all spilt on the floor." She clung to her daughter weeping uncontrollably.

"Will you be alright Miss?" The ambulance driver placed a sympathetic hand on Rachel's shoulder.

She stared at him through a mist of tangled emotions. "Yes, thank you," she said, and led her mother inside as the ambulance drew slowly away.

A few days later at her father's funeral she watched them lower his coffin into the grave, and reflected on the terrible irony of life. She had abandoned her baby son so as not to jeopardise her father's life, and less than thirty-six hours later he had died anyway. It was too late now to undo what she had done, and even in her most determined moments she knew it would be an almost impossible task to find her son now. There had been no report of his finding in the papers or on the news. It was as though he had simply vanished. Her grandmother had come to stay to help with the twins, who didn't really understand what had happened. Rachel had returned to work, hoping to spot the woman whom she had seen taking Daniel; but so far there had been no sign of her on the factory bus, and Rachel even found herself doubting that it was the same woman – somehow it all seemed so distant and indistinct now.

Her milk had dried up and she had begun to squeeze back into her normal clothes; but nobody noticed. A dreadful pall hung over the whole household and Rachel bore her additional grief alone, finding it hard to support her mother and her brothers who had no idea what she was going through. She would lie on her bed and wonder what she had done to deserve such a cruel blow – *why couldn't her father have died two days earlier?* Then she would recoil in horror at her own monstrous thoughts – what was she becoming?

TEN: MOVING ON.

Spring was slow to show its face that year. The weather reflected the mood in Rachel's home – it was sombre, dull, and dreary, the temperature remaining below normal for the time of year. Rachel returned to work at the factory after her father's funeral. She kept searching the bus for the woman who took Daniel; but there was no sign of her. On Sundays she would take a walk in the park hoping to see the woman and her dog; but with no luck. She would sit on the circular bench in the little green folly and reflect on the events of the past few months, and wonder what she could possibly have done to deserve this heartache that at times overwhelmed her and robbed her of the will to live.

The weeks dragged by and she could see no light on the horizon of her humdrum existence. It was now almost exactly a year since she first met Dan. She wished she had never gone to the Flying Horse that night, or at least that she had stayed with her girlfriends and resisted the temptation of the handsome stranger who would later destroy her life. She had no social life any more; she had lost touch with her friends and didn't feel able to make new ones who might ask her questions she couldn't answer without opening the wound left by her parting with Daniel.

She would see groups of girls her own age passing her house going out on the town at weekends, giggling loudly and clattering down the road in their platform shoes. She felt alienated from them; they lived in a world that no longer existed for her. She had grown up the hard way and didn't know how to laugh and have fun any more.

Her mother thought it was all down to the death of her father.

"Rach," she pleaded, "I wish you'd go out with your friends sometimes. Your Dad wouldn't have wanted you to mope around like this. For goodness sakes girl; you're only young once and you should make the most of it while you can – look at you, you're wasting away!"

"I'm ok Mum. I just don't feel like going out much, and I'm tired after my shifts."

"Well, I wish you'd make the effort and get a better job and get your life back. It's not helping me seeing you so miserable you know."

One morning at the beginning of May a notice went up on the factory notice board. There was a job going in the office for a Girl Friday; mainly typing and ledger work to begin with, but after training there would be opportunity for promotion to a marketing or human resources post which would carry a better salary than her factory wage whilst still being essentially nine to five, five days a week. If she could get it, she would escape from the boredom of the assembly line, and her mother, she knew, would be pleased that she was using the skills she had learned at college.

After finishing her shift she went along to reception to pick up an application form. The receptionist smiled encouragingly at her as she rummaged in a drawer for the form. She was a little older than Rachel, with sleek blonde hair and bright red lipstick that matched her perfectly manicured nails. She was dressed smartly in a navy mini skirt and red blouse, and Rachel by comparison felt dowdy in her shapeless factory overall, and at odds with the sumptuous feel of the office area. She took the application form and turned to go.

"What's your name?" asked the receptionist. "Just in case you get the job that is. We'd be working together some of the time."

"I'm Rachel," Rachel replied hesitantly.

"I'm Kate; good luck Rachel; I hope we'll meet again."

Rachel thanked her and left, clutching the form. She hurried down to the bus stand where the bus was just about to pull away. She slipped into a seat near the front and read through the form. It seemed straightforward enough; she would fill it in when she got home and send it back in the post; she didn't want to face Kate again in her overall. The applicants would be shortlisted and invited for interview in a week's time, and the successful one would start on the ninth of June after the Queen's Silver Jubilee celebrations. She decided not to tell her mother in case she didn't get the job – no point in raising her hopes only to have them dashed.

All week she hugged her secret to her. She sorted through her wardrobe for some suitable clothes to wear for an interview. She was, if anything, smaller than before she got pregnant, and everything fitted but nothing looked right. She remembered Kate's simple sophistication and realised that her pre-Daniel style was perhaps more tarty than she cared to admit. If she were to have any chance of getting this job, she would have to go shopping. If she didn't get an interview this time she was now determined to apply for other jobs.

"I'm going down town Mum," she called to her mother as she put on her coat. As she closed the door behind her and set off down the road, Rachel felt her spirits lift a little at the prospect of the new challenge that lay ahead. A blackbird was singing, perched on one of the TV aerials that clung uniformly to the chimneys along the terrace, the crystal notes soaring freely over the rooftops. A plump ginger cat lay stretched out on the wall at the end of the street soaking up the morning sun. She paused to stroke it, and was rewarded with a rumbling purr. The avenue of red May trees between her street and the park was laden with blossom, and through the railings she could see tall red tulips still in bloom, interspersed with multi-coloured Primula and tall, spiky grasses.

She realised that she had been blind to all these things for weeks now; only seeing the dull red brick houses with the smoke rising from their chimneys blighting the air, the chewing-gum speckled pavements, and the ceaseless flow of traffic along the dirty grey streets.

It was a while since Rachel had been shopping; the last time was for baby things from Mothercare. She walked quickly past the big double-fronted shop with its displays of prams and baby clothes in the window, averting her eyes but not avoiding the stab of pain that penetrated her heart. She had to put Daniel behind her for now and get on with her life, so that should she ever find him she could provide a decent home for him. She had run out of options in her search for him, but she would never give up. The woman who took him must surely live nearby, and one day she would find her and ask her what happened to him.

She went into C&A where she bought a pale blue chevron patterned A-line dress with a halter neck, a navy and red tartan mini kilt, and a red short-sleeved skinny-rib jumper for cooler days. Next door to C&A was a Dolcis shoe shop, where she bought a pair of navy suede platform soled shoes – not too high, and comfortable enough to wear all day. Happy with her purchases, she went in search of a hairdressers, and booked a cut and colour for the following Monday afternoon.

When the letter came, she opened it with trembling hands. She had been selected for interview. She was to report to reception at ten a.m. on the following Wednesday, and bring her college diploma with her along with the letter.

Her mother stood at the window and watched her leave. She was wearing her kilt and jumper, and her new shoes, with her tired bleached out hair now coloured rich chestnut brown as nature intended, and cut in a stylish Purdey bob. She turned and waved, then hurried through the park to the bus stop on the far side. She would have to walk from the end of the road to the factory, but if she got the job there was a factory bus that would pick her up at the end of her road and take her all the way there.

She arrived with ten minutes to spare and approached the reception desk. Disappointed to see that Kate wasn't there, she addressed the middle-aged woman in a tweed skirt, a twin set, and horn-rimmed glasses, who took her letter and her diploma from her wordlessly and told her to sit in the waiting room next to reception. There were two other women sitting there already; both older than Rachel. She took her place alongside them feeling sick with nerves. They looked as though they had more experience than she did, and she was beginning to regret her choice of outfit as they were also rather more conservatively dressed; their skirts longer, their shoes

125

flatter. Her confidence evaporated as she sat there sensing their hostility.

A buzzer sounded and a disembodied voice called for the first interviewee, who entered the inner sanctum, reappearing after twenty minutes or so with what Rachel thought was a self-satisfied smirk on her face as she swept past like a yacht in full sail and left without a backward glance. After five minutes or so the second one disappeared in turn. Evidently there were only three candidates, since Rachel now found herself alone. Relieved of the scrutiny of her fellow candidates, Rachel began to feel much better. After all, she was just as capable as they were; and Kate was living proof that you didn't need to be dull and dowdy in order to do your job well, she thought. Just then, as though summoned magically by Rachel's thoughts, Kate popped her head round the door.

"Hello again; I thought you might be here," she said, smiling and giving Rachel the thumbs up. "Best of luck, you look fab!" she said, and winked broadly before disappearing again before the startled Rachel could reply. Glowing with pleasure, she waited her turn with renewed confidence. Evidently she had made a good impression on Kate; so why not whoever was interviewing her? She was properly qualified, and she would just be herself.

The second interviewee emerged from the office a little red-faced, and hurried away. *Didn't go so well then,* thought Rachel. Almost immediately the door opened again and the lady with the horn-rimmed glasses beckoned her inside. There were two interviewers; Horn-rims and a man who looked to be in his thirties with blonde hair and blue eyes; wearing dark trousers, a blue shirt, and a purple tie with white polka dots. He leaned forward in his chair that had his jacket draped over the back of it, and smiled.

"Good morning. Please sit down Rachel." He indicated the chair facing the desk. He exuded sophistication, and she observed that he had used her name without having to refer to his notes.

Rachel sat upright, her knees together, her legs at a slant with her ankles crossed and her hands resting in her lap as she had been taught on her course.

"My name's Michael Fenton. I'm the Chief Executive Officer of this firm; and this lady is Isabelle Brunt, the office supervisor," the man said. He sat back in his chair now, his hands clasped across his chest.

"We're quite informal around here; we like to keep a happy ship," he continued. Isabelle smiled indulgently, but the smile never reached her eyes and Rachel wondered if she was a somewhat reluctant party to this policy.

"I see you achieved distinction in your college diploma, and we're pleased to see that you completed a full two years, as opposed to the more usual one year course, which tends to leave out some of the important aspects of office work and simply concentrate on typing and dictation skills. We have a general policy of advancement throughout the office, and the extra skills you have acquired should stand you in good stead should you be appointed. Isabelle would like to ask you some questions now." He glanced sideways at his colleague, who cleared her throat imperiously and peered over her glasses at Rachel.

"I see you have no experience of office work since you left college. Why is that?" she asked. *Straight for the jugular then,* thought Rachel wryly.

"Just after I finished my course, my father became ill," she replied, stretching the truth slightly. "I had to take shift work here at Eagle so that I could help my mother care for him and my two small brothers. I have been working in the factory here since last summer. Sadly, my father passed away at the beginning of February, and when I saw this position advertised on the notice board it seemed an ideal opportunity to do what I was trained to do; what I have always wanted to do," she said.

"I see," said Horn-rims, looking singularly unimpressed. "This is a very busy office, and you would be required to undertake a variety of tasks. How do you think you would cope with this; and what do you feel are your particular strengths and weaknesses?"

Rachel thought for a moment. She remembered her mock interviews at college, and that just such questions had arisen; she was well versed in the answers. She looked directly at Horn-rims as she spoke.

"I should enjoy a varied working day, and I'm happy and able to learn new skills. As you can see, my typing and shorthand speeds are excellent, I have had extensive training in public relations and I might add I make excellent coffee, but my specialty is hot chocolate." She watched a slow smile spread over Michael's face.

Isabelle remained poker-faced. "Have you ever worked a PBX switchboard?" she asked, giving Rachel a look that said *I've gotcha there!*

"I haven't; but I would love to learn to, and I'm sure it can't be that difficult. Would that not be part of my training?" she finished, turning the tables on her interrogator.

"Indeed it would," Michael butted in. He sat upright, and turned to Isabelle. "I think we've heard all we need to, don't you?" he said. Horn-rims glared at him, but nodded briefly. He addressed Rachel again, "Is there anything you would like to ask us?"

"Thank you, no." she replied.

"In that case Rachel," Isabelle said, "you may go now. You'll be hearing from us in due course."

128

Michael smiled warmly, "It was very nice to meet you," he said, and looked as though he actually meant it. Rachel rose from her chair, her knees trembling slightly, but managed a confident toss of her new hairstyle as she walked to the door.

"Thank you," she said, and smiled back at Michael. As she left through reception, there was no sign of Kate. Instead, a tall woman in her thirties manned the desk, and smiled at Rachel as she passed. *Apart from Horn-rims,* thought Rachel, *Everyone seems really nice.*

She set off back along the road through the estate towards the main road where she would catch a bus home. A sleek motor drew up beside her, and she recognized Michael at the wheel. He leaned over and spoke through the open window.

"Hello again. Can I give you a lift anywhere?"
Rachel hesitated, but not for long; her shoes weren't really made for long walks and it was getting a little too warm now that the sun was high in the sky. He opened the door and she climbed in, conscious of her posture and smoothing down the kilt as she sat.

"Thank you," she said. "If you could drop me off at the bus stop that'd be great."

"Wouldn't dream of it." He smiled sideways at her as the car moved off silently. "I'm going your way, so I'll drop you off; it's the least I can do. You acquitted yourself very well in there you know; not everyone can handle Isabelle. She's ok once she gets to know you as long as you toe the line. I think you'll fit in very nicely, and you definitely got my vote. Our head receptionist gets the decider, because she's the one who ultimately has to work with you."

Rachel's heart leaped. "Is her name Kate?" she asked, hardly daring to hope.

"That's right; have you met?" Michael responded sounding a little surprised.

"She gave me my application form, and we seemed to hit it off," replied Rachel. "She also came to the waiting room to wish me luck," she finished. Michael raised an eyebrow,

"Well, it sounds like she has already made her choice, so it's a good job you lived up to her expectations. She's a good judge of character is Kate, and a good person to have on your side. She's friendly enough, but she generally likes to keep her distance; so frankly you're honoured."

They were approaching the avenue of trees that led to Rachel's street. "I'm not sure exactly where Albion Road is; so sing out when we get there," said Michael.

"It's just here," said Rachel. "The first road after the trees; we're number twenty-six, about halfway down on the left."

Michael drew up just outside the house and Rachel was aware of some twitching of net curtains, including her own, at the sight of such an impressive car pulling up in their modest neighbourhood.

"Thanks for the lift," she said, smiling and reaching for the door handle.

"It's my pleasure; and between me and you, the job is almost certainly yours. It's been nice meeting you Rachel; our paths won't cross much from hereon so I'll wish you well."

Rachel waved at him as he pulled away. *The job's mine!* she thought with a rush of excitement. Her mother was standing in the hallway.

"Who was that then?" she asked, eyeing Rachel with suspicion.

"It's ok Mum, that was my new boss; it looks like I've got the job!"

"Huh!" said her mother, with an arch look, "I wonder why?"

"Hey! That's not very nice! It's not like that at all; my interview went really well. I remembered everything they told me in college and Michael was just being polite because he saw me walking for the bus. What's for lunch Mum? I'm absolutely starving!" Her mother gave her another piercing look, not convinced, but she was glad to see some enthusiasm in her daughter and together they went into the kitchen to make a sandwich for lunch.

"Shall we go and eat them in the park, like we used to?" her mother asked a little uncertainly. Rachel seemed to prefer to avoid the park these days.

"Ok, it's a lovely day; but I'd better change out of my work clothes first. Won't be a minute." Rachel took the stairs two at a time; she felt happy for the first time in months. In the end she just changed her top, putting on a short-sleeved summer blouse that went well with the kilt, and a wide navy belt with a gold buckle.

They sat on their usual bench in the park, near the duck pond and well away from the little green folly. There was the usual assortment of dog-walkers, elderly people, and mothers with toddlers and babies in prams. They munched their sandwiches and Rachel gave her mother a blow-by-blow account of her interview and of her conversation with Michael in the car. Now convinced that all was above board, her mother hugged her and said she was proud of her.

"Your Dad would be chuffed," she said. "He always said you were going places."

Suddenly, Rachel froze. She had spotted a young woman pushing a pram towards the duck pond; a large coach built pram with a fringed sun canopy over the top. She had long brown hair, and at her heels trotted a black Labrador type dog. It was *her!* Rachel felt sick. *Was that her Daniel in the pram?* She couldn't be sure. The woman might have a child of her own; she might have left that child at home with her husband on that cold Sunday morning in January that now seemed so long ago.

"What's up Rach? You've gone as white as a sheet," said her mother anxiously.

"I'm ok Mum; I just feel a bit sick. You stay here, I'll have a little walk over to the ducks; they can have the rest of my sandwich."

"Hang on, I'll come with you," said her mother and began to gather up her things.

"No Mum!" said Rachel, a little too sharply. "You stay there and finish your lunch; I'll be ok in a minute." Her mother sat back down, a slightly hurt expression on her face. Rachel had no time to notice; she was halfway to the duck pond. She stood near the woman with the pram and broke her sandwich into small pieces to prolong her stay as long as possible. The ducks crowded round fussing and squabbling, making little squeaky noises in their eagerness to feed. Rachel moved closer and at last dared to glance towards the pram. The baby in it, propped up on pillows, looked to be about three or four months old. Dressed all in blue, his dark hair sticking straight up on his head, he was smiling and chortling happily beneath his sun canopy. Rachel's heart lurched sickeningly – it was Daniel, she was sure it was; after all, a mother must know her own baby. She bent and peered into the pram.

"What a lovely little boy," she told the woman. "How old is he?"

"He's nearly four months," the woman replied, smiling at the compliment. "His name's Danny. He loves to watch me feed the ducks. We come here often now that the

132

weather's a bit better; it was such a long winter, wasn't it?" Rachel heard herself agreeing but her mind was full of the sight and sound of her baby; so near, and yet so far. She had found him, and she wasn't sure whether to laugh or cry.

"Do you have any other children?" Rachel asked. The woman appeared to be in her late twenties; perhaps Daniel had an older brother or sister. A shadow fell across the woman's face and she hesitated for a moment before replying.

"I had a little girl, Danielle. I called him after her; she was Dani too. She died of meningitis when she was four. When Danny came along it was as though she had come back to me. I don't know why I'm telling you this; I don't usually open up to strangers, I'm sorry."

Rachel was dumbfounded. What twist of Fate had decreed that this woman should be the one to find her son – someone who needed him just as much as she did? For months now she had planned what she would do if she ever found him; how she would engineer to take him back now that it wouldn't harm anyone. Her greatest worry had been how to justify abandoning him in the first place. Now however, she looked into this woman's eyes and saw a mixture of pain and pure happiness that tore at her heartstrings, and she knew she could never take him back. Was this yet another cruel twist? Or simply the best result she could have wished for? She was undecided.

"It's nice to meet you – and Danny," she said at last. My name's Rachel; I live just over there." She indicated the direction of her street.

"It's nice to meet you too," the woman smiled, but didn't venture her name. "We'd better go now; Danny will be wanting his feed. I'll see you around I expect." She turned the pram, and calling her dog to heel moved away along the path towards the gates on the far side of the park.

Rachel stood watching them go until they were almost out of sight before returning to her mother.

"Who was that Rach?" her mother asked.

"Oh, I didn't ask her name; but she has the cutest little boy called Danny," Rachel replied, fighting back the tears that threatened to well up in her eyes; tears of mixed emotions ranging from deep regret to immense relief.

"Oh! Same as your young man you had last year," exclaimed her mother. Rachel looked at her sharply – did she suspect something? *No, don't be silly, that's just your guilty conscience talking,* she chided herself.

"Whatever happened to him Rach?" her mother was asking now.

"Oh, I don't know Mum, he just dumped me; I'm better off without him. I haven't clapped eyes on him since before Dad got ill."

"Never mind; perhaps you'll meet someone nice now that you're not working all those funny hours. It'd be nice to see you settled now."

"You mean married and off your hands," Rachel laughed. Suddenly she felt light hearted and euphoric. She had found Daniel; he was well and happy, he was living nearby, and she knew she would see him again. What a day this was turning out to be; she would never forget it. She linked arms with her mother as they set off home together.

Mariana turned at the end of the path, and watched Rachel walk away, arm in arm with a woman she took to be her mother. There was something about her, she thought; she shook her head, her brow furrowed – what was it she just couldn't put her finger on? Danny began to whinge; he must be tired, and probably hungry too; she had stayed out longer than she intended.

She and Kate had taken Danny down to the registry office to register his birth when he was six weeks old. She had telephoned first and told them that his father had died, and they asked her to bring her marriage certificate and Terry's death certificate with her. When asked where the birth took place she said he was early and unexpected and was born at home, and they accepted this without question. She emerged shortly afterwards triumphantly bearing his birth certificate; a small sheet of paper that made Danny officially her child, hers and Terry's. She named him Daniel Matthew Harding, taking his middle name from her father.

"That was easy," said Kate as they got into the car.

"I thought they'd see me shaking," said Mariana as she studied the birth certificate. "He's mine now; this makes it legal," she said.

Right from the start she had wheeled him out in his pram on a daily basis; most days down to the park so that Alfie could have his run. There was no use hiding away; she just had to run the gauntlet of the inevitable remarks – *You kept that one quiet,* was a favourite, to which she replied that it had come as quite a surprise to her too. People seemed to accept that after Terry died she hadn't realised she was pregnant until the last minute – after all, grief does strange things to people. She was worried that Alfie would be jealous of his new rival for her affections, but there was no need. From day one he appointed himself Danny's guardian, trotting close behind her when they went for their walks and lying alongside the pram outside the corner shop whilst she went in to buy bread, milk, or nappies. If anyone approached the pram he would treat them to a long-drawn-out throaty growl and they would beat a hasty retreat.

She often wondered about Danny's real mother. Who was she, where was she, and did she know that he was loved and cared for? As the months went by she stopped wondering if every young woman who stopped to admire him was his real mother, and sometimes she even forgot that he wasn't really hers. She grew accustomed to the comparisons people tended to make between her and her baby; *Oh, he looks just like his mummy,* they would say, and some who were acquainted with Terry even thought he was the spitting image of his dad. She settled happily into the routine of having a new baby and often thought how she was getting the best of both worlds, remembering that when her daughter was born she had struggled with tiredness for the first few weeks and was often weepy and emotional, much to Terry's annoyance. *There are certain advantages,* she thought wryly, *to having a baby without actually having to go through childbirth!*

As spring approached, she would put him out in his pram by the back door. The back garden was private; enclosed by larch-lap fencing and a small gate with a bolt on the inside. It was full of flowers and shrubs and near the gate was a small flowering cherry tree that Mariana had planted in Dani's memory along with the rose bed under the living room window. She had long since given up trying to stop Alfie cocking his leg irreverently against the tree – she didn't think Dani would have minded. The garden was always sunny, as though her daughter's spirit warmed it.

She sat at the kitchen table and fed Danny, thinking how much her life had changed in the past eight months. For some time after Terry's death she had been haunted by dreams, brought on she supposed by her own guilt at feeling nothing but relief that he was gone from her life forever. She couldn't shake off the fear that somehow he would return, and the changes she made were slow and gradual at first. Slowly however, the dreams subsided and she began to find her feet. When Terry first died Lorna had invited her to stay with her down in Sussex, but she declined; it would have felt like running away and there was no need for that now; this was the beginning of a new life for her. *Thank goodness I didn't take her up on her offer,* she thought now. *I never would have got Alfie, and I never would have found Danny.*

ELEVEN: KATE.

Kate had worked for Michael for five years, ever since she left secretarial college at eighteen in 1972. Although he was almost twenty years older than her, he was, she thought, undeniably attractive in a way that powerful men often are and also by merit of his actual good looks – fairly tall, blonde and well-proportioned, with impeccable dress sense and a warm personality. Regrettably, she soon learned that he was also married with two young children.

Eagle Electronics was a modern electronic components factory with a large workforce and a busy office. When Kate started there she was the office junior; but she was determined that would change, and worked hard to make it happen. Her boyfriend Scott worked as an engineer for the same firm, except that he worked shifts, whereas Kate's job was nine to five, five days a week. Scott earned twice as much money as Kate and made it quite clear that, because of this, he considered himself her superior. Nevertheless he was also generous with his money, and Kate decided that his slightly overbearing manner was just a man thing, and went along with it, allowing him to make all the decisions in their relationship. She had met him when he came to the office to do some repairs and had accepted his invitation to have a drink with him later that week. He was the perfect gentleman. He picked her up in his purple Triumph Stag and drove her to a cosy bar uptown with atmospheric lighting and comfortable plush seats. They drank cocktails and chatted easily. She told him she used to live in Manchester, and at the weekend he drove her there for a nostalgic day out. They wandered the streets window-shopping and he bought her a necklace in one of her favourite stores, Kendals. They had dinner at an Italian restaurant, and then went on to Tiffany's nightclub where they danced and drank the night away. She didn't question it when he said he'd booked them a room for the night in a hotel near the station. Kate was no fool; she had known there would be strings attached to such extravagance, and she had been on the pill since she was seventeen. Scott was good-looking and good fun, and she was happy to be his girl. They began to date regularly, and she even took him home to meet her parents towards whom he was charming and courteous. A year later he asked her to marry him.

"I'll have to think about it," she told him, "I don't think I'm old enough to get married."

"Well, don't think too long," he replied, somewhat tetchily. "There are plenty of girls who'd be happy to be asked, I'm sure." All her friends were envious. They had met him when he took her out around Manchester. He had impressed them with his slick sophistication, and they were almost unanimous in urging her to accept his proposal. Her mother, too, was glad that she appeared to have landed on her feet, if slightly disappointed that the wedding was to be in a registry office, and not in church. Therefore, she pushed aside her vague misgivings, and agreed to marry him.

They were married in late May and had an idyllic honeymoon in Italy. When they returned Scott handed Kate the keys to their new flat which he had bought as a surprise. The flat was newly-converted; modern, and very bare and masculine looking. Kate looked around, thinking how it really needed a woman's touch, and the following weekend when Scott was working she made up her mind to begin work on its transformation. She decided to start in the bedroom, and having bought some paint and brushes, she spent the day painting over the magnolia walls in two shades of purple; pale lilac on three walls, and a deep plum colour on the wall behind their bed. She moved all the furniture back into place, and put the finishing touches in place with a matching plum coloured bedspread and ready-made curtains. She stood back and admired her handiwork – it looked spectacular; she couldn't wait for Scott to see it. She was going to enjoy being a home-maker, she decided. Exhausted from her efforts, she curled up on the sofa to await his return.

"What the fuck have you been doing?" Kate shook herself awake. Scott was standing over her; he didn't look happy.

"Don't you think you should've asked me first before making my flat look like the fucking Casbah?" She had never seen him like this before. *'His' flat. That didn't sound right somehow.*

"I wanted to surprise you," she said. "I thought you'd be pleased."

"Well, I'm not, you silly bitch. Don't you think I might have liked a say in things? If you want to live here you need to get a few things straight lady." Kate stared at him in disbelief. She could scarcely believe what she was hearing. She had never seen him like this before.

"I actually thought it was *our* flat," she retorted, "and if that's your attitude, I'm really not sure if I do want to live here at all!" She scrambled to her feet. Heading for

140

the offending bedroom she dragged her suitcase down from on top of the wardrobe and began emptying the drawers of her clothes. Scott grasped her arm, swinging her around to face him. "Don't go Kate," he said, "I'm sorry. I over-reacted. It was just a bit of a shock seeing everything changed like that. I chose everything myself, and I thought you liked it," he finished, lamely.

"You mean you actually chose to have wall to wall magnolia and beige? I never realised you were so bloody boring!" Kate retorted. "You never asked if I liked it; I suppose you thought I'd just be grateful to be here. Well I'm not – in fact, you're the one who should be grateful!"

The blow took her by surprise and sent her reeling onto the bed, her face stinging. She put a hand up to her face; it was hot, and she could see in the dressing table mirror that it bore the imprint of Scott's hand in a bright red weal. He stood by the door, his face twisted in an ugly sneer. It was like looking at a stranger, and suddenly she was very afraid.

"I should be grateful should I? For what Kate? Grateful that a pathetic little dogs body like you condescended to be my wife? You could never have any of this without me you little bitch. I've a bloody good mind to teach you a lesson you won't forget." He stepped towards her menacingly, and she stared in disbelief as he slowly removed his belt and twisted it around his hand. She had once known a girl at school whose father used to give her the belt. It had sickened and disgusted her that anyone should have to endure such treatment from those who were meant to protect them. She would rather live on the streets she thought, where such behaviour would be a criminal offence, than be subjected to it in her own home that was supposed to be her sanctuary. She held her breath, watching him approach and waiting her chance. Just as he almost reached the bed, the belt held taut between his hands, she launched herself off the bed, taking him by surprise as she pushed him aside and made a run for the door of the flat, only pausing to grab her handbag in passing before slamming the door behind her and racing down the stairs two or three at a time.

She never returned to the flat for her clothes. When she confessed to her parents what had happened they told her they were proud of her for standing up to him, and relieved that she hadn't allowed him to hoodwink her into staying. They wanted her to report him to the police, but she said she wanted nothing more to do with him. Her father drove her to work the following week ready to face up to him, but he wasn't there; he had chucked his job and left her clothes in a suitcase in the office. She never saw him again.

So it was that Kate found herself divorced at twenty, and she moved back in with her parents. Some months later she received a letter from Scott apologizing for his behaviour and telling her that he was getting married again. *Good luck with that,* she thought, *I hope she likes magnolia!*

Soon afterwards, Kate met Mariana. She had come to the office to collect her wages, because somehow they had not been included in the usual batch that were pigeonholed on the wall at the entrance to the factory.

"I'm sorry," said Kate, as she retrieved the brown pay packet from the out tray on her desk. "I don't know how that happened."

"It's okay," Mariana smiled, "I'm just relieved nobody nicked them – you never know, do you?" Kate looked at this woman who was probably not much older than her. In her overalls she looked dowdy and plain, but her hair was a rich lustrous brown, and she had kind eyes. Kate had never really spoken with anyone from the factory floor before.

142

"Hey, what's it like in there?" she asked, jerking her head in the direction of the factory. Mariana hesitated momentarily, then replied,

"Oh, you'd never believe it! We're chained to our benches throughout the shift, and we're not allowed to talk to one another. If you don't tie your hair back, the supervisor comes round and chops it off." She looked at Kate with a tortured expression, and Kate didn't know what to say. Suddenly, Mariana began to laugh, her eyes creased at the corners, her cheeks like red apples, her shoulders shaking with mirth.

"Oh I'm sorry," she gasped through her laughter, "I couldn't resist – don't tell me you fell for it?" Kate blushed violently – how naïve must she seem! She glanced at the pay packet in her hand bearing the name of Mariana Harding, and on a sudden impulse said,

"D'you fancy a coffee? You can tell me more about the Dickensian conditions on the factory floor, and perhaps then I can persuade my boss Michael to make a few improvements."

"Okay. I've got twenty minutes before my bus goes; but I'm buying, it's the least I can do after making you look s'daft."

"Oh, no you're not – I've seen your pay packet don't forget! It's my treat; that's the best laugh I've had all day, even if the joke was on me! I'm Kate, by the way." She smiled at Mariana; she had a feeling she had just made a friend.

Now that she was single again Kate turned her thoughts back to Michael. The hierarchy structure at Eagle was a fairly loose and informal affair, and everyone tended to muck in. Since they now had a new office junior named Lucy, Kate's endless filing and tea-making days were more-

or-less over, and instead she frequently found herself stationed on the PBX switchboard or called upon to take dictation from Michael. As bosses go, he was easy to live with. He presented a friendly face and appeared pretty laid back, and although he must have pots of money, you would never have known it from his demeanour. He spoke to everyone as though they were his equal; he was friendly and informal, and everyone liked him. She had never seen his wife, but he had a picture of her on his desk, blonde and smiling, with two very pretty children, their nine year old twins Kieran and Molly. Kate had long straight mousey-blonde hair that she often wore up for work. She had it lightened and cut into a sleek Sassoon bob. A smart dress code was required for the office and Kate soon became known for her stylish pencil skirts and tailored blouses, making her look sophisticated beyond her twenty years. The first time she entered his office after the transformation he looked up from his desk, did a double-take, and smiling said,

"For a moment I thought I had a new secretary. You look very nice today Kate. Is it a special occasion?" Kate felt herself blush and replied,

"No, not really, I just thought I'd give myself a make-over to celebrate being single again."

"Well, I'm sure you won't be single for long," Michael replied. "Now then, where was I?" He drew some papers from his in tray and began to dictate a letter, and the moment had passed.

"Kate, that wasn't a 'moment', he was just being polite. You know he's married." Mariana hated to burst Kate's bubble, but she didn't want her getting hurt either. "You need to be careful, you wouldn't want to jeopardise your job over a wild fantasy would you?"

"I suppose not," Kate replied a little sulkily. It was strange how quickly Mariana had become her confidante, and also, being four years older, her advisor in many things. Mariana was very good at giving advice, but not so brilliant when it came to taking it, and Kate knew that she was having some serious problems with her husband Terry.

"You're married aren't you? But you're not happy, so if someone came along that you fancied you might be tempted don't you think?"

"Oh Kate! It's not as simple as that, I've told you! Besides, I think from what you've told me Michael is happily married, and apart from that he has kids. I just don't want you getting your hopes up because he's naturally nice to you. You'll meet someone soon who'll make up for what happened with Scott, I'm sure." Kate knew she was right; she had fixated on Michael because she knew he was trustworthy and kind, but if he were to have an affair with her wouldn't that mean that she was wrong about him anyway? It was a no win situation and gradually she overcame her crush on her boss.

A few months later Michael's wife Susannah upped and left him, taking the children with her to Australia with her new boyfriend. It was all over the factory, how she must have been having an affair for years, and had planned her escape without him having a single inkling what was going on. Kate's heart went out to him – how could anyone do that to him? But far from opening a door for her it seemed that now more than ever she must back off so as not to appear opportunist. Mariana agreed with her.

"You don't want to look like a vulture Kate, you might just end up scaring him off for good. He won't be looking for anyone else right now and the best thing you can do is to help to keep things normal. He'll be dead

145

embarrassed as well as hurt you know. If you or I get dumped it's nobody else's business, but for him it's public humiliation, and everyone will be wondering what he did to deserve it. Just be your normal self and let him be the one to make the first move."

So Kate made herself indispensable, kept her appearance immaculate and made it her personal remit to provide him with cups of coffee. One day, she noticed the photograph had gone from his desk, replaced with one of the children alone, smiling and tanned, sitting on some far-distant beach presumably in Australia. On impulse, she said,

"How are your children Michael? Do you miss them terribly?" He looked slightly taken aback. She could see him examining her face, questioning her motive for asking such a personal question. She burned with embarrassment, regretting her outspokenness; what must he think of her? Then a smile spread over his face and he answered,

"They're fine Kate. They seem very happy. They write to me and send me pictures, and Susannah has said they can come to me for Christmas next year. I do miss them, but one has to make the best of things, and I shall spoil them rotten when they come here make no mistake!" He hesitated then added, "Thank you for asking. As a rule people avoid the subject so that it becomes the elephant in the room. Your candour is very refreshing Kate." He smiled at her again and she smiled back as she made for the door.

"Oh, Kate!" She turned quickly in eager anticipation, her heart pounding. "Some biscuits would be nice," he finished. She mumbled assent and hurried from the room. Closing the door behind her she leaned against the wall burning with embarrassment, pressing her flaming cheeks with her hands that were inexplicably cold. Had he noticed

146

her faux pas, she wondered? She sent Lucy, the new office junior back in with the plate of biscuits. After that she determined to push her feelings for him firmly aside so as not to make a fool of herself, and gradually they formed a tacit friendship that was to last for many years.

TWELVE: MICHAEL.

Michael watched the door close behind Kate, and smiled inwardly. Her discomfiture was plain to see and his heart went out to her, but not in the way she would like it to, he thought. Kate was a nice girl – he cringed at the clichéd adjective that he had mentally attributed to her, but it was true. She *was* nice; attractive, kind and thoughtful, and she would make someone a lovely wife one day he was sure, but not him. He had known she had feelings for him since she first came to Eagle. It wasn't unknown for employees to have crushes on him; it went with the territory and he found it mildly flattering, but didn't take it very seriously since normally, it quickly wore off. With Kate it had lasted longer, several years now in fact. He had been painfully aware of it at first and careful not to give out the wrong signals.

Then Kate had got into a relationship with someone else and Michael hoped that she might settle down, young as she was, and forget about her unfortunate crush; it could have been awkward since they sometimes had to work closely together. She married Scott, and his relief was tangible. He gave her a hundred pound bonus as a wedding gift.

Unfortunately the marriage ended after just over a week. Isabelle the office manager confided in him that

Kate's new husband had, in fact, been violent towards her. Michael felt deeply shocked by this revelation. He knew that Scott was an Eagle employee, and would have dismissed him forthwith had he not quit his job anyway without word or notice. This was proof enough to Michael of his guilt. Soon afterwards Kate gave herself a makeover. He felt she was being exceptionally brave and wanting to be supportive, complimented her on her appearance. As soon as he had spoken he realised his mistake, when a violent flush spread over her face and he quickly moved on to dictating the letter and avoided her gaze for the rest of the day. After that he sensed her withdrawal, and hoped that the whole awkward situation had now been avoided.

Soon afterwards, his wife dropped the bombshell of her imminent departure with the twins (on the morning before they left). Michael was devastated; not only because of her leaving and taking his children with her, but also by the fact that he hadn't realised that anything was wrong in their marriage. She had been having an affair for nearly three years and he had had no idea. In addition he felt his humiliation deepen since it inevitably became common knowledge at Eagle that he had been well and truly done over by his wife. He immersed himself in work and slogged through the days on automatic pilot, spending the evenings alone with only a glass of whisky for comfort. His friends for the most part were also Susannah's, and he couldn't help but wonder if they had known something, if not all about, her affair – it's probably harder to hide such things from one's friends than one's husband because, he supposed, of the need to manufacture alibis and spurious reasons to spend nights away with girlfriends in crisis. He tried to remember such occasions but he had probably paid them little attention, seizing the opportunity instead to have a night out with the boys or a quiet evening in with his children, a bonding opportunity that was always welcome given that his work kept him away from them so much. He had trusted his wife implicitly; he would never have dreamt of cheating on her and had assumed that she felt the same.

Michael was no fool; he knew that the gossips would be chipping away at his integrity – there must have been *some* compelling reason for his wife to turn to another man when she had a husband with reasonably good looks, a generous salary and a nature to match. He was aware of the talk on the factory floor amongst employees who barely knew him from Adam, but he was also aware that the office staff were behind him one hundred percent; he had earned their loyalty, and he was glad of that now. So when Kate began dancing attention on him with cups of coffee and unsolicited work-based favours such as tidying his desk and sorting through his somewhat chaotic filing system, he was too wrapped up in his grief to attach any importance or hidden meaning to it.

The weeks went by and sadly he realised that his children seemed to be settling down very happily into their new life. They sent him drawings of their new home, their school and their friends, and brief letters describing the places they had visited with Gordon at weekends. Oh yes; their new stepfather was certainly pulling out all the stops. He was older than Susannah – a fact that somehow compounded Michael's humiliation. To be replaced by a younger man would at least have provided him with an excuse and revealed his wife to be just another shallow woman flattered by the attentions of such a man. No; Gordon was fifty-something, and whatever attracted Susannah to him it was clearly not his age nor his looks, and she had no need of his money, so he must have possessed some fundamental endearing quality that Michael evidently lacked. He decided also that Kate was just being kind; she was that sort of girl and Isabelle, who was a sound judge of character if a little prickly, had nothing but praise for her, trusting her with even the most confidential tasks around the office. She was now deputy head of personnel and frequently had the casting vote when new staff members were recruited.

So when Kate asked about his children, he allowed his guard to drop and responded warmly, happy to talk about them since most people studiously avoided the subject. As she left the room he saw that he had reopened an old wound and he wanted to call her back and explain to her that he thought highly of her, just not in that way. He lost his nerve however, and simply asked for some biscuits instead. After that day he was more careful in his dealings with Kate. Gradually their relationship took a new direction and he eventually realised to his relief that she had finally pushed aside her romantic feelings for him. Life became easier, if dull, and Michael had no reason to suppose that it would improve any time soon. It would be a long time he knew, before he allowed anyone else into his heart.

Indeed, for almost three years, nothing changed for Michael. He worked, drank and slept, and little else. Some of his and Susannah's former friends gradually drifted back into contact, but he wasn't prepared to trust them any more, and he wasn't even sure what he had liked about them in the first place; so for the most part he declined their invitations to venues and events that belonged in another life. His children visited him regularly, bravely flying alone to spend the summer holidays with him, and every other Christmas. He engaged a temporary nanny named Louise in the summer; a large, inelegant girl who came with excellent references and an obvious way with children. She lived just

151

down the road and arrived on her first morning in a tiny car that only just accommodated her ample proportions. She was, however, cheerful, competent, and an excellent cook, and the children adored her. Life settled down into a reasonably pleasant routine and Michael was in no hurry to complicate it with a romantic encounter.

Then Rachel came into his life. One of the junior office staff was leaving and Michael decided to advertise within the firm as well as through the job centre. Isabelle trawled through the two dozen or so applicants appraising their qualifications and their possible merits and settled on three for short listing, all with similar qualifications, all in their thirties, and all with a minimum of five year's office experience. At Eagle the office junior held a great deal more responsibility than was usual and might almost immediately be required to stand in for more senior staff at a moment's notice. Isabelle chose carefully, drawing on her many years of handling the factory's personnel department. There were only a small number of applicants from the factory floor and these she laid aside after barely glancing at them; after all they were hardly likely to be suitable applicants, and if they wished to better themselves, they were not going to do so at her expense. She laid out the chosen three on Michael's desk and awaited his approval, never doubting that he would grant it automatically.

"I'm a little concerned," Michael said wearily after perusing the three letters of application, "that these three women actually appear to be one and the same person."

Isabelle eyed him suspiciously. *What was the man wittering about, was he losing his grip?*

"I'm sorry Michael, I don't quite get your drift," she said pointedly. "I've selected three candidates for interview as you asked. They all have considerable experience, excellent qualifications and impeccable references. Is that not what was required of me?"

"My dear Isabelle; I'm not questioning your judgment of any of those things, but I can't help wondering if these ladies might be just a little dull. I like to think we're a forward-thinking firm, and our office staff really ought to reflect that don't you think? I've given Kate the casting vote on this one and she was quite taken with one of the girls from the factory floor, a certain Rachel Steele. I think perhaps we should grant her an interview at least, since she will be working under Kate's supervision."

"Very well," Isabelle answered in frosty tones. "Far be it from me to veto Kate's choice. You'll have to decide which one to throw out from the three I've recommended; I am washing my hands of the whole thing." With that she swept majestically from the room like an exiting prima donna, slamming the door behind her. *Whoops,* said Michael to himself, *that's torn it!* He sighed wearily, and picking one of the three applications at random, dumped it unceremoniously in the waste paper basket. He hoped he was doing the right thing.

As soon as Rachel walked into the room, he knew he had found his salvation. She entered the room with a slightly defiant tilt of her head. Michael guessed that she had been comparing herself to the two previous interviewees and perhaps feeling that she may be prejudged to be too young and inexperienced in the comparison. She was dressed fashionably. Her short skirt, tight jumper, and platform shoes paid no homage to the kind of strict propriety favoured by Isabelle, but neither were they offensively provocative. She sat neatly; her back straight, her knees together, legs positioned sideways and ankles crossed. Her hands were still, resting lightly on her lap, and gave no hint of nervousness although Michael knew she must be feeling it. He smiled at her approvingly, conscious of Isabelle's penetrating stare taking in his every move. He addressed her only briefly then handed her over to Isabelle who immediately set about attempting to undermine her confidence and expose the inevitable failings in her suitability for the job. From her answers however, it soon became clear that she was intelligent, kind-hearted, and loyal. The addition of grim determination and a well-developed sense of humour meant that she was perfect for the job. Michael knew it; and he knew that Isabelle knew it too – *she'll get over it,* he thought, *you can't win 'em all.*

It seemed only polite to offer Rachel a lift when he came upon her walking down the long dusty road towards the bus stop. The sun was high in the sky, and as he drew up alongside her she wiped the perspiration from her brow before turning and recognizing him. She accepted his offer and sat decorously in the passenger seat, smoothing her skirt down to cover her knees. Her home was a modest red brick terraced house on the outskirts of town. An avenue of trees lent it an air of grandeur that belied its lowly origins. The avenue was like Rachel, he thought; there was more to it than met the eye; its rather flamboyant surface concealing the quiet dignity of the humble but well-maintained properties beyond. He caught a brief glimpse of a face at the window as he returned Rachel's wave goodbye.

It was several weeks before he saw her again. A warm dry May gave way to a cool wet June failing, however, to dampen the spirit of the great British public as they celebrated the Queen's silver jubilee with street parties and concerts. Michael closed the factory from Saturday night until Wednesday morning so that everyone could join in the festivities and watch the royal procession on

154

television on the Tuesday. Wednesday morning was Rachel's first day and Michael felt duty bound to welcome her into the fold in person. She was busying herself with some filing at Kate's instruction, her hair falling over her face as she worked so that she didn't see Michael come into the room. She was wearing the same outfit as she had for the interview and he guessed that she didn't have many to choose from. Her smile was spontaneous and genuine when she turned at his greeting.

"Welcome to Eagle, Rachel," he said, extending his hand politely.

"Thank you Sir," she replied, giving his hand a brief squeeze. He couldn't help noticing her hand was soft and yet firm, her grip confident but with no trace of arrogance. "Actually, I've been here for quite some time, just not in the posh part," she finished. – *There was that sparky sense of humour again,* thought Michael.

"Of course, I forgot. I hope Kate has shown you round alright."

"She has, and the office is much bigger than I thought. She's going to allow me to make the coffee this morning, having made me a list of everyone's preferences."

"Ah! Kate has her priorities right. I hope she showed you where the biscuits are aswell."

"She did; and she also mentioned that they're only allowed on Fridays, by order of Isabelle who is seriously concerned for your waistline," Rachel laughed.

"Isabelle is a tyrant, and you have my express permission to disobey her in this instance," rejoined Michael, enjoying this light exchange of banter. "I think you should be allowed carte blanche as it's your first day, so I'll leave it up to you."

"That's not a decision I really want to make," replied Rachel, with mock seriousness, "since Isabelle is my

155

immediate superior, and you are asking me to disobey her orders on my first day. I'm sorry Sir, but you'll have to get your own biscuits if you really want them."

"Really? Well, thank you Rachel, that's me told – oh, and by the way, it's Michael if you don't mind. I really think 'Sir' has rather Dickensian overtones, and Kate assures me that we are all equals under the skin although I doubt if Isabelle agrees; she clearly believes herself to be superior to all of us!" With that he winked at Rachel and left the room. She stood for a moment staring after him. *What a lovely man,* she thought. *I'm so lucky to have a boss like him.* Later that day she took him his coffee and, after relating their conversation to Kate, a chocolate biscuit.

"Isabelle wouldn't like it," said Kate, "but there again she ain't gettin' it. Go on Rachel, risk it for a biscuit!" They giggled together at the thought of defying Isabelle's strict edict.

Rachel tapped gently on the door of the inner sanctum.

"Come in," Michael called, and she entered with her forbidden victuals.

"Rachel! I'm surprised at you!" Michael exclaimed as he caught sight of the biscuit. "Disobeying an order on your very first day! Lucky for you Isabelle isn't back from London yet or your position might have been short-lived indeed."

"I didn't realise she was away," admitted Rachel. *So that's why things seem so relaxed around here today,* she thought to herself. Evidently Michael was merely the titular boss around here; the person in charge in reality was Isabelle.

"She went to watch the parade – no huddling round the telly for our Izzie – oh, and don't ever call her that to her face. You'll find things a little different tomorrow so make the most of it. Kate knows how to handle her and I'm sure it won't be a problem for you either, once you get to know her. Thank you for the coffee; and now believe it or not, I have work to do." She glanced over her shoulder as she left the room. He was rocking back in his chair with his fingers clasped over his chest, thumbs touching, smiling thoughtfully as he watched her go.

THIRTEEN: A FINE ROMANCE.

"Well? How did your first day go?" Rachel's mother asked her when she got home.

"It was brilliant Mum, I'm really going to like it there. Kate and I get on great."

"And what about Michael then; did you see him?"

"Oh Mum! Get off my case. Of course I saw him. I took him his coffee and a biscuit and we had a laugh because he's not allowed a biscuit on a Wednesday but the office manager's away, so Kate and I decided he should have one." Her mother frowned slightly with a puzzled air; *what on earth was she babbling on about biscuits for?* Noticing her pursed lips and questioning stare, Rachel laughed,

"You had to be there Mum, sorry. What's for tea?"

Rachel settled happily into her new job, although with the return of Isabelle the following day there was a little less banter and a lot more work going on. She and Kate were becoming friends, and most days took their lunch breaks together. Kate told her of her brief but disastrous marriage and inevitably quizzed her about her love life in return. It was a long time since Rachel had talked of Dan, or even allowed herself to think of him; it opened up too much of a wound and brought memories of Daniel flooding back in.

"By the sounds of things Rach, you were better off without him," Kate said, referring of course to Dan. "Just be thankful you didn't make the mistake of marrying him."

Rachel wondered what Kate would say if she knew the truth. Sometimes she longed to unburden herself to someone, and it had been such a long time since she had a friend. Should she confide in Kate? She decided not and resolutely pushed the thought away. She tried not to dwell on the negative aspects of her life; how just a few hours had needlessly separated her from her son forever, and how she would now have had the means to care for him properly since her mother would happily have minded him whilst she worked. No; she must concentrate on the present, anticipate the future, and not dwell on the past she told herself firmly.

Michael was quite right, she observed, when he said that their paths wouldn't cross a great deal, as he spent much of his time out of the office, and when he was there he remained closeted in the inner sanctum, calling occasionally for Kate to take dictation.

"Michael asked after you today Rach," Kate informed her one morning. "I have to go to Manchester next week for a couple of days so you'll be standing in for me taking dictation. You'll be pleased to know that Isabelle recommended you; I actually think she's impressed with you."

That weekend Rachel went shopping again for a new work outfit. If she was to take on Kate's duties she had better look the part. In the end she settled on a sleek jersey dress in midnight blue, with three-quarter sleeves and a wide scarlet belt that showed off her figure, now fully restored to its pre-Danny proportions. She contemplated a

159

stunning pair of stilettos in soft red leather that perfectly matched the belt. She had never worn stilettos but immediately she could see that they lent a certain sophistication to the outfit, and decided that the discomfort would be a small price to pay. A man like Michael was worth the effort, she decided.

Kate came in on the Monday morning to run through everything with her. She did a double take when she saw Rachel's new look, then narrowed her eyes and remarked pointedly,

"Hmmmm! If I was a betting woman, I'd say someone is hoping to impress Michael with rather more than her secretarial skills."

Rachel felt herself blushing violently. *Was it that obvious?* Kate grinned at her discomfiture,

"Don't mind me," she said. "That ship sailed a long time ago. Michael's a good man, but I warn you, he's a hard nut to crack. Still, I have a feeling you just might be on to a winner." She leaned across and squeezed Rachel's hand,

"Good luck kid," she said kindly. "You can tell me all about it on Wednesday."

The carpet in the inner sanctum was thick and springy and Rachel felt her heels sinking into it as she walked into the room. The floor of the anteroom was tiled in the same way as the corridor and the stilettos had click-clacked a path across it that sounded shockingly loud, making Rachel feel she ought to tip-toe. She tried to, but fearing that she may overbalance, gritted her teeth and approached the door to the inner sanctum boldly. Michael, hearing the sound of stilettos on the tiles outside, felt a sudden pang of disappointment. Kate, it appeared, had changed her mind about her trip to Manchester. He

160

therefore didn't look up as the door opened until Rachel was halfway across the room.

"Wow!" The exclamation was out of his mouth before he could stop it. Gone was the fashionably dressed but nevertheless rather gauche young girl whom he had interviewed back in May, and in her place was a veritable doyenne of sophistication, the knee-length skirt and scarlet stilettos making her appear several inches taller; sleek, well-groomed and ladylike in the nicest sense of the word. She smiled at him suddenly; her soft brown eyes lighting up with pleasure at his involuntary exclamation of approval. He composed himself and said,

"It's nice to see you Rachel; please take a seat. I need you to take a letter for me." He dictated the letter to her, pausing now and then to collect his thoughts. She wrote swiftly in shorthand, her pen flying across the page of her notebook faster than he could think, pausing momentarily every now and then as he contemplated his next sentence. He noticed that her hands were small and delicate, the nails cut quite short and painted in a pale pearlescent varnish that matched her lipstick. Kate, he thought, would have worn red lipstick with that outfit; he felt that Rachel had instinctively known that would have been too much for someone as young as she.

"Will you have dinner with me Rachel?" There, he had asked her. He hadn't meant to ask her so soon, but somehow the words just escaped from his mouth of their own volition. She hesitated; his heart sank. What if she refused; how would he overcome the embarrassment and maintain a working relationship from now on. She was staring at him; he wished he could read her mind.

"Thank you Michael, I'd love to." She answered at last, and he breathed again.

"Are you free tomorrow evening?" he asked now, wishing he dared say 'this evening', but knowing that women generally preferred a little prior notice of these things.

Rachel thought quickly. It wouldn't do to jump at the offer and appear gauche and over-eager, and besides, she needed some advice on what to wear.

"Thursday would be better," she answered. "May I ask where we're going?"

"To be honest I have no idea," Michael replied with a smile and a rueful shrug. "Where would you like to go?"

"We-ell," Rachel replied, a little hesitantly. She wasn't used to posh restaurants and wouldn't feel comfortable. "A country pub would be lovely, one that does nice food — if that's alright with you that is."

"Perfect!" replied Michael emphatically. "I think I know just the place. I'll pick you up at seven. Are you on the phone at home? Just in case anything crops up." Rachel gave him her phone number and he wrote it in a small black diary that he kept in the breast pocket of his jacket. The rest of the afternoon passed quickly, and considering that they were working, pleasantly. The sexual tension between them was almost tangible and Rachel had to check her work carefully afterwards for errors. However, it didn't seem to have been unduly affected.

"You're what?"

Kate was astonished when Rachel told her she was to have dinner with Michael.

"My, you're a fast worker," she laughed. "I only turned my back for five minutes!"

"You don't mind, do you Kate? If it's going to spoil our friendship I won't go."

162

"Don't be s'daft! I told you; that ship has sailed, and my head was getting sore from banging it against a brick wall for years. He needs a woman in his life Rach, and if it can't be me, then I'm glad it's going to be you. Go and enjoy yourself and stop worrying about me for goodness sake; you'll be giving me a Cinderella complex!"

Wednesday and Thursday dragged interminably and Rachel now wished she had been less circumspect in responding to Michael's invitation.

"What are you wearing?" asked Kate.

"I don't know; what do you think I should wear? We're going to a country pub for a meal."

"Oh, smart casual then, definitely. If it wasn't your first date I'd say jeans and a nice tee shirt, but perhaps you'd better glam up a bit more than that. What about that blue halter neck dress? You've only worn it here once and I think you look really nice in it. You might need a cardi or a jacket though, it's not so warm in the evenings now." August had been disappointingly dull and cool and already there was a hint of autumn in the air.

"I'll just take a cardi; I can sling it over my shoulders if I need to. Oh Kate, I'm so nervous! What if it's a disaster? I still have to work with him, after all."

"It won't be, trust me. I've sensed something between you two since that first day. Michael isn't one to rush into things hastily; believe me he will have given it a lot of thought before taking the plunge. Just enjoy it and see what happens, yer daft cow." She gave Rachel a quick reassuring hug.

"Thanks Kate," Rachel said, "You're a true friend."

Thursday evening was warm and sunny without the autumnal feel that had pervaded of late. Rachel's mother fussed around her. Rachel had decided in the end to tell her about her date with Michael.

"Remember, he's your boss, so mind your ps and qs; you don't want to jeopardise your job girl."

"Mum, he's my boss at work fair enough, but I'm not going to be taking dictation tonight – or making the coffee!" Rachel laughed, and hugged her mother. "Don't worry, I won't do anything to get me the sack."

"You can laugh young lady, but they say you shouldn't mix work and pleasure, don't they?"

Michael's car drew up outside and she dropped a kiss on her mother's cheek and made for the door. When she opened the door she was surprised to see that Michael was on the doorstep.

"You look nice," he said. "Good evening Mrs. Steele, it's a lovely evening."

"Oh, please call me Eileen Mr. Fenton."

"Only if you'll call me Michael," he rejoined. "It's very nice to meet you Eileen; you've done a fine job in raising this young lady."

"Oh, thank you, I do my best," her mother replied, self-consciously smoothing down the folds of her pinny. *What a charming man,* she thought. "Have a lovely evening."

"We will," answered Michael over his shoulder as he opened the passenger door for Rachel. He waved at her mum as he climbed into the driver's seat and drove away. Eileen smiled in satisfaction as the net curtains along the street twitched back into place. *Charming, good-looking, and the perfect gentleman – Rach has fallen on her feet this time,* she thought as she closed the door.

"I think you just gained a fan," laughed Rachel as they drove away down the tree-lined avenue past the park. Rachel glanced briefly towards the folly, which you could

164

just make out in the distance if you knew where to look. That January night seemed like another lifetime now.

He took her to a charming waterside inn where they sat outside in the garden with ice-cold gin and tonics whilst they waited for their table. The river flowed lazily by and the air was fragrant with the scent of cut grass. Rachel fingered her glass a little nervously wondering if she was going to be out of her depth.

"Your mum's nice," said Michael. How is she coping without your father?"

"Oh, she copes. She's a strong woman and she has the twins to think of. I think they were a bit of a shock when they arrived, but she's glad she has them now; they help her focus on the present instead of dwelling on the past. My Nan helps out; she lives in the next street."

"You seem a close family; there's a lot to be said for that," Michael observed. "Funny that we both have twins in our families. Mine are a little older than your brothers though; they'll be thirteen next year – teenagers. I'm not looking forward to that!"

They chatted about everyday things. There was an easy rapport between them and Rachel began to relax and enjoy his company. The meal was delicious, as was the wine that accompanied it, chosen by Michael since Rachel had little knowledge of such things. *I could get used to this,* she thought.

They lingered after the meal over the rest of the wine, moving to the lounge where a bright fire burned in the grate, for the evening had turned chilly as dusk drew in.

Afterwards he drove her home, pulling up outside her house. He kept the engine running and said,

"Thank you Rachel, for a lovely evening. Can we do this again?"

"Thank you too; I'd love to," she answered, her heart beating so loudly she thought he must hear it above the purr of the engine.

She expected him to kiss her but instead he took her hand and said,

"I think we have an audience Rachel. Would you have dinner with me at my home on Saturday? I'm not a bad chef though I say it myself."

"That would be lovely," she replied. *At his home – wow!*

"I'll pick you up at six. You can explore the place whilst I cook; it's a rambling old house but quite interesting. I'm out of the office tomorrow, which is probably just as well. I'll see you on Saturday."

Rachel's mother was waiting for her in the hallway.

"Well, how did it go? Are you going to see him again?" Rachel laughed,

"Of course I am Mum. He's my boss, remember?"

"Very funny! You know what I meant. I must say he seems a very nice young man – lovely manners."

"Yes Mum, he is, and I'm going to his house on Saturday for dinner." *Young man,* she thought, *he's only a few years younger than Mum!*

The next day at work, she told Kate all about her evening and her impending date with Michael.

"Wow! Dinner at home? You'll love his house, it's enormous."

"Have you been there then?"

"I have. I went there once when he left his briefcase at work. I could have rung him but I was curious, and it was in the days when I still had hopes of him. He was really kind; showed me around and made me coffee in his kitchen. He said he had thought of selling up and getting somewhere smaller but he wanted it to be somewhere familiar for his children to come home to when they visit. He's kept their rooms for them just as they were when they left. He must rattle around in there like anything all on his own."

On Saturday Rachel was ready and waiting long before six o'clock arrived. Following Kate's advice she dressed casually in jeans and a bright silk blouse that draped softly over her curves. She had her hair trimmed to refresh her sleek Purdey bob and treated herself to a pair of gold hooped earrings from H Samuel's to complete the look. A quick spray of her favourite Goya Wild Silk perfume, and she was ready.

"Should I take anything with me?" she had asked Kate, "A bottle of wine or anything?"

"I should forget the wine," laughed Kate, "Michael has enough of that to float a battleship; but you could take some after dinner mints or something – that would be a nice gesture." Rachel settled for a box of After Eight mints.

"You look nice love," said her mother approvingly. "What time will you be home?"

"I don't know Mum, but don't wait up will you," Rachel answered. She had no idea what Michael had in mind for her, but whatever it was, she would be more than happy to go along with it. She heard his car pull up outside, and giving her mother a quick hug she hurried to the door, then walked to the car with as much nonchalance as she could muster. Michael, to her relief, was also wearing jeans, with an open necked blue shirt that intensified the blue of his eyes. He smelt delicious.

"Do I smell of cooking?" he asked.

"Not at all. At least, if you do, I'm a little concerned about what we might be eating," she replied. "Good job I brought some of these." She handed him the mints, and he laughed. There was that unexpected dry sense of humour again that he enjoyed.

"I did splash on a bit of extra aftershave as a precaution," he said as the car pulled away. He turned to wave at her mother, who stood at the window watching them go.

Michael's house was indeed enormous. The gracious mellowed red brick building stood at the end of a quiet country lane surrounded by fields and meadows and accessed by a long tree-lined drive. The grounds were enclosed with post and rail fencing at the front and a low sandstone and flint wall at the side that encompassed a small stable yard. In the paddock next to the stable yard two ponies grazed, one dappled grey and the other a dark glossy bay.

"They belong to Molly and Kieran," he told her, following her gaze. There's a girl who comes to ride them from the village to keep them in shape for when they come home in the holidays. I'll never sell them, they'll live their lives out here."

Inside, the house was cool and serene with a mix of antique and strikingly contemporary furniture. The floors were mainly polished oak, covered in varying rugs of mainly oriental extraction. A long sweeping staircase rose in an arc from the large panelled entrance hall, and several doorways afforded glimpses of the rooms beyond. A long corridor led to the vast farmhouse kitchen where Michael led her. The kitchen was warm and welcoming, pervaded by some delicious aromas of cooking which appeared to emanate from the triple Aga cooker that stood in an

168

inglenook on one side of the room. Beside it a rustic pine breakfast bar jutted from the wall, flanked by tall bar stools. The walls were lined with free-standing antique pine furniture except for along one side where built in cupboards topped with slate housed a large butlers sink and wooden draining board. A long heavy pine table ran almost the length of the room, and at the far end windows extended the height and breadth of the room, with heavy wooden shutters at their sides. Nothing was new; everything looked as though it had grown there from the limestone flags beneath their feet.

"Would you like a drink Rachel?" Michael asked her, reaching down to open the oven door and checking the contents. "If you don't mind we'll sit in here, otherwise I'd have to abandon you whilst I finish cooking."

"It's nice in here. Can I do anything?"

"No thanks, I'd only get confused. I can cook, but I have to do everything in a certain order or I'm stuffed. You can sit there at the breakfast bar and chat to me – it's a long time since I've had any company in the kitchen except for the cats, and they're only in here for what they can scrounge. After we've eaten I'll show you around; that way you won't get lost."

"How long have you lived here?" she asked him.

"Most of my life," he replied. "I was raised in this house and when my father retired, he bought a villa in Spain and gifted me the house – I'm an only child, and he said I may as well have it whilst he was alive rather than get stung for inheritance tax. He founded Eagle, and he also owns two other electronics factories: Kestrel in Manchester, and Falcon not far from London. He and my mum have lived in Spain for over ten years now."

"So where did you live before he gave you the house?"

169

"When I married Susannah we bought a new build near Chester. Susannah liked the idea of no one having lived in it before and enjoyed making it hers. I say hers, because with hindsight, that's really what it was; I had very little say in anything. Susannah could be very persuasive and I was too involved with learning the finer points of the business so that I could take over from my father. Two years later the twins came along, and by the time they were three years old and tearing round the house and garden like things possessed, the house began to feel a bit small and the shine was beginning to wear off. We were spending most weekends here and the twins had their own room, so when Dad told me his plan it was a small step to take. The old place has changed a bit since we moved in, some of it down to Susannah, although she was never terribly keen on the house if I'm honest. I haven't really done much to it since she left; I never had the heart somehow."

"I think it's lovely," said Rachel, thinking Susannah sounded awfully spoiled. "You could fit most of my house into this room!" Michael laughed.

"That's all very well when it's got a family in it, but it gets awfully lonely when you're rattling around in it with nobody to talk to."

The meal was delicious. They had prawn cocktail for starters, because Rachel had said it was her favourite, and Michael had remembered. This was followed by roast pheasant; accompanied by vegetables and delicious sautéed breadcrumbs, and a gravy made from red wine that Michael informed her was called a jus. This was followed by a wonderful concoction of summer fruits, cream, and meringue that she learned was called an Eaton Mess. They had red wine with the first course and white with the dessert. They ate in a small dining room just off the kitchen. Michael had drawn the curtains across to shut out the dull and drizzly late August evening and a welcoming log fire blazed away in the marble surrounded fireplace. Candles burned in silver candlesticks on the table and also on the mantelpiece, their flames reflected in the sparkling crystal wine glasses and gleaming cutlery. Rachel felt like a queen; she had never known such luxury. *I wish my mum could see this*, she thought. As if he had read her mind, Michael said,

"Why don't we bring your mum over for tea tomorrow; and the twins. They can even have a ride on Kieran's pony – not Molly's though; he's young, and a bit more of a handful. Jester's getting on a bit now, and he's pretty docile. I can rustle up some sandwiches and cake, but we'll have to nip into the village for some pop I'm afraid."

"Michael that's a lovely idea. Are you sure? The twins can be a bit of a shock to the system when you're not used to them. They're not allowed pop by the way, it makes them go ape; so you can save yourself a shopping trip since they only drink water or squash at home."

Michael laughed, "Must be a twin thing – mine were exactly the same, though they've calmed down now I'm happy to say. That's settled then; you'd better give your mum a ring and tell her. Oh, and while you're at it, you'd better tell her you're staying here tonight. I've had far too much wine to be driving. I'm not propositioning you; I've a very pretty guest room, and I'm sure she'll be pleased to know that is where you'll be sleeping. The phone's in the hallway, so go and talk to her and then I'll show you around."

Michael was as good as his word, and after showing her around the rest of the house, including the guest room that had an ensuite bathroom and was equipped with everything you could need for an impromptu stay, they settled down in the drawing room and drank wine and chatted until late. He was easy company, and quite expert at extracting information from her regarding her likes and dislikes and her interests. She found herself telling him about her frustrated interest in art, history, and poetry, which she had given up on leaving school in favour of perfecting her secretarial skills.

"I'm glad you did," he said quietly, "Otherwise we should never have met."

They sat on the sofa by the fire, his arm resting easily about her shoulders. He asked her about former boyfriends. She said there had never been anyone serious, and wondered with a jolt what he would think if he knew the truth about her, how she had been easy prey for a man who clearly didn't feel she was worthy of any respect. Oh how she regretted all that now; how she wished she had been more circumspect and less of a pushover. She barely recognized the girl she was back then, the girl who certainly wouldn't be sitting here now with this lovely man. She suddenly felt terribly weary. If only she could turn the clock back. She stifled a yawn.

"Hey, you're tired. Why didn't you say? It's so nice to have someone to talk to that I got a bit carried away. Off you go to bed now; I'll wake you when breakfast is ready." He pulled her to her feet, and took her into his arms.

"Thank you so much Rachel, I can't remember when I enjoyed an evening more." Before she could answer, he bent and kissed her gently. She melted into him and returned the kiss, feeling his arms tighten around her. At last they broke apart.

"Goodnight, lovely Rachel," he said, smiling.

"Goodnight Michael; I've had a wonderful evening." She turned away from him and climbed the long staircase, turning near the top to wave, feeling like Scarlett O'Hara in Gone With The Wind.

Rachel and Michael were married in the village church at Farnley on Christmas Eve. They postponed the honeymoon because Kieran and Molly came over for the wedding, as did Michael's parents, and Molly was Rachel's flower girl. It was a small wedding. Rachel wore a simple dress in cream lace with a long white velvet hooded cape. Her mother bought a soft woolen dress and matching coat in sage green, and had her hair cut and styled. On the eve of the wedding, Michael presented her with a splendid mink coat that had once belonged to his mother, (she said she had no use for it in Spain) and to Rachel he gave an exquisite sapphire necklace that had belonged to his grandmother.

"Something old and blue my love," he said.

Rachel's gran immediately stepped in and purloined the green woolen coat. It went, she said, very nicely with her cherry red mohair hat. Secretly, Rachel thought she looked rather like a radish, but she was happy, so what the hell.

"Mum you look fantastic," said Rachel. "I always said I'd get you to ditch the pinny sometime!" Johnny and Jimmy were on their best behaviour and Kate was the only bridesmaid, wearing a deep red dress and a shorter version of Rachel's cape with a stand-up collar instead of a hood. Isabelle was there too, although she refused their invitation to the party afterwards, saying that she needed to get home to her cats.

"They'll be upset if I don't light the fire for them on Christmas Eve," she said.

"I never knew she had cats," said Kate. "Well, you learn something about people every day!"

173

Afterwards they all returned to the house, where Michael had arranged for caterers to provide the wedding buffet. Fires blazed in all the rooms, and they danced the night away to a DJ in the great hall where a ten foot Christmas tree stood in front of the tall window.

At the end of the evening Rachel and Michael sat by the fire in the drawing room after everyone else had either left or gone to bed. She reflected on how her life had changed in the past twelve months. This time last year she was eight months pregnant and her future looked bleak. She was a different person now; she had been given a second chance, and she would always be grateful for that.

"Merry Christmas Mrs. Fenton," said Michael gently as he took her in his arms.

"Merry Christmas," she replied happily.

FOURTEEN: FIVE YEARS LATER, (1983).

Mariana waited anxiously outside the school gates. The first stampede of children exiting the school was over and now they appeared in dribs and drabs, the ones who were not so eager for home for reasons probably known only to themselves. Danny, apparently, was one of them. Now only one other mother remained, and Mariana didn't recognize her, so she merely smiled at her and didn't try to make conversation. After what seemed like an eternity Danny appeared, hand in hand with his teacher whose other hand clutched in its turn that of a little girl with golden hair who was dabbing at her face with an enormous handkerchief. Mariana could hear the sobs from halfway across the playground. Clearly, something had upset the little girl terribly.

"Oh, no, not again," thought Mariana.

"Mrs. Harding, Mrs. Crofts, I'm sorry we have kept you waiting," the teacher called out, relinquishing her hold on the two. The little girl ran to her mother and buried her face in the folds of her dress, sobbing with renewed vigour. Danny approached more slowly to stand beside Mariana, silent and unflinching, regarding his teacher with a look of defiance.

175

"Has something happened?" Mariana asked the teacher anxiously. The other mother occupied herself trying to placate her offspring. The teacher reached the gate; she was flushed and a little breathless.

"That's what I've been trying to ascertain," she said. "I found them in the cloakroom. Chloe was crying and says she hates Danny, but they won't tell me what has happened. Perhaps one of you can get some answers before tomorrow since clearly Danny has upset Chloe in some way, even though neither of them is prepared to part with any information as to what happened.

"I'm sorry," said Mariana, moving her gaze from mother to teacher. "I shall do my best to get to the bottom of it. Come along Danny, you and I have some talking to do!" She took his hand and hurried away. Glancing back, she saw the teacher and the other mother still deep in conversation.

"Are your ears burning Danny?" she asked, "Because mine are! What did you do to Chloe?"

"Chloe's stupid, and I didn't do anything." Danny was sullen and recalcitrant, refusing to look his mother in the eye. They walked home in silence whilst Mariana pondered how she was going to tackle him, and Danny pondered how he was going to talk his way out of this one. Mariana couldn't help wondering where her lovely sunny-natured baby had gone. Ever since he reached the age of four he had been changing, becoming moody and unpredictable and not seeming to care how much he upset her. She had hoped that school would sort him out, but after a year in Miss Radcliffe's class, the situation was going from bad to worse and he seemed to be constantly falling out with the other children, although it was never clear why. She decided she must tackle it now, before he got any older; it was surely only going to get worse otherwise.

They sat facing one another over the kitchen table and mugs of hot chocolate. Alfie settled down next to her, resting his chin on her feet.

"Ok Danny, are you going to tell me what's going on? This is the second time this week." She looked her son in the eye and he glared back unflinchingly.

"No," he said, quietly but firmly. He buried his face in his mug of chocolate, drained it quickly and made to rise from the table.

"Oh, no you don't!" Mariana said sternly. "I want answers Danny; I don't know what's got into you lately."

"Too bad," he answered with a shrug, "you can't make me." He walked off without a backward glance, leaving a stunned Mariana sitting there alone. She sunk her head into her hands; Alfie pushed a damp nose against her arm and pawed at her anxiously.

"Oh, Alfie! What am I going to do with him?" Mariana sighed. She felt weary, defeated; she had no-one to turn to for answers except a dog. She cast her mind back over the years since Danny appeared in her life as though by magic. They had become a completely self-sufficient little unit, the three of them – herself, Danny and Alfie. They didn't really need anyone else and her friendship with Kate had gradually dwindled to the occasional day out in Kate's car on a Sunday, not even once a month any more. They had grown apart and Kate had new friends now, in particular a girl at work named Rachel whom Mariana had never met. Lorna had two children now and although she and her husband George were Danny's Godparents along with Kate, it seemed that the occasional phone call, and presents on birthdays and Christmas were all they felt necessary to fulfil their obligations, and she could hardly blame them, she thought. No, there was no help, she would have to ride this one out in the hope that it was just a phase.

That night, the dreams began again. She awoke in the early hours to feel runnels of sweat trickling between her breasts and down her arms. The dream had seemed so real. There was Terry, leering at her from the doorway, his eyes glittering with venom in the half light. She had a strong feeling that he had been standing there for some time, watching her sleep, but when she turned on the bedside light, there was nobody there and she realised it had been a dream. It was nearly six o'clock, and a pale dawn was spreading slowly across the allotments at the back of the house. She stood at the window and watched the rooks gathering in the trees opposite, squabbling and jostling for position. Then she caught a sound coming from Danny's room. She tiptoed onto the landing and stood listening outside his door. He was talking to himself in low, hushed tones as though he didn't want to be overheard. She leaned closer, straining her ears to try and catch what he was saying. A floorboard creaked beneath her feet and the talking ceased. She opened the door gently and peeped in. He was to all appearances sound asleep, his face flushed with warmth, his breathing deep and even. He looked completely relaxed. Perhaps she had dreamed that too, she thought, and made her way downstairs for a cup of coffee. Alfie rose from his place on the rug beside her bed and followed her, his tail waving slowly, uncertainly.

"It's alright boy," Mariana bent to ruffle his ears, "nothing for you to worry about." The wagging increased and he ran to the door, tugging at his lead that hung there.

"Later boy, after Danny's gone to school," said Mariana, opening the door onto the back garden to let him cock his leg as usual against Dani's tree that now spread its canopy halfway across the garden. In Spring, its blossom would fill the air with delicious fragrance.

She supposed she had got off lightly really. The terrible two's and three's had passed un-noticed and the fearsome fours' only kicked in right at the end, in fact just after he started going to school the term before his fifth birthday. It had begun in small ways – he had kept things from her, not wanting to join in with school activities, so that she didn't find out about things like the harvest festival concert, the autumn bring and buy or the school nativity play until it was too late. Danny therefore failed to contribute to any of these and Mariana felt that the teachers held her responsible. She asked them in future to give any newsletters and notes directly to her, as putting them in his school bag didn't guarantee that she would ever receive them. She had asked him what happened to them, but he insisted that he had never received them in the first place. She knew he was lying; once or twice would be a credible oversight, but *every time?* Mariana didn't think so!

She had to make allowances for him, she told herself. He had no father figure to look to, after all. Little boys, she was finding to her cost, are a whole different ball game from little girls, and she had no idea how his mind worked much of the time. It was worrying, because it could only get worse as he grew older. She had consciously avoided making friendships among the other mothers, still painfully aware of the secret she carried and afraid that one of them might turn out to be Danny's real mother and perhaps want him back. At the school gates they all had their cliques and she hung back, only smiling politely and avoiding engaging in conversation. It was easy; no one really noticed her because Danny would run happily into school without any of the clinginess displayed by many of his classmates and she would be well on her way home

179

before most of them had finished saying goodbye to their offspring. So there was nobody she could confide in or ask for advice and she just had to muddle through somehow, trying her best to be both mother and father to her son who was becoming more and more distant the older he became. It was just a phase, she told herself; he would grow out of it, and at least he was healthy and never caused her any worries on that score.

In the end, Mariana gave up her attempts to get to the bottom of Danny's run-in with Chloe. It was futile, as she was to find repeatedly over the next few years; there was no way of forcing Danny to account for his behaviour.

All through primary school, Danny remained a constant cause for concern. He never made any friends amongst the other boys, preferring the company of girls, but inevitably falling out with them in spectacular fashion after a few weeks. The teachers didn't seem to know how to handle him, and he was accused of almost every misdeed that occurred, or so it seemed to Mariana, so that she had no choice but to defend him – after all, he couldn't possibly be to blame all the time! She knew what they all said about him behind her back, and it cut her to the quick. After all, surely everyone is entitled to a few mistakes. By the time he was ready for secondary school, Mariana was glad she would no longer have to stand by the school gates and bear the brunt of the other mothers' complaints about her son. In spite of his appalling behaviour, Danny was a beautiful boy and Mariana found it hard to stay mad at him for long, feeling sure that he was merely misunderstood. She didn't want him travelling on the school bus with the other boys from his school whom she knew were often unkind to him. She made the decision to move to somewhere where his troubled boyhood wouldn't follow

FIFTEEN: DANNY.

At eleven years old Danny decided that he didn't fit in anywhere, never had, and never would. He couldn't explain his feelings, not even to himself, but he knew he was different.

Danny had never known love, although he would have found that a difficult statement to qualify since his mother was devoted to him and went to great lengths to prove it. Nothing was ever too much trouble, and every night of his life had he allowed it, she would have tucked him up in his bed with a cuddle and a kiss and told him how much she loved him. He in turn would have answered mechanically, "I love you too Mum," although he didn't really comprehend what that was supposed to mean since he had never felt love for anyone, therefore the concept was completely alien to him.

He soon put a stop to all that, however. When he was eight years old and the nightly declarations of love from his mother became an embarrassment he began barricading his door when he went to bed.

When he was nearly five, just before he started school, his mother had told him about his sister Danielle who had died of a sudden illness when she was only four. She told him that when he came along she had named him after his sister, and how lucky she had been to be given a second chance at motherhood. She showed him photographs of Danielle, a cute little dark-haired girl, laughing and playing, being pushed on a swing by their tall, handsome father who had also died without ever knowing Danny. There was even a photograph of her taken on her last day dressed in a pretty sparkly pink party dress, surrounded by other children, smiling and happy, apparently unaware that anything untoward was about to happen.

It seemed that Danielle had had everything he would never have; two parents who adored her, a capacity for love, and no one to compete with for it. He was absolutely convinced that even though she was somewhere way out of reach, he was still second best and always would be. Had she lived, he believed she might have proved to be less than the perfect angel her mother remembered; she would have had faults like any other child. You can't compete with a ghost he decided, so he didn't even try, but became increasingly sullen and withdrawn, spending most of his time alone in his room. Nevertheless, his mother loved him dearly, and made sure to tell him so whenever he allowed it. His mother was also (quite understandably,) somewhat overprotective of him, and he was never encouraged to mix much with other children or allowed to go to parties – not that he was ever invited anyway, nor indeed would he have wanted to go. She still escorted him to and from school until the day he went to secondary school which was too far from their home to walk to, and his mother had never learned to drive. His father had died at the wheel of his car. His grandparents, too, had been lost in a tragic car crash along with one of his aunts, so he understood his mother's dislike of cars. He had never met any of his father's family, and doubted that they even knew of his existence. His mother said that they had fallen out with his father long before she even met him. When he asked about his father, she told him that she didn't want to talk about him. He was not a good man, and best forgotten, and that was all she wished to say on the subject. Danny wondered what his father might have done to elicit such revulsion in someone as mild-mannered as his mother. After showing him the pictures, she replaced them carefully in the box and returned it to the attic. Danny was left with his questions unanswered and a huge gap in his identity that would blight his life.

Soon after his mother told him about Danielle, the voices had started. He would wake in the night and she, Danielle, was there inside his head talking incessantly, asking questions and telling him to do things. It was her idea to hide the notes from school, and when he complied, for a while she left him alone, until his mother discovered his deceit and forgave him as always. Then she was back, telling him precisely how to bully little girls, for he had no idea they were so easily upset. This time, however, there was no let up, and he had to recount his deeds in detail each time in order to satisfy her. Danny believed that she was jealous of his victims; they were alive, and it simply wouldn't do for them also to be happy. He went along with her wishes because they were little girls, and he hated little girls. As he grew older however, it became increasingly difficult to carry out her demands because everyone grew wary of him and avoided his company. Danny became a loner, and the other children soon turned the tables on him, ganging up against him and calling him names like Freak and Weirdo.

That was when she told him to bully poor Alfie instead. Danny knew Alfie meant the world to his mother.

When she was unhappy because of Danny's behaviour it was inevitably Alfie she turned to. She would pour her heart out to him whilst he sat by her side resting a paw on her knee, his soft brown eyes gazing into hers with deep consternation. She would hug him and he would lick the salt tears from her face. Danny witnessed these moments many times without them knowing. It was clear to him that Alfie, like Danielle, occupied a place in his mother's heart that he could not.

"What are you waiting for Danny," whispered Danielle. *"You know what to do."* Danny knew that if his mother found out, she would find this harder to forgive than anything he had ever done, so he was very careful – after all, Alfie couldn't talk, but he could cry out, so again there was no physical harm involved. Instead, at every opportunity, Danny would crouch in front of him, holding his head firmly and looking him straight in the eye. In menacing tones, he would tell him what a bad dog he was, and how stupid and worthless. Alfie may not have understood the words, but the tone and the implied threat were unmistakable.

Gradually the bouncing, extrovert Alfie changed and became cowed and nervous. He began chewing his feet constantly. Mariana took him to the vet, who said there was nothing physically wrong and the chewing was most probably stress-induced. He asked if anything had occurred to cause this, but Mariana could think of nothing and it remained a mystery. The vet prescribed long walks and some mild tranquilisers. She took him to the park daily whilst Danny was at school. She would take a sandwich and sit near the duck pond whilst he ran free seeming completely normal. As soon as he was back in the house however, it started again, and much as Mariana adored him, the chomping and slurping was impossible to ignore, so

184

that eventually she was forced to banish him from her bedroom where he had always slept, confining him to the kitchen at night. Danny reveled in the success of his mission, and Mariana grew increasingly unhappy, as did Alfie. *It's this house,* she thought. *It's never been a happy house, I should have moved when Terry died.*

SIXTEEN: A NEW BEGINNING.

"You're moving?" said Kate. "When? Where to?"

"I'm not going far, just to Farnley. I want Danny to go to a country school. Farnley seems like a nice place and I've found us a two-bedroomed house with a garden overlooking the river. The school bus goes from just down the road, and the school is only five miles away. It'll be a fresh start for both of us; he's never fitted in at school and every time he got into trouble I would find myself wondering if his real mum was somewhere around and whether she knew I was bringing him up all wrong. If we move I won't be wondering any more if every woman I see is her come to take him back. This has never been a happy house for me Kate, and not for Danny either. A fresh start – the more I think about it, the better I feel."

"I'll help you move M; you'll need someone with a car for the bits and pieces. Just give me a ring when you're ready."

"Thanks Kate. I'm sorry I haven't seen so much of you lately. It's been hard with everything that's been going on. I hope we'll keep in touch after I move."

"Of course we will you daft cow. As a matter of fact, it's not far from where Rachel and Michael live so perhaps I'll introduce you some time. You should see their place, it's stunning."

"Oh, I don't know, I'm not really one for socialising. When are you going to find yourself a nice man Kate, and start a family of your own instead of being everyone else's kids' Godmother?"

"Nice men are pretty few and far between M, as you'd know if you hadn't shut yourself away all these years. I had high hopes of Michael once, but I'm afraid Rachel managed to beat me to it."

"And you're still friends? How come?"

"Oh, I don't know. I just took a liking to her, and it wasn't her fault that Michael picked her. She lost a child too you know; Mickey had a stillborn twin, so you and Rachel have something in common. I really think you'd like her.

"Well, let me find my feet first Kate; I'm not ready for introductions yet. I'm hoping Alfie will get better when I can walk him along the river every day. I might need you to run me to the vet's with him sometimes and I've heard there's a good one near Danny's school"

"Of course, just say the word. Poor old Alfie; he used to be such a livewire. Let's hope they can get to the bottom of it soon. I'll have to shoot off now but don't forget to ring me when you know your moving date." They hugged each other and Mariana felt happy that they would continue to be friends. Perhaps the new place would be the end of her isolation, and Danny's.

They were moving to the countryside. Danny felt a mixture of excitement and fear. Excitement because this was, as his mother told him, a new start. He was going to a new school; he would meet new children and be taught by teachers who didn't know of his past misdemeanours.

Perhaps everything would be different; perhaps Danielle would leave him alone when he no longer slept in her room. The fear was that nothing would change and he would continue to be an outcast and a slave to her demands. He threw himself into helping his mother with the packing, sorting out all his stuff and packing it in boxes. Looking around at the empty room he thought how good it would be to have a room that was entirely his and not his sister's old one that she refused to relinquish. Surely, he would be leaving her behind in this room that just wasn't big enough for the both of them. His mother had taken him to see his new home. His room overlooked the river; you could just make out the silver ribbon through the intervening trees that at night rustled and danced in the light of the street lamps. No cars passing, and no late night revelers; it was peaceful and felt like a sanctuary. He and his mother discussed how they would decorate it, replacing the magnolia walls with deep blue like a midnight sky. She promised it would be the first room they decorated. He felt something lift from his shoulders as he stood at the window of his new world.

Their new home was a small modern terraced house on an estate at the edge of the village situated well away from the main road. The back of the house overlooked the river, with a narrow path that ran along the entire row giving direct access to the riverside meadows. It would be ideal for walking Alfie who was getting too old and arthritic now to go far, but would still attempt to chase a rabbit when he got the chance. There was a grocer's shop, a butchers, and a farm shop all within walking distance, so Mariana would have little need to venture back into town; but should she wish to do so there was a regular bus service. Near the end of the summer term Kate had taken

188

them to visit the school that was on the outskirts of a larger village a few miles away. Mariana was favourably impressed and the children appeared friendly and well-behaved. Danny even acknowledged their greetings with a shy smile and a nod. Perhaps here he would at long last make some friends. Although Mariana knew that the school would probably have received a report on Danny's somewhat appalling behaviour from his primary school, there was no hint of reticence in the welcome the teachers extended to him. She thought he looked relieved – things must have been getting on top of him more than he would care to admit, she thought, her heart going out to him.

They moved on a fine day in mid August, with the help of a large removal van and Kate's car. Mariana had spent the past few weeks gradually packing up their belongings into boxes and labeling them carefully. She and Danny cleared out the attic together. There was a box in there already sealed and labeled *Dani*. It contained the mementoes of Danielle that Mariana had used to go through every so often, the last time when Danny was four. Now she felt a sudden longing to look through it again, and determined that once they were settled in she and Danny would go through it together so that he could learn a little more about his sister. Saying nothing to Danny about it – he was busy packing up some of his old toys to go to the charity shop, she placed it carefully in the back of Kate's car; she would surprise him with it later, she thought.

They worked hard and by late evening everything had been transported to the new house and the removal van had departed.

"Phew!" said Kate, plonking herself down on the sofa that was surrounded by boxes and bags. "I wouldn't fancy doing that again!"

"Me neither," agreed Mariana. "Hopefully we won't ever need to unless I win the pools!"

Danny was in his room, already unpacking his stuff and arranging his bedroom to his liking. Mariana had taken him shopping the previous week for new bedding and curtains, the first he had ever chosen himself. His curtains and duvet cover were themed from Star Wars and they would go well with the planned midnight blue walls.

"He seems happy about the move M," Kate observed.

"He does, doesn't he?" mused Mariana. Indeed, she hadn't seen Danny so upbeat in years. "I really hope this move will be the making of him."

Kate volunteered to make the short trip to the chippy in the next village and came back with fish and chips all round. Danny bounded down the stairs to join them. Alfie rose from his bed beneath the kitchen table and approached him cautiously, yawning and stretching.

"What d'you think Alfie old boy?" Danny bent and fondled the old dog's ears. "Are we going to like it here?" Alfie's tail thumped slowly on the floor in agreement and cautiously he licked Danny's outstretched hand for the first time in months, before settling back down in his bed with a long sigh.

SEVENTEEN: AN ACCIDENTAL DEATH.

The respite lasted less than a year. Danny settled in at his new school, and after the first couple of weeks, no one really noticed him. Out of habit, he kept himself to himself, he didn't want to risk his new-found equilibrium and he was happy to remain anonymous. His classmates were curious at first, but soon lost interest and left him alone. He might have been popular if he hadn't been so cautious, but from choice, he had no friends. Out of school, he would spend hours exploring the countryside around his new home with Alfie, who had suddenly taken on a new lease of life and would bound across the meadow and plunge into the river for a swim, returning to shake his wet coat over Danny. Mariana smiled to herself as she watched them from the bedroom window. *I should have done this years ago,* she thought.

Their first Christmas in the new house was the best they had had since Danny was small. Kate came over for Christmas lunch with them and afterwards Danny went out on the new bike that Kate had bought him.

"You shouldn't have Kate," Mariana told her, "It's far too much!" Kate shook her head.

"No it's not M. You two have been through a lot and Danny seems so much happier now. He'll get good use out of that bike around here. I've been neglecting him lately and after all he is my godson, so just be pleased he likes it so much." Mariana pushed aside her vague feelings of jealousy. Money was tight these days, she had not sold the old house for as much as she had hoped, and she realised that finding a job nearby wouldn't be easy, but nevertheless she was going to have to look for one soon. The new bike, however, was definitely a hit with Danny, who used it to explore his surroundings in a way he hadn't yet been able to, since they had no car. Mariana was happy that he was out and about all weekend instead of spending all his time locked in his room as he had done for years in the old house.

For his twelfth birthday she bought him a Walkman cassette player, and then wondered if she had done the right thing since he barely used it after the first few days, and it had cost more than she could sensibly have afforded. He seemed, however, happier than she had seen him since he was a toddler. Her only concern was his apparent lack of any need for companionship, apart from Alfie, who now followed him constantly, even running alongside his bike sometimes, although these days he couldn't keep it up for any great distance. Her son still seemed to be a bit of a loner, and it worried her.

"Why don't you invite one of your friends round for tea on Saturday?" she asked him.

"No thanks, Mum, I'd rather not," was his answer, and she thought it best to respect his wishes. She rang the school and enquired about his progress and his behaviour there. They informed her that he had settled in well, and they had no concerns with either.

"Danny seems to have left all his past issues behind him Mrs. Harding," the headmaster assured her. "He's a little quiet, but that might be viewed as a good thing considering his previous record, don't you think? I'm sure he will come out of his shell as he progresses through the school." Mariana could see his point, and pushed aside the nagging doubts that still assailed her. Winter gave way to spring, and as the new leaves on the trees began to obscure the view of the river, the garden came into life, revealing crocus, tulips and daffodils in abundance. Mariana decided to plant a new tree for Danielle. She arranged for Kate to run her to the nearby garden centre where after much deliberation they chose a pretty weeping tree with pale pink scented flowers. Heaving it onto the flat metal trolley they wheeled it through the shop to the checkout, where they saw a notice: *'Part time staff wanted, please take an application form.'* Mariana took a form and put it in the pocket of her jeans. The garden centre was within easy walking distance of home and she really needed a job; any job. Kate promised her a reference from the factory.

"I know it was a long time ago, but we can bend the truth a bit I'm sure," she said with a wink.

Together they dug a large hole in the centre of the lawn ready to take the tree and poured water into it as the man in the garden centre had instructed them. Then they left the pot containing the tree to soak in it and went inside for a cup of coffee.

"Thanks, Kate," said Mariana, "I'd never have managed that by myself."

"Where's Danny?" asked Kate.

"He's gone fishing; took his lunch and Alfie and went about seven this morning. I hardly ever see him at weekends to be honest Kate; he's always out and about these days, either fishing or on his bike."

"That's good isn't it?" Kate asked, unsure whether or not her friend was pleased.

"Oh, yes, it's so much better than mooching around in his room all day like he used to. It just seems a pity he's always on his own instead of with other lads his age. Still, it's his choice I suppose, and he seems perfectly happy. I rarely have to walk Alfie nowadays; he gets plenty of exercise with Danny, and he's stopped that terrible habit of chewing his feet."

They finished their coffee and returned to the task of planting Danielle's tree. As they began filling in the hole Mariana looked up and saw Danny coming down the road. He was carrying something, staggering slightly under the weight, and as he drew nearer she could see that it was Alfie, his head dangling lifelessly, his tongue lolling out of his mouth. Then she saw that Danny was crying, with great wrenching sobs that wracked his body, the tears flowing down his face relentlessly.

"Oh God!" she exclaimed. "Danny, what's happened?"

"Alfie," Danny sobbed, and sank to his knees on the garden path allowing his precious burden to crumple to the ground. "He's dead Mum, he's dead!" Mariana saw blood seeping from Alfie's head, his ears matted with it, and the white patch on his chest stained dark red.

She drew Danny into her arms. "What happened?" she whispered. Danny's sobs increased as he tried to explain what had happened, but his words were incomprehensible. Kate stood slightly apart from the tableau on the ground, aghast, not knowing what to say or do. Mariana cradled her son and her dog, gently stroking first one then the other with grief washing over her in waves of nausea. Minutes passed before Kate pulled herself together and came over. She helped them slowly to their feet and with Mariana now carrying Alfie's lifeless body, she led them indoors.

Danny, it turned out, had decided to return home through the village instead of cutting up the path at the back of the house so that he could stop at the shop and buy some sweets. When he reached the bridge that carried the main road at the end of the riverbank path he called Alfie to him, intending to clip on his lead. Alfie however, saw another dog on the other side of the road and ran to greet it. A squeal of brakes and a sickening thud told Danny that Alfie had been hit by a car. He ran up the slope to the road and found Alfie lying there with the owner of the other dog bending over him. The lady was distraught, and clearly Alfie, who had taken a blow to the head, was dead. The driver of the car, the lady said, sped off immediately and was gone over the narrow bridge before she could take his number.

"I'm sorry son," she told Danny. "He just ran out; there was nothing I could do to stop him. Do you want me to walk home with you?" Danny shook his head. Numb with shock, he gathered poor Alfie in his arms and set off home. He held back the tears until he saw his mother and they began to flow relentlessly with grief, guilt, and remorse. They would never know who was driving the car. They buried Alfie under the new tree and it became *Alfie's tree*, not *Dani's tree* as Mariana had originally intended. Mariana had a small brass plaque made and set it at the base of the tree.

'Here sleeps Alfie,' it said simply.

Danny retreated into himself and stopped going down to the river. He left his fishing rod where it lay, and never went back for it. Mariana went to look for it the next day, but it had gone as she had expected it would. Danny didn't care; he would never go fishing again.

"I'm baaack!" Danny sat up suddenly, instantly awake, staring into the darkness. She was back; Danielle. Inside his head she was talking to him again. He fell out of bed, dazed and stupefied, fumbling for his school bag. The Walkman was in there somewhere. He dug deeper; it must be right down at the bottom. Her laughter echoed in his head, he pushed his fingers in his ears but it only made it louder.

"Oh Daaaaaneeeee! What's the matter, aren't you pleased to see me?" The mocking tone was lower now, lilting, whining and cajoling, *"Who's been a naughty boy then – that's my Danny. Did Mummy cry for Alfie then?"*

"Shut up, *shut up!*" Danny turned on the bedside light. There was his Walkman on the shelf above his bed. He snatched it down and hunted frantically again in his bedside cabinet for a cassette tape. Putting on the headphones he turned the volume up and let the pulsating tones of Guns 'n' Roses obliterate Danielle's voice from his consciousness. Turning off the light he crawled back into bed and lay in the darkness, the music pounding at his skull, his body bathed in a cold sweat. *Please God, not again!*

The next morning Danny stayed in his room until it was time to go to school. Mariana stood at the bottom of the stairs calling repeatedly, but he didn't respond. She climbed the stairs to his room.

"Danny, it's gone eight; you'll have to go without your breakfast or you'll miss the bus." There was no reply. She tapped gently on the door and pushed the handle down – Danny had locked it.

"*Danny, come on!*" Angry now, she banged on the door loudly. *What was he doing in there for God's sake!* As she turned to leave the door burst open and Danny hurtled past her, down the stairs and out of the front door, his school bag slung over his shoulder, his headphones on. She could hear the rhythmic thump of some heavy rock music – he must have the volume turned up full blast. The door slammed behind him and he was gone.

With a heavy heart Mariana witnessed her son slide back down into his own private hell. Try as she might she couldn't reach him. He began to spend all his time in his room as he used to, with his Walkman now seemingly glued to his head. He would go for days barely eating at all. She began leaving his meals outside his door on a tray since he refused to eat with her, and sometimes it was still there when she went to bed. She tried talking to him, reasoning with him, pleading with him, and once she lost her temper and shook him, tearing the headphones off his head and threatening to destroy them. Snatching them back, he pushed her away roughly and retreated into his room once more locking the door firmly behind him.

Later she listened outside and heard him sobbing; great heart-rending sobs that seemed to continue for hours. He lost weight, his already slight frame becoming almost ethereal, like some elfin being with enormous blue eyes that were beset with a permanent crazed stare. She made an appointment at the doctor's but he refused to go. Slight as he was, he was also strong, and Mariana was helpless to enforce her will on him. She waited with a feeling of dread for the letters to start arriving from the school.

The weeks passed however, and no such letters materialised. In the end, unable to bear it any longer, she telephoned the school again and asked how Danny was doing. The headmaster assured her as before that he was doing fine; he was a little quiet and withdrawn but not causing any trouble as such. *Let sleeping dogs lie,* he seemed to think. In fact, he did have some concerns, but he didn't really feel he could confide these to the boy's mother. Danny was now known as the Freak throughout the school, but having questioned him, he was sure it was just a passing phase.

"I understand his dog died, Mrs. Harding, and he felt in some way responsible," he continued. "Such events can have a profound effect on boys his age, but I'm sure he'll get over it in time if we just let him deal with it in his own way. I can refer him to an educational psychologist if you're really worried, but I don't think there's any undue cause for concern." *An educational psychologist? What was he implying?* Mariana thanked him and said she didn't think that was necessary. She put the phone down and decided it was time to call Kate.

She hadn't seen Kate since the day Alfie died. She was seeing someone, and as is often the case, everything else had taken a back seat. Mariana was glad that at last Kate seemed to have found some happiness, but right now she needed a friend more than she had for years. She dialed Kate's work number but a stranger answered. Kate had popped out for a minute, she informed Mariana.

"Can I give her a message, or will you ring back?" the person asked. "She shouldn't be more than a few minutes."

"Can you just tell her that Mariana phoned; there's no message thank you."

Mariana put the phone down, the tears pricking at her eyes. She couldn't recall ever having phoned Kate at work before. She had given her the number 'for emergencies only' a few years ago. *Why couldn't she be there when I needed her?* Mariana thought. Overwhelmed by despair, she sank onto the sofa and wept bitterly.

An hour later Kate's car pulled up outside.

"What's up M? Emergencies only we said, so I thought I'd better come straight over," she said as she burst through the door like a breath of fresh air. Mariana burst

198

into tears again. Kate gave her a hug then went into the kitchen to put the kettle on.

"Tea, coffee or wine?" she called through the kitchen door. It was only five-thirty, so Mariana settled for coffee.

"When Isabelle said you rang I knew there must be something drastically wrong," said Kate. "What's happened; is it the job?" Mariana had been working at the farm shop for almost a month now. It provided her with a welcome break from the house and a modest income.

"No, the job's fine – it's Danny."

"Danny? Is he alright? Has something happened to him?"

"You could say that. A couple of weeks after Alfie was killed he started getting all weird again – like he used to be but without the agro at school. He shuts himself in his room for hours on end and he hardly eats anything, although the headmaster says he appears to eat at school ok. He won't talk to me; he's barely said two words to me in weeks, and he has that damn Walkman glued to his head day and night with the volume on full blast. I was passing his room the other night and I could hear him talking. It sounded like he was arguing with someone and I heard him say 'fuck off', I'm sure I did, only there can't have been anyone else there. The headmaster said he could arrange for him to see a psychologist; but surely there's no need for that Kate. You don't think he's going crazy do you?" Mariana began to cry again.

"No, of course I don't," Kate assured her friend with a great deal more conviction than she actually felt. He's probably just missing Alfie you know; they had become so close, hadn't they. Have you thought of getting another dog?"

"No, not really. It's not so easy now that I'm working. We couldn't have a puppy; I wouldn't have time to even house train it. Alfie was special, but it's always a risk getting a rescue dog; I might not be so lucky next time."

"Well it wouldn't hurt to try; you could always take it back if it didn't work out. Look, why don't we go and see what they've got on Saturday – or are you working?"

"No, I swapped my Saturdays after two weeks because I didn't want to leave Danny here alone all day. I just didn't feel I could completely trust him – not that he ever comes out of his room, but if I wasn't here – well, who knows," she finished with a shrug. "Alright, I suppose it wouldn't hurt to have a look, though I doubt if we can persuade Danny to go with us," she added ruefully.

'Well try M. It'll be his dog this time. Perhaps if he feels he has something of his own to take responsibility for he'll make more of an effort. I'll come over Saturday morning. Jeff's going to some god-awful football match anyway. What is it with men and football? It's the one thing I'd change about him, and the one thing, with hindsight, that was good about Scott, since he never bothered with it! Do you feel a bit better now that we have some sort of plan?"

"I do; even if it doesn't work, at least we'll have given it our best shot."

"Ok, I'm off-skis. Tell him tonight M, it'll give him something to think about for the next few days."

"I'll try, if I can get him out from under those blasted headphones for long enough. Thanks Kate, you're a true friend!" They hugged, and Kate sped off in her little red car as Mariana waved her out of sight.

Danny showed not a glimmer of interest when Mariana told him of their impending visit to the re-homing centre; but on Saturday morning when Kate's car drew up outside, he came out of the house and climbed in the back

200

wordlessly. As they drove through the countryside back towards their old home the headphones remained glued to his head as he sat slumped in the back seat gazing out of the window. The re-homing centre was just the other side of town. Mariana remembered the last time she went there, not long after Terry died. She had walked the two miles or so there and returned home an hour later with Alfie. She couldn't help feeling it would be a miracle if she were to bond with another dog so soon after losing him.

The kennels stood in rows of galvanized pens with a run down the middle, at the end of which was a large covered exercise yard. Beyond that open meadows stretched in undulating rolls of verdant green. As they pulled up outside the offices a cacophony of barking broke out, interspersed regularly by one long-drawn-out mournful howl.

"Shut up Bowker!" a shrill voice came from the other side of the kennels. "Why do you always have to make the loudest noise?" A girl appeared from behind the galvanized pens. Wiping her hands against the front of her jeans, she pushed her hair back behind her ears and scrutinised the trio standing before her; Danny leaning against the side of the car looking disinterested, Kate in her inevitable stilettos, and Mariana gazing around anxiously as though she expected the Hound of the Baskervilles to suddenly emerge from one of the pens. Suddenly the girl's face lit up in recognition.

"Alfie," she said, smiling at Mariana. "You're Alfie's Mum aren't you?"

Mariana nodded dumbly. She had no recollection of this girl, who must have been only a slip of a kid when she came here for Alfie.

"He was my favourite," announced the girl. "I was here on work experience and he came in looking really depressed and nervous. I spent hours sitting with him and walking him so that he was fit to rehome. How is he?

"He's dead," said Danny. Everyone turned to stare at him. Mariana wished the floor would open up and swallow her.

"Danny!" she hissed, her cheeks burning.

"Well, he is, isn't he!" retorted Danny and strode off down the yard along the rows of pens, his hands in his pockets.

"I'm sorry; my son can be a little direct at times. He was really upset by Alfie's death; he'd never known life without him," Mariana said by way of explanation. "He was with him when he got run over and blamed himself, but it was just an accident. The only person who should feel guilty is the driver, because he didn't stop."

"Oh, I'm so sorry; how awful! Poor Alfie. So you've come to get a replacement?" the girl surmised cheerfully.

"Well not exactly," replied Mariana. "As far as I'm concerned Alfie's irreplaceable, but Kate thought it might be good for Danny to have a dog of his own and I'm quite happy to give it a go. Just a small one perhaps." She glanced down the row of kennels. Danny was walking slowly down the far side now, peering into the pens and stopping every now and then to crouch and stroke a nose or fondle some ears.

"Someone's coming round to the idea," whispered Kate encouragingly. Danny was sitting on the ground now, his arms clasped around his knees, his fingers through the wire netting. As they approached, they could see that the occupant was a large copper coloured Irish Setter.

"That's Bowker," said the girl. "He was the one singing when you arrived. He isn't coping with being in kennels, but he's a bit of a handful, I'm afraid. Now, what about Benjy next door to him?" She indicated a small

202

brown dog with appealing eyes and a furiously wagging tail. Mariana thought he looked ideal; he was small, quiet, and manageable. She bent to pat him and he licked her hand.

Danny spoke,

"I want this one," he said. Mariana and Kate exchanged glances. So much for a small, manageable dog. This was not at all what they had had in mind. Danny looked up at Mariana, his blue eyes shining and intense. "Please Mum," he said, and that was that. Shortly afterwards Mariana signed the papers, handed over forty pounds, and the girl said someone would be round to do a home visit in a few days.

"Since you've had one from us before, you can take him now. We just need to check out your new place, but it sounds as though Bowker has fallen on his feet.

"Paddy," said Danny. "His new name's Paddy."

"I like it," said the girl. "Much more fitting really for an Irish guy. He was brought in not as a stray, but because his owner couldn't cope. The poor guy's an author, and Bowker devoured most of his manuscript one day! Perhaps he'll be better behaved when he has a more sensible name. Anyway, if you have any serious problems, give us a ring and we'll do our best to help. Poor Bo – er I mean Paddy's been here far too long." She stood by the gate waving as they drove away with Paddy happily ensconced on the back seat with Danny.

EIGHTEEN: PADDY.

Paddy was glorious in his unruliness. He stood above Danny's knee; he was big-boned and his coat was the colour of ripe conkers with extravagant feathering down his legs and along his deep chest and his elegant flag of a tail. All the way home in Kate's car he stood with his head out of the window, the wind blowing his silken ears back like some Hollywood starlet in an open-topped car. His eyes were golden brown flecked with amber; soft and appealing – it was impossible to be angry with him even though he did much that otherwise might constantly have got him into hot water.

Clearly he had never had a day's discipline in his life, nor had he been introduced to the word 'no'. He followed Danny from the car and gamboled into the house in great excitement. He then ran up the stairs and immediately availed himself of the water in the toilet bowl, drinking it down in noisy gulps. Danny hared after him, pulling him away and banging down the lid. Paddy then raced from room to room, jumping on the beds and standing at the windows to survey his new surroundings before racing downstairs and continuing his exploration with little regard for anything low enough to be swept away by his furiously wagging tail. His last port of call was the kitchen, where he stood on his hind legs and investigated the contents of the draining board, wolfing down the remains of Mariana's breakfast. At last Danny managed to make a grab for him, and sat him down on the floor by the table just as his mother and Kate appeared in the doorway having made their way more slowly from the car, deep in conversation. He pulled away from Danny and ran to Kate, joyously thrusting his nose up her skirt.

"Paddy you pervert, get off me!" she squealed, cementing her knees together firmly against the invading wet black nose. "For goodness sakes Danny, you're going to have to train him in the art of decorum, or I'm going to have to wear jeans every time I come here!"

"Sorry Auntie Kate," said Danny, red-faced, and held on tightly to Paddy's collar as the two women stroked and fondled his silky head.

"He is lovely," said Mariana, "but I'm afraid he's going to be trouble. You'd better take him for a good walk but I'd keep him on the lead for a few days til he gets used to you Danny, otherwise he might run off."

"After you've walked him," said Kate, "I'll take you to Petsmart and we'll get him one of those extending leads and a dog whistle so you can start training him – my treat."

"Thanks Auntie Kate. He's just excited; he'll calm down in a day or two; and I will train him, I promise Mum."

Mariana surveyed her son's eager face. The haunted look had gone from his eyes and they were shining with a new light. Whatever trouble this dog was going to be he was worth it, she decided. They took him with them to Petsmart and Danny kept a firm hold on him as they made their purchases, although he still managed to cock his leg contemptuously against a large bargain bin containing tins of cat food. As well as the extending lead and the whistle, they came away with an enormous bag of complete dog food, feeding bowls, a brush, and a large dog basket that Mariana intended he should sleep in.

"You can put it in the space under the stairs," she said. "That'll be a good place for him to sleep."

That night however, she made no objection when Danny took the dog to sleep in his room; and when she carefully opened his door later to peek in, the shaft of light from the landing showed her son's dark head on the pillow next to the copper silken dome of his newfound friend. They looked utterly peaceful and neither of them stirred as she gently closed the door. *Just for tonight,* she told herself.

Danny and Paddy formed an immediate bond and were inseparable. The next day being Sunday, Danny was up and about before Mariana was even awake. He took Paddy down to the river on his long lead. The meadow was bathed in early morning sunlight, and droplets of dew hung on the grass and bejewelled the myriads of spider webs that festooned the hedges at its border, transforming them into exquisite swirls of crystalline lace. Paddy gamboled through the long grass as far as his lead would stretch leaving dark green lines where he disturbed the dew, criss-crossing in a tireless pattern as he cast to and fro, his nose to the ground. A fisherman sat by the water's edge with his creel at his side. Paddy bounded up to him as Danny frantically tried to reel him in before he reached the small canvas bag on top of the creel, which no doubt contained the man's breakfast.

"Fuck off!" the man shouted irritably and made a swipe at Paddy with his free arm, holding on tightly to his rod. Luckily Danny regained control just in time.

"Keep your bloody dog under control kid," snarled the man.

"I am," replied Danny. "Good morning to you too," and pulling Paddy to his side he continued along the river

206

keeping a sharp eye out for more fishermen. When they reached the sandbanks at the far end of the meadow he let the lead out to its furthest extent again and began Paddy's training. He made him sit, and walked away slowly keeping his hand raised and saying 'stay' in stern, commanding tones. He was only feet away when Paddy bounded after him, jumping up excitedly to lick his face.

"No Paddy," said Danny, and led him back to his spot. "Not til I blow the whistle." He sat him back down and repeated the exercise. It took almost an hour, but finally Paddy remained at his station until Danny blew his whistle, then bounded over joyfully to receive his reward from Danny's pocket.

"That'll do for now mate," said Danny, and they headed for home.

Every morning before school, come rain or shine, Danny took Paddy for his walk and his training, rising just after dawn and returning for his breakfast at eight. His patience was endless and gradually Paddy learned to obey him. After a week he dispensed with the lead, keeping a short one in his pocket to use when necessary, and although recall was never instant, two or three long blasts of the whistle would bring Paddy to his side more times than not. However, it was only Danny who could control him; he took no notice whatsoever of Mariana. She daren't let him out during the day when Danny was at school and was forced to tie him to the rotary washing line on the back lawn, where he remained until his master's return. When it rained and when she was at work, she shut him in the kitchen with his basket and his water bowl, first making sure that everything was secured against his foraging. At first, when she went to work he would howl intermittently for the whole morning, but gradually he learned her routines and the howling ceased, as did the complaints from the neighbours.

Occasionally he would escape, chewing through his restraining rope and clearing the four foot fence with ease. She would later find him tied up to the gate by whatever unfortunate person had found him rooting through their dustbin, or devouring food from their kitchen intended for their own pets. It wasn't safe to leave your door open on a sunny day when Paddy was about, and soon everyone in the village knew whose dog he was.

Once he came home with a mouthful of sausages destined for someone's barbecue. Mariana saw him rounding the corner of the garage at speed, the string of sausages trailing after him, just like an illustration from a strip cartoon. She couldn't help but laugh and then waited anxiously for the knock on the door from an irate and hungry owner. However, none came; he must have seized them stealthily and their disappearance must have remained a complete mystery, much to Mariana's relief.

It wasn't safe to wear a skirt either unless you wished to be treated to Paddy's cold wet nose probing your nether regions, and after the first day's experience, Kate always wore jeans when she visited.

None of this mattered however. In Danny's eyes, and therefore in Mariana's also, Paddy was worth his weight in gold.

Besides Paddy, the other great love of Danny's life was the river. He would sit on the bank for hours and watch the water flow. In the summer it was slow, clear, and languorous; eddying gently around the weeping willows that hung in its shallows and the rafts of flotsam caught against its banks. Lines of ripples marked the currents at its centre that carried everything in their path swiftly down river. Mallard and coot, and the occasional pair of swans paddled and dabbled along its edge, or sailed majestically along with the current. Herons fished at intervals on reeded knolls along its banks, and sand martins swooped low above its surface and chattered tirelessly, clinging to the sides of their sandy burrows in an endless loop of hunting and feeding. Sometimes, especially early in the morning, Danny would catch a glimpse of a jewel-bright kingfisher flashing its iridescent turquoise wings.

In winter; the river was swift and turgid, dark and threatening, careening at breakneck speed carrying its plunder of torn branches and the occasional dead mallard and depositing them against the ancient sandstone bridge that straddled the border between England and Wales. Often the river burst its banks, spreading over the sodden meadow where it would lie for days in a gleaming slick before miraculously draining away again seemingly overnight. Danny knew its every mood, every colour and form, every ripple and eddy.

He and Paddy were often its only companions, the other neatly-clad dog walkers with their brightly coloured leads not venturing beyond the somewhat slippery wooden walkway in winter, and the fishermen staying away cursing the swollen waters that rendered their leisurely vigil fruitless and impossible. In summer, especially at weekends the riverbank thronged with families, teenagers, and lovers during the afternoon and evening, and Danny would rise before dawn in order to claim the few hours of solitude that were precious to him. When people began to filter onto the riverbank, he spoke to no one, lowering his head as they passed by. Often, they would pause to pat and admire Paddy who would wag his tail ecstatically and accept their attentions gracefully before returning to lie at his master's feet.

When Danny needed solace it was the river he turned to, and the river knew all his secret innermost thoughts. The river didn't judge, advise or scold; the river was just there, always, and it never divulged the secrets it was entrusted with.

Now he had everything he needed – his music, his dog, and the river. They were the only entities in his life that accepted him for what he was, and didn't seek to mould or change him into something more socially acceptable. As Danny entered his seventeenth year, he couldn't imagine that he would ever need anything or anyone else.

NINETEEN: SEEDS OF DOUBT.

The day the girl disappeared Danny was walking by the river with Paddy as always. It was winter; the first week in February, and Danny was just sixteen. The fields were shrouded in a blanket of freezing fog. Through its swirling wraith-like layers dark stems of dried-up purple loosestrife and cow parsley emerged eerily in tall black and silver frosted spikes topped by frothy plumes or umbrellas of spent seed heads. Vast ice-glazed puddles punctured by swirls of perennial rye grass or spiky crop stubble glistened on the meadow where the lying floodwater had frozen days earlier. Walking down the lane at the back of the house in the early morning Danny heard the gunshot report of the ice cracking as the air began to warm, although the rise in temperature was as yet barely perceptible. A strange and unearthly stillness hung with the fog, punctuated only by the crackling ice and the isolated cawing of a solitary rook in the bare branches of a ghostly white tree.

He saw the girl sitting on the rough-hewn earth steps formed from tree roots and rocks that led down to the riverbank. He had to deflect around her as she sat with her head resting on her arms, the hood of her purple coat pulled up to hide her face. He glanced at her in passing but pushed aside the sudden urge to approach her and ask if she was alright – clearly she wanted to be alone. *If it were me,* he thought, *I shouldn't want to be disturbed.* Paddy, however, had no such reservations, and ran to nuzzle her hand as it rested on her shoulder. She pushed him away and Danny called him to heel sternly.

"Sorry," he said; but the girl didn't look up or acknowledge his presence. He shrugged, and moved on down the steps.

They walked along the riverbank for a mile or more. Paddy running in wide circles over the frozen meadow, occasionally putting up a mallard or coot that was taking shelter in the reeds along the edges of the ditches that separated the swathes of land. Shattering the frozen air with his joyous barking, he pursued them to the water's edge where they took off over the ice-laden shallows and out into the dark, sluggishly flowing water in the centre. Danny followed, crossing the ditches via the narrow bridges formed over drainage pipes to facilitate the farm machinery. He breathed in the icy air reveling in the sharp shock of it hitting his lungs and relishing the intense joy of living. Gradually, since the advent of Paddy nearly four years ago now, the voices had receded and rarely bothered him any more, except occasionally in the dead of night. He still kept his Walkman handy in case he should have need of it but for the most part it was merely for insurance, and not out of necessity.

The girl was gone when they returned to the steps an hour or so later. Danny wondered what demons she was struggling with, and half wished he had stopped to ask, but by the time he reached home, all thoughts of her had vanished from his mind.

The following day at school, an announcement was made in assembly. A girl from the second form was missing after a row with her parents the day before. The

212

headmaster asked whether anyone had seen her after she left her home sometime on Sunday morning. She was wearing jeans, and a purple coat with a hood. Her name was Hayley Price, and she was twelve years old. With a jolt, Danny realised that it must have been the same girl that he had seen the day before. He decided however, that discretion was the better part of valour, and said nothing about their brief and wordless encounter.

Later that day, a search party discovered her body hidden in the undergrowth below the path, where the branches of a fallen tree swathed in flotsam left by the floodwater had concealed it from view. The post mortem on the dead girl revealed that she had died of exposure after receiving a blunt trauma to her head that would have rendered her instantly unconscious. A full-scale murder hunt was now under way.

The police came to the school and interviewed the teachers and the girl's known circle of friends in order to try and glean some inkling as to why this might have happened. As well as feelings of grief for their colleague, an air of excitement tinged by fear pervaded the school, and nervous parents kept their children from going out in the evenings. The girl's father was taken in for questioning, because the neighbours had heard an argument taking place early on the morning she disappeared. Her distraught mother defended him loyally; arguments were a normal part of family life, especially where young prepubescent girls were part of the equation. After being grilled for almost two days, he was released without charge, and they turned their attention to the general male population of the village, including anyone over sixteen in their house-to-house enquiries.

When the policeman who'd been assigned to their road asked Mariana where her son was on the morning concerned she lied and said he had been in his room for most of the day, only emerging to eat his Sunday lunch. Danny sat at the top of the stairs listening to his mother lying through her teeth, and wondering why she thought it necessary. It was unlikely that anyone would have seen him at that time on a cold and foggy February morning, so when the policeman asked him he collaborated with her statement – what choice did he have?

"That's a nice dog you've got," observed the policeman as he rose to leave. "Bet he needs some exercise though." Danny and Mariana exchanged glances.

"He does," Mariana agreed, "and it's a good job I don't mind doing it; you know what teenagers are like!" The policeman laughed, and Danny breathed again.

"Why Mum?" he asked after the policeman had gone. His blue eyes regarded her steadily, full of aggrieved accusation. "Why did you lie to him? Do you honestly think I might have had something to do with this?"

"No Danny of course I don't, it wasn't that. I just didn't want you getting hauled over the coals. You've been through enough and so have I, and I didn't want it all starting up again. I thought if they questioned you they might not believe you and mud, as you well know, has a nasty tendency to stick. I'm sorry if I've upset you; I thought it was for the best."

"Well, we'll just have to hope nobody saw me go, or they're really going to think I have something to hide. Thanks Mum, thanks for nothing! You know, it's bad enough at school with them all whispering behind my back – but you? I tell you, I didn't even know the girl, and I never touched her!" He stormed back to his room, slamming the door and locking it. Mariana sank down onto the sofa, the tears pricking at her eyes. Paddy climbed up beside her and laid his head on her knee. "Ah! Paddy, if only you could talk," she told him sadly.

"Do you really think he could have done it M?" Kate asked, having rushed over in response to yet another 'emergency' phone call. Mariana shook her head.

"Oh, I don't know Kate. Not really I suppose; but you know how strange he is sometimes; you just never know what's in his head, and his track record with girls isn't good, is it?"

"Yes, but *murder?* Good God M, you don't honestly think he's capable of that do you?" Mariana shrugged, and gave her friend a despairing look.

"I just can't be sure. Does that make me a terrible mother? I've lived with his moods for so long, and things have been so much better since Paddy; but he's such a loner Kate, and I know there are a few people who wouldn't be surprised. I know what people say about him; that he's weird and not like other lads, and he did used to be a bully, although I think that stopped when we came here. I'm scared Kate. What if it *was* him. After all, we don't really know who he is or where he came from, do we."

"It doesn't matter where he came from M; you're the one who brought him up, and that has to count for something surely. Where is he now?"

"In his room. That's what worries me too sometimes; it's almost as though he doesn't trust *himself*, as though he doesn't want to be the way he is, but can't help himself. Since this happened, he's spent all his time in his room, and I'm having to walk Paddy now every day, which wasn't why we got him. I don't know how to help him Kate."

"Let me talk to him; he might find it easier to open up to me. It might be worth a try, don't you think."

"Well, I don't suppose it can do any harm; except that he may resent my having confided in you. Still, if that's the case, it'll be me gets it in the neck, not you. Go on then Kate; do your worst. If you can get him to come out of his room for more than half an hour, you'll deserve a medal, won't she Paddy?" Paddy's tail thumped against the floor and his long silky ears cocked forward as he listened to Kate climb the stairs to Danny's room.

Danny lay in his room, the curtains closed, and the headphones firmly attached. The past week or so had been hell on earth. At school, everyone called him The Freak and gave him a wide berth, and he knew there were whispers behind his back – *wasn't there some trouble between him and girls at his primary school? Wasn't he constantly being punished for bullying them, and wasn't that why his mother moved away from there and came to live in Farnley?'* There was no one to speak up for him since he had no friends, and suddenly everyone wondered why. He would walk into a room and the conversation would come to an abrupt end, everyone staring at him without greeting him or even acknowledging his presence. *How had they found out about him?* The teachers treated him as they normally did, *but there again,* he thought to himself, *that's what they're paid to do.*

School however, wasn't half as bad as the ordeal he faced when he was alone at home.

"Oh, *Daaaaaaneeeeeeee!*" She was back again the night after the visit from the police; taunting him in her sly, cajoling tones. *"Have you been a naughty boy again then? What did you do to Hayley Danny? Was she pretty? Don't you remember Danny?"*

Danny turned up the volume on the Walkman. No, he didn't remember. He had thought he did; had thought he had walked past the girl without speaking and returned an hour or so later to find her gone, but he couldn't be sure. *Why did his mother lie to protect him? Did she know something he didn't?* Why was Danielle back if he had done nothing wrong? Time and time again he cast his mind over that morning's events and remembered the girl sitting silent and motionless on the steps, moving only to brush Paddy away when he attempted to nuzzle her hand. The sound of the crackling ice, and Paddy's disembodied barking echoing through the fog. He retraced his steps in his mind's eye down to the sandbanks then back along the riverbank that was completely deserted. He was sure he had seen no one and heard nothing except the raucous cries of some rooks that rose suddenly into the air from the trees on the steep-sided embankment at the edge of the meadow near the steps, just visible through the fog that was now beginning to lift. At the end of the wooden walk-way he had called Paddy to heel and kept him close as he always did as he climbed the steps back up to the lane, and he had been relieved to see that the girl was no longer there. The fact remained however, that he had not admitted to seeing her at all, and that his own mother had lied about his whereabouts on that morning, and they must both have had their reasons.

"Danny, can I come in?" Faintly, through the pulsating sounds of Nirvana on the Walkman, he heard a knock on the door.

"Go away!" he shouted, then took off the headphones – perhaps it was something important.

"It's me Danny, Auntie Kate. Can I come in please?" Danny was fond of his Auntie Kate. She had always been there, and she had been instrumental in many of his mother's better decisions concerning him, especially where Paddy was concerned. *Paddy!* He felt a huge surge of guilt.

217

He had been neglecting him lately he knew, and Paddy didn't deserve to be neglected. Oh, he knew he would be fed and walked, but his mother had never really loved him; he was Danny's dog.

"Alright," he answered at last and went to unlock the door.

They sat on the bed together; Kate leaning on the headboard, Danny sitting cross-legged at the foot.

"What is it Danny?" she asked. Her eyes were full of concern. "What's wrong with you?"

Danny had never told anyone about the voices; they might think he was mad and lock him up. How could he explain when he couldn't tell her about the constant torment from his sister whom he hated now with every fibre of his being. He had done bad things because of her and he was afraid of what else he might do, or may even already have done unwittingly, whilst under her influence.

"Mum thinks I killed that girl." He heard her sharp intake of breath and knew that his mother had told her. "Do you think so too?" he asked, watching her closely.

"No Danny, I don't; not even for a moment." She leaned forward and reached for his hand, gripping it firmly and looking him directly in the eye. "Do you?"

The question took him by surprise, and he withdrew his hand, recoiling.

"What d'you mean?"

"Danny, you haven't even denied it. Your mum knows you were out down the river when the girl disappeared, and when you came home from school after the police had been there you began to act strangely again. You haven't been outside since; not even to walk Paddy. Your mother is afraid that you may have something on your conscience."

"I saw her," he said quietly. "Hayley. I saw her sitting on the steps; but I never went near her I swear. I took Paddy down along the river, and when I came back she was gone. But I swear I never touched her Auntie Kate, I'm sure I didn't."

"What do you mean you're sure you didn't? That sounds as though you aren't sure at all." Kate took his hand again. "Talk to me Danny; tell me what it is that makes you think you may have done this thing."

"Danielle," he said. Kate frowned, not understanding.

"Danielle?" she asked. "What about Danielle? What can she possibly have to do with this?"

"I can't say, you'd tell my mum."

Kate thought for a minute or two. This was awkward, to say the least. Clearly Danny needed help, and he seemed to trust her and want to confide in her, but if he did she would have to lie to her best friend in order not to betray that trust. This was a horrible dilemma.

"Danny why can't you tell your mum? You know she loves you and would do anything for you."

"Not when it comes to Danielle she wouldn't," he said sullenly. "It doesn't matter; there's nothing you can do anyway. Just forget it."

"Ok, I'll make you a deal. You must tell me everything, and then you have to come out of your room and try to act normally. I'll do whatever I can to help you, and I promise I won't tell your mother anything unless you want me to. Is that a deal? It won't be easy I daresay, but it's the best I can do."

"You promise you won't tell, no matter what?"

"I promise Danny. We're going to have to trust each other."

They talked for an hour or more., whilst Mariana sat downstairs, hearing the murmur of voices, and longing to climb the stairs and listen outside the door but knowing

219

that if she was discovered it could jeopardise Kate's plan, whatever that was. Danny poured his heart out to Kate. It was like a great burden lifting from his shoulders. Kate sat motionless except for the occasional encouraging nod.

"I don't know who I am," he began, and Kate's heart contracted as he echoed his mother's earlier statement.

"Mum won't talk about my dad. I've asked about him, but all she said was that he wasn't a good man. There are no pictures of him except in Danielle's box – pictures of him and Danielle together. Mum says he used to drink a lot, and he would hit her for no reason. She says we're better off without him, and she even blames him for Danielle's death because he stayed out all that night and Mum couldn't get the doctor. I don't know if it's all true; but if it is – what if I'm like him? Is that why she doesn't love me like she loves Danielle, because I might turn out to be like my dad? Is that why she called me Danny instead of naming me after him? I'm named after my sister, and I bet she would've been happier if I'd been another girl."

Kate's heart ached for him. All his life he had worried about turning out like the man who wasn't even his father. If he had been his father, she knew Mariana would never have disrespected him to Danny, no matter what he had done. What should she do? Should she tell him the truth? No, she couldn't betray Mariana's trust, but she would have to try and persuade her friend to come clean about her son's birth, for all their sakes.

"After Mum told me about Danielle, I started to worry that she didn't love me, and that's when she started on me – Danielle, that is."

Kate gave him a puzzled look. What did he mean by that?

"She talks to me," he said, and heard again a sharp intake of breath from Kate. She had heard of this sort of thing before. She was beginning to feel out of her depth.

"All those things I did in primary school; it was Danielle. I was doing it for her; to make her leave me alone. I wanted to punish Mum too I suppose, for not loving me. I knew if Danielle was here she would have loved her more than me, but she was wrong to, because Danielle was never the little angel Mum thought she was. She's an evil little witch, and she made me do things so that I would look bad and she would look good. She even made me hurt Alfie just to upset Mum. I think Danielle is like my dad; after all he was her dad too. When we moved here I thought I'd left her behind – until what happened to Alfie."

"Danny that was an accident. You can't blame yourself, surely?"

"I was supposed to be looking after him. I wouldn't even have gone that way if I hadn't wanted something for myself. No, Danielle told me I let it happen just to upset my mum because she loved Alfie more than she loved me."

"Danny *no!*" Kate intervened. "That simply isn't true. Your mum never blamed you for Alfie's death, not one little bit! Of course she loves you; she loves you more than life. Why d'you think she's never had another relationship in all these years? It was because you are her whole world, and she could never trust anyone to do right by you."

"I thought it was just because she hated men after my dad. I'll be a man myself soon and then she'll hate me too." Danny's eyes blazed with anger and frustration. "It's not fair!" he cried.

"Look Danny," said Kate. "You need to talk to your mum. There are things you should know that I can't tell you; only your mum can do that. I have told her she must

221

tell you, but I can do no more than that, it's not my place. You're growing up now and you need to know who you are, and only she can tell you."

"What do you mean, who I am?"

"I've probably said too much and I'm certainly not saying any more. Danny, you must forget about your sister. She's dead. She's been dead for nearly twenty years. If you're hearing her voice, it's coming from within you, and you have to stop using her as an excuse for everything you do wrong, and especially everything you imagine you've done wrong. You had nothing to do with Hayley's death. You should've admitted to seeing her, but I can understand why you didn't. Now, promise me you'll stop listening to Dani. If you don't listen to her, she can't make you do anything. If you need someone to talk to, I'm always there. Have you got a pen and paper?" Danny hunted through his school bag and handed her a piece of paper torn from an exercise book, and a pen.

"Here's my number at Jeff's, and my work number too. If you need to talk, ring me. If I don't answer just say it's you and I'll get back to you. Don't face this alone any more Danny; together we can rid you of your sister. You mark my words, they will find out soon enough who killed that girl, and it sure as hell won't be you."

Two weeks later, Hayley's nineteen-year-old brother was arrested and charged with her manslaughter. He had gone out to look for her after overhearing her arguing with their parents, and tried to drag her home. She refused to budge, they struggled, and she fell from the path and hit her head on the fallen tree. He thought she was dead and panicked, dragging her into the undergrowth and leaving her there. She must have died soon afterwards. He couldn't live with what he had done, especially when it became clear

222

that had he gone for help instead of concealing her, she might have lived. His confession and his obvious remorse bought him a lesser sentence, but he would live with his guilt for the rest of his life. Danny wondered what he himself would have done if he had discovered the girl only minutes later. Would he have done the same? Would he too have panicked and left her there to die unknowingly? He was thankful that he didn't have to answer that question.

TWENTY: MICKEY.

'On either side the river lie
Long fields of barley and of rye,
That clothe the wold and meet the sky;
And thro' the field the road runs by
To many-tower'd Camelot.'

(Excerpt from 'The Lady of Shalott', by Alfred Lord Tennyson)

Mickey woke early, and throwing off the covers made her way to the window, pushing the curtains aside to let in the morning sunlight. Mist wraiths drifted pale and wispy over the fields at the bottom of the garden, and the grass sparkled with the heavy dew of autumn. Crows jostled and squabbled in the faded yellow oak trees, and the Japanese maples that lined the garden path were a blaze of orange and pink. October would soon give way to November, and the colours would fade, leaving the dull grey sheen of naked trees in their place. She pulled on some socks and a dressing-gown over her pyjamas and tiptoed down the long sweeping staircase to the warm and welcoming kitchen. An enormous Aga dominated the room, and three cats were stretched out on the limestone flags in front of it. She poured some milk into a pan and lifting one of the heavy chrome covers, placed it on the Aga, mixing chocolate powder, sugar and a drop of cold milk into a froth in a mug whilst she waited for it to heat. When the milk threatened to rise above the rim of the pan she snatched it off the heat and poured the steaming liquid over the mix in the mug, stirring it vigorously to a rich creamy head. She hauled herself up onto one of the tall bar stools that stood alongside the breakfast bar and sat sipping her hot chocolate with relish and thinking about Danny.

She had met him a few weeks earlier. One Monday afternoon soon after the beginning of term she had gone to the library at school to find a book to help her with her art project. She found what she wanted and took it to one of the study booths together with her notebook. There was a boy sitting in the booth; he had his nose buried in a book, and didn't look up as she slid into place on the bench opposite. He was tall and slightly built, with lank dark hair that hid his eyes as he bent over his book. They sat in silence opposite each other poring over their books. Mickey tried hard to concentrate on the life of Michelangelo, but felt her eyes drawn to the boy across the table who seemed oblivious to her. The bell went for the end of study period and simultaneously they closed their books. The boy looked up and their eyes met and locked. Mickey's heart skipped a beat as she looked into his languid blue eyes fringed by long dark lashes. He had a wide mouth in a thin face with well-defined cheekbones and a square jaw. Mickey was captivated as a slow smile spread over his beautiful face.

"Hi," he said.

"Hi," Mickey replied, swallowing the large lump that had lodged firmly in her throat. She searched for something to say but it was too late.

"Gotta go," he said, and picking up his book he strode away, a slight figure whose presence nevertheless filled the room.

After that day she looked out for him around school, but as a whole week passed with no sign of him she began to wonder if she'd dreamed him up in her imagination. On Friday afternoon she skipped her maths lesson and went to the library again in the hope that this was a regular haunt for him too. There was, however, no sign of him in any of the booths. Disappointed, she wondered what to do. She didn't normally skip lessons, and she had got her friend Sophie to cover for her and say she had gone home sick at lunch-time. Knowing her luck she thought, she would bump into Mr. Lawson her maths teacher and blow her cover; she would have to spend the rest of the afternoon dodging him. She decided to stay in the library until home time to minimize the risk. Choosing a book on the romantic poets of the nineteenth century she settled down in her usual place and was soon lost in the immortal words of Christina Rossetti.

A sudden shadow fell across the table and she looked up. Her heart lurched almost painfully – it was him.

"Hello again," he said, sliding onto the bench beside her.

She pulled herself together quickly.

"Hi" she replied in what she hoped was a casual way, at the same time summoning what she hoped was a dazzling smile. The languid blue eyes lit up as he smiled back.

"I'm Danny," he said, "who are you?"

"I'm Mickey," she replied. "Well, Michaela really, but my friends call me Mickey. I'm named after my father so it could've been a lot worse I guess," she finished ruefully.

226

"I'm named after my sister," replied Danny, "so I know exactly what you mean. I haven't seen you around before; what form are you in?"

" 4A – you?"

"Oh! I thought you were older. I'm in the upper sixth, should've been doing my A-levels this year but I had to do re-sits. I'm gonna be drawing my pension before I get to leave school!" He made a rueful gesture, "Do you live nearby? I haven't seen you on the bus either."

"My mum runs me to school. I live in Farnley – well, just outside really; our house is the big red brick one down Crow Lane End."

"Wow!" Danny looked impressed. "Your old man must be loaded!"

"He is," sighed Mickey. "He's CEO of a big firm on the industrial estate. He's not stuck up though. My mum used to work in the office there before they got married. What about yours?"

"My dad's dead," Danny replied in a matter-of-fact tone.

"Oh, I'm sorry!" exclaimed Mickey, mortified.

"It's okay silly; I never knew him; he died before I was even born and so did my sister Danielle. There's just me and my mum, and my dog Paddy. We live in Farnley too, on the old council estate; my mum bought our house four years ago."

Mickey fell silent, unsure what to say now. How lucky she was she thought, to have two parents as well as three grandparents, a half sister and brother, and her two uncles, all of whom she adored, and not forgetting Sparky, her pony."

The shrilling of the bell announced the last lesson.

"Aren't you going?" Danny asked, puzzled.

227

"No, I'm not supposed to be here; my friend Sophie told Mr. Lawson I'd gone home ill, so I'll have to hide out in here now until it's time for Mum to pick me up."

"Well I hope you don't get caught," remarked Danny with a chuckle. "I'll have to go; I'll see you around."

She watched him go, hoping he would turn to look at her, but he didn't. She hadn't seen him again since that day, except glimpses of him in the distance. She had been to the library several times but there was no sign of him, and she daren't miss any more lessons.

Today was Saturday, and she felt almost liberated by the fact that she wouldn't be on tenterhooks all day wondering if she would bump into Danny again, rushing to the toilets several times a day to check her hair looked okay. Her hair was rich chestnut brown, long and glossy. She brushed it hastily now, twisting it into two plaits and securing it with elastic bands. She dressed quickly in jeans and a polo-necked sweater. Snatching her waxed jacket from behind the door and pulling on her riding boots she made her way down to the paddock at the end of the tree-lined path to find Sparky. He was down at the far end munching grass, but her soft whistle brought him trotting up to the gate. Sparky was bright chestnut, with a flaxen mane and tail, a white blaze, and long white stockings on his forelegs. His companion, a dapple grey with dark legs, mane, and tail, continued to munch the grass without pausing. Mickey slipped a halter on him and led him through the gate. At the side of the house was a small stable yard with several loose boxes and a tack room arranged around a courtyard that had an ornamental pond in the middle. She led Sparky into the nearest loose box and tied him to a ring in the wall. Fetching a dandy brush from the tack room she hastily brushed the mud from around his withers and flanks before heaving a saddle onto his back and fastening the girth loosely — she knew he would puff out his stomach and she would have to tighten it anyway before she could mount. He resisted the cold steel of the bit momentarily as she slipped it between his teeth and drew the bridle up over his head, slipping off the halter. "Come on Sparky, be nice," she told him. He turned to gaze at her with his limpid brown eyes,

"Hrrrrmph!" he said conversationally, gently nuzzling her arm.

She rode out of the yard and down the drive to the narrow country road beyond. Mickey wondered if she dared ride down to the council estate, which would mean crossing the main road. She glanced at her watch; it was still early, only just after eight; but it would be busy coming back. There were three housing estates in Farnley; one on the right as you entered the village, with tree-lined avenues of neat red brick three and four-bedroomed houses; another on the road going out of mainly bungalows; and Danny's estate. White painted half-rendered or pebble-dashed semi-detached houses, nearly all privately owned these days, but still referred to as the Council Estate by the locals. Further down the road, the houses were more modern, arranged on both sides of the road in terraces on one side, and semi-detached on the other. These in turn led to a final terrace of two-bedroomed houses overlooking the river. Having no idea which part Danny's house was in she decided not to venture across the busy road, but turned right instead down a narrow lane that lead to the riverbank. Here she urged Sparky into a canter and rode along the river to where the sandbanks sloped gently downward to the water's edge. In the summer she would slip his saddle off and let him wade into the water, but today she sat on the grassy bank and let him graze whilst she ate the somewhat soggy jam toast she had wrapped in kitchen roll and stuffed in her pocket before leaving the house. She gave him the crusts and he munched appreciatively on the sweet sticky offering.

Mickey loved the river. On the opposite side the neighbouring Welsh village sprawled down to within a field's breadth of its banks, contained by a low sandstone cliff. She ignored the modern housing estate that had invaded the meadow higher up the river and concentrated her mind on the church tower, with it's silver flag pole sporting a large green and white flag emblazoned with a red dragon; and the jumbled mix of tall red brick and elongated grey stone houses that flanked the main street. This was Camelot – not in reality; but in Mickey's imagination. She would visualize the shallow boat carrying the doomed Lady of Shalott to her death beneath the walls and the imagined turrets beyond the river; pale and ethereal, shrouded in her floating white robe with diamond clasp, her arms folded over the parchment missive lying on her still breast. If she concentrated hard she could almost see Sir Lancelot on the far bank, the morning sun glinting on his armour as he rode along on his fiery charger with its bright bejewelled reins and gleaming burnished saddle, oblivious to the great lady who was dazzled and doomed by his vision.

The church clock struck nine and she shook herself back to reality and remounted her pony, urging him into a canter again until they reached the narrow track where she slowed him down to cool off. Someone was approaching in the distance along the lane. She pulled Sparky to a halt in a convenient gateway and waited. As the figure drew nearer she realised with a jolt that it was Danny, with a large copper coloured dog at his heels. He bent down and clipped a lead to the dog's collar. With the dog stopping to sniff every couple of yards, it took him several minutes to reach her. She let Sparky eat grass and wished that she looked more presentable and didn't have her hair in plaits. *Typical,* she thought, *All these weeks of dolling myself up, and now he turns up when I'm looking like Looby Loo!* Her heart pounded wildly against her chest as she watched him approach, apparently unaware of her waiting there; his head down, his dark hair falling over his eyes. Then the dog saw Sparky, and began to bark. Danny looked up, seemingly annoyed, and looked straight into her eyes. He bent down and grasped the dog's collar,

"Paddy, shut up, you'll scare the horse y'daft old Irish bugger." Paddy stopped barking and Danny smiled up at her, pushing the unruly locks of hair out of his eyes.

"Hey Mickey, I didn't recognize you," he said brightly. Mickey felt herself colour; a hot flush spreading up her neck and face making her feel even more gauche. "Is he yours?" Danny was stroking Sparky's neck now, squinting up at her through the hair.

"This is Sparky. I had him for my tenth birthday, so I'm growing out of him now really, but I'd never sell him. My dad says we can keep him anyway when I get a bigger one," answered Mickey. A shadow fell over Danny's face.

"D'you always get what you want then?" he asked, his eyes flashing.

"What d'you mean? It's not my fault my dad's got money." Mickey felt tears pricking at her eyes. Why was Danny taking that attitude with her?

"Spoilt little rich girl Michaela. I'll see ya. Come on Paddy." With that, he walked off down towards the river without a backward glance. Mickey rode slowly home with a heavy heart. What was wrong with him? One minute they were getting along fine, and the next it was like a door shutting and she didn't know why. She dismounted in the yard, pulled the saddle off and led Sparky back to his paddock. She took him through the gate and stood for a moment, hugging his neck. He nuzzled her gently, waffling at her tears with his pink speckled lips and blowing his warm breath in her face, which only made her cry all the more.

"See you later Sparky," she told him, wiping her nose on her sleeve and reaching over his head to remove the bridle. He wandered off down the paddock towards his companion; head down, shaking himself from head to tail. In the kitchen her parents were having breakfast. She left her coat and boots in the utility room and checked her face in the mirror by the sink, composing herself and dampening a corner of a towel to wipe away the teary smears.

"Nice ride?" her father asked, looking up from his newspaper as she entered the kitchen.

"There's bacon in the warming oven love," said her mother. "Shall I do you an egg?"

"No egg thanks Mum; I had some toast before I went out." Mickey cut two slices off the crusty loaf on the table and spread them liberally with butter, followed by three slices of bacon and some tomato ketchup. No boy was going to spoil her appetite, she told herself.

At school the following Monday she sat with Sophie in the canteen at lunchtime, and told her about her encounter with the mystery boy.

"What's his second name?" asked Sophie. There were a few Danny's in the sixth form and you could rely on Sophie to know them all.

"I don't know, I never asked him," replied Mickey with a sigh. He's tall and skinny, but he's soooooo good looking. He has these amazing blue eyes and when he smiles it's like the sun coming out."

"Hmm, very poetic. You've been in the library again haven't you Mickey," laughed her friend. Maybe he only exists in your imagination."

Just then Mickey looked up, and there he was. He was standing by the window on the other side of the room looking towards her. Was he looking at her or beyond her at something else? She couldn't tell, but her heart leaped.

"Sophie, there he is!" she whispered, tugging at her friend's sleeve. "Don't stare, but he's over by the window."

"Oh my God," her friend said. "That's Danny Harding, the Freak. Is that who you've been stressing over for weeks Mickey? He's the one everyone thought killed Hayley Price, remember?"

"I didn't realise. I didn't take much notice at the time. Anyway, he didn't kill her did he? It was her brother. For God's sake Sophie, you can't go round saying stuff like that about people when it isn't true."

"Well it's your funeral, but I wouldn't touch him with a bargepole if you want my opinion."

"Well, I don't," retorted Mickey. She looked up and Danny had gone.

"I thought you were my friend Soph," she said as she rose from her chair and hurried from the room.

He was leaning against the wall behind the canteen. She walked up to him, trying to look casual, her heart thundering in her chest as she drew nearer.

"Hey," she said, "I thought it was you."

"Mickey – hi. I didn't think you'd be speaking to me," he answered slowly. He lowered his eyes; she could see he was embarrassed.

233

"Don't be daft," she reassured him, "I suppose you were having a bad day, and I'm used to people thinking I'm just a spoiled princess."

"I didn't mean it," he said. "It's not your fault your dad's rich. I like your horse."

"Sparky's not a horse; he's just a pony. I like your dog, he's gorgeous!"

"He is, isn't he?"

"Is he yours then or just the family dog, like our cats?"

"No, he's mine, and I trained him myself. When we got him he was mad; but he's cool now, though my mum still can't handle him." He hesitated,

"Would you like to meet him properly?" He gazed at her uncertainly, his eyes narrowed, anticipating her rejection.

"Yes please," she said eagerly, "I'd love to!"

'Ok. Meet me at the top end of the lane where I saw you last time next Saturday morning. What time d'you get up?"

"Well I usually take Sparky out about eight o'clock, but your Paddy didn't seem cool with him so I could get out earlier if you like, and take him afterwards."

"Ok, how about I meet you there at seven then."

"Ok. My parents don't get up til about nine on a Saturday so they won't even know I've gone."

"Saturday then. See ya Mickey." She watched him walk away and a sweetness seeped into her very bones at the thought of their Saturday rendezvous.

Saturday dawned dry and bright. Mickey set her alarm for six, and put it under her pillow so that it wouldn't wake her parents. She didn't need it, however, she was awake long before it went off. She made herself some toast and chocolate, then dressed in jeans and a green cowl-necked jumper and brushed her hair til it shone. She put on her waxed jacket and her Timberland boots, and set off for her assignation with Danny.

He was waiting at the top of the lane with Paddy at his side. She knelt down and gave Paddy a hug, resting her head against his silky-coated flank.

"You're lovely," she told him, and he acknowledged her words with an enthusiastic lick and a wag of his tail.

Danny stood watching her. She and Paddy were almost the same colour; her hair mingling with his coat so that it was hard to tell where one ended and the other began. She looked up at him smiling shyly; her brown eyes soft and gentle, and Danny felt a warmth creeping through his entire body and a sudden urge to hold her close. He had never felt like this before. Girls were unknown and unwanted territory, but there was something about this one.

"He likes you," he said, his voice coming out a little gruff. She smiled again as she rose to her feet.

"He's lovely Danny," she said, wrapping his name around her tongue as though she didn't want to let it go.

"I usually take him along to the sandbanks; d'you want to come?"

"Ok. I take Sparky there too; it's a wonder we haven't bumped into each other before; we've been going there for the last three years."

"I've seen you in the distance," admitted Danny. "I don't usually like to talk to people." *Oh, but I like talking to you,* he thought. She was tiny; she had looked bigger perched on her outgrown pony.

They walked down the lane and turned left into the meadow at the bottom. To the right the ground rose sharply, and Danny led her up the hill until in the distance you could see his house, his bedroom window just visible above the hedge that bordered the meadow, and through the line of trees, mainly ash, whose leaves were thinning now leaving bunches of keys dangling from their bare branches.

"That's my house," he pointed towards it. The one on the end with the blue curtains; and that's my room. I can see the river from it, except in the summer when the trees hide it a bit."

"Wow! You have an even better view than I do. I can only see fields from my room – and Sparky of course," she grinned at him.

"I love the river," Danny said. "It never changes, yet it's different every day, if you know what I mean."

"I think I do," replied Mickey thoughtfully. "Do you like poetry Danny?"

"Never really thought about it. I s'pose some of it's ok."

"I love it. I'll teach you some of my favourites if you like."

They descended the hill and set off towards the sandbanks, away from the houses. Paddy was running across the meadow now, a tiny copper speck in the morning sunlight. A mist clung along the riverbank hiding its mirrored surface from view. Paddy put up some mallard from their hiding place in the reeds and pursued them enthusiastically, leaping after them as they rose way beyond his reach in a clatter of wings. Mickey laughed, her laughter echoing across the wide sombre meadow sprinkling it with the sheer joy of living.

Suddenly Danny could no longer resist the urge to hold her, and he threw his arms around her and lifting her slight body, twirled her in circles until they were both dizzy, falling into the damp grass. Their eyes met and their lips locked. Hers were warm and soft, sweet as peppermint creams. His were firm and searching, drawing her very soul deep into his being as they obliterated everything else from her consciousness. They broke apart, breathless and speechless, and lay still in each other's arms heedless of the dampness of the grass, staring silently at the swirling sky with no need for words.

Paddy bounded over, searching for them anxiously. He nudged them with his nose then plunged onto them licking their faces.

"Paddy!" Danny pushed him off, laughing. The moment was broken; but not the spell. Paddy backed off then danced around them, barking furiously.

"He makes a good chaperone," laughed Mickey as Danny pulled her to her feet. There was no awkwardness between them now; it was as though they had always been this close. Paddy, satisfied that they were unharmed and merely behaving strangely, ran back down towards the riverbank.

They walked on to the sandbanks, Danny's arm around her. He told her how he had got Paddy from the rescue centre and what a hooligan he used to be. Mickey laughed as Danny told her of his antics when he first had him.

"He's calmed down a bit now, he's six years old; but I daresay he'll always be a bit of a lunatic – not that I mind."

"My dad won't let me have a dog; he says they're too much of a tie. We have three cats, Sparky, and my half-sister's old pony. There's a girl who comes and looks after them when we go away, but she doesn't go in the house; just rides Sparky and feeds the cats in the tack room. They're always glad to get back in the house when we get home. What d'you do with Paddy when you go on holiday?"

Danny laughed, "Holiday? What's that? We've never been, except once to visit my aunt Lorna in Sussex, but that was before I had Paddy. We had a lab cross in those days called Alfie. We left him with my mum's friend Kate, but he was no bother; she'd never cope with Paddy in her high heels!"

"My mum has a friend called Kate too. I wonder if it's the same one – she always wears high heels, she's got blonde hair and she's dead nice."

"Sounds like Auntie Kate. She's been my mum's friend for donkeys' years."

"How weird is that! Our mums have the same best mate; and yet they've never met one another, or you and I might have met up years ago."

"I'm glad I've met you now," said Danny. "It might not have been the same if we'd met years ago." They sat down on the sand bank and he drew her into his arms. She rested her head against his chest, relishing the feel of his arms around her. She felt warm and protected. The morning mist was dispersing from the river and the sun gleamed on its rippled surface. Paddy splashed in the shallows by the bank happily. They sat in silence for some minutes, Danny playing with a lock of her hair. She looked up at him, at his thin but handsome face and those haunting blue eyes. She was overwhelmed with feelings she had never had before. Danny met her gaze, noticing the amber flecks in her brown eyes, and the freckles that peppered her nose and cheeks; her soft wide mouth and her chestnut hair that gleamed in the sunlight. He thought he had never seen anything more beautiful. They kissed again tenderly, passionately, and completely in tune with one another. He knew he wanted more but he was afraid of scaring her away, so he settled for the kiss; after all they had all the time in the world.

The week before Christmas they took their relationship to another level. School had broken up and Mariana was working in the farm shop every day in the run-up to Christmas. Danny and Mickey met in the lane as usual. It was cold and damp, and rain threatened.

"Come back to mine with me," said Danny. "We'll have the place to ourselves; my Mum's at work all day."

"Ok," said Mickey. "But we'd better go the back way so no one sees us. I really don't think my parents would think I should be your girlfriend; or anybody's girlfriend come to that."

"But defo not the village freak; isn't that what you mean?"

"No Danny; stop being paranoid. I'm only fourteen remember. They got me a pony so that I'd be a late developer! I'd hate them to know their little plan didn't work!" She giggled, and Danny was reassured.

They went down the lane then turned right over the rising ground to the stile at the top that lead into the lane at the back of Danny's house. He let them in through the back door. His mother had left some rolls and a tin of hot dog sausages for his lunch.

"I'll be eighteen next month and she still doesn't trust me with the chip pan," laughed Danny. "I hope you like hot dogs."

"As long as there's plenty of tomato ketchup," Mickey replied.

"D'you want to see my room?"

"Of course I do," she said, and followed him upstairs. He closed the kitchen door behind them, and Paddy sank to the floor under the table with a heavy sigh.

Mickey moved around his room as he watched from the doorway. It was still midnight blue; the walls, the carpet, and the curtains, but the Star Wars theme had long gone. It was like some celestial bower or perhaps the depths of the ocean. She examined his collection of CDs – turning each one over to read the legend on the back.

"Wow Danny! I've never even heard of some of these bands, except The Cure and Nirvana. Haven't you got anything a bit more cheerful?"

"Kurt Cobain was a fucking genius," Danny said. Have you ever listened to his music?"

"No, not really. I'm more Take That and East 17; though I do have a Guns 'n Roses CD; my Uncle Jimmy gave it to me for my birthday." She moved over to his bookcase.

"Oh-oh. I wouldn't go there if I were you," he said; but she was poring over the titles, every now and then sliding one out to examine it further. She pulled out a hard-backed volume of Paradise Lost.

"Have you read this?" she asked. "I thought you didn't do poetry."

"Some of it. I love the illustrations; Blake and Dore were geniuses too," he said with a somewhat apologetic grin. She flicked through it.

"I can see what you mean, and I quite like Blake's poetry," She reached for another volume – the complete short stories of Edgar Allen Poe.

"Hey, I really like his stuff;" she said eagerly, "but my dad doesn't approve; he thinks I should still be reading Enid Blyton I think. Danny, I didn't realise you were into literature. We must swap books and we can learn from each other." Danny sat on the bed and watched her rifling through his books; the books his mother didn't understand; books on art – William Blake, Theodore Gericault, Richard

Dadd, and H R Giger. She ran her fingers over the illustrations almost reverently, then carefully replaced the books and came to lie beside him on the bed. His heart was thumping; there was something intensely erotic about watching this lovely girl absorbing his private passions that no one else understood. He took her into his arms and they kissed, gently at first then with gathering momentum, his hands searching her body as she pressed herself to him. Before they even realised it they had undressed and were enveloped in the searing passion of first love.

Afterwards she rested in his arms with her head on his chest and listened to the pounding of his heart with a smile of contentment on her softened lips.

"Danny, I love you," she whispered.

"I love you too," he replied.

"My parents like art. My dad has a couple of original paintings by contemporary artists, and my mum's favourite is The Kiss, by Gustave Klimt; she bought a print of it years ago before I was born. She left school when she was sixteen and went to secretarial college, so she never studied beyond the fifth form. She says she's glad she did because otherwise she would never have met my dad."

"Your mum sounds nice; do you look like her?"

"Quite a bit; she's got hair like mine. So's my Uncle Jimmy; he and Uncle Johnny are Mum's younger twin brothers – they're really cool."

"I wish I had a brother, or even a sister – a live one that is. I don't even have a Grandma; just Auntie Lorna and my two cousins Ellie and Georgia that I never see, and my Auntie Kate who isn't really my aunty at all, but my mum's best friend. I wonder if she really is the same Kate your mum knows? No way we can ask though without them finding out about us."

'We can't risk that. I don't know what my dad would do to you if he knew we.... you know."

"It won't always be like that Mickey. When you're sixteen they'll have to let you off the lead a bit, won't they?"

"I wouldn't count on it; they'll still think you're too old for me."

"Well," said Danny, laughing, "you're sure as hell never going to catch up with me, so we'll still be sneakin' around in ten years' time!"

They ate hot dogs. "Mum'll think I'm a right piggy today," remarked Danny. The threatened rain had passed over, and the day was cold and bright. They returned to the lane the way they had come, and there Danny kissed her goodbye before continuing down to the river with Paddy.

"Meet you here tomorrow?" he asked, suddenly feeling uncertain for reasons even he didn't understand. Perhaps this escalation of their relationship would be too much for her. He needn't have worried.

"Of course. Is your mum working again?" she gazed at him eagerly, and he pulled her to him, laughing.

"Mickey Fenton! You're not as sweet and innocent as you look, are you?"

"Not when I'm with you Danny Harding." She kissed him quickly on the cheek and pulled away, running towards home and turning to wave before disappearing from sight.

TWENTY-ONE: THE TRUTH WILL OUT.

In just over a week's time Danny would be eighteen. Mariana stared at the photograph she had taken of him on the day she found him. It seemed like only yesterday, and yet a lifetime away. It hadn't always been easy, and even now she was never sure when something might trigger the strangeness in him again, but he seemed happier now than he had ever been. It was Sunday morning and he was out with Paddy as usual. He still spent most of his time down by the river, but when he was home he was calm and relaxed, and sometimes even affectionate towards her. Gone was the rather sullen, distant boy who would eat his meals in silence and speak only when spoken to. The new Danny asked her how her day had been, complimented her on the meals she cooked, and sometimes even gave her an impromptu hug as he left with Paddy for their evening walk. Perhaps it had just been a phase he was going through, and now he had outgrown it and was becoming an adult. She still worried that he had no friends, and she had asked him once if he had a girlfriend. He shrugged, and said,

"No one special Mum; I'll let you know if I do." She decided not to pry any further but still, such a beautiful boy surely ought to have a girlfriend.

A few days earlier she had gone into his room to retrieve his washing when she noticed a book on his bedside cabinet entitled *Romantic Poets of the Nineteenth Century*. *Strange,* she thought. *I had no idea he was into poetry.* She allowed herself a quick peek inside. One or two of the pages were turned over at the corner marking the place. At the top of one someone, not Danny, had written *'Favourite poem'*. She read the poem; it was by someone named Christina Rossetti. It was haunting and sad, entitled 'Remember'. The next one was marked *'Second favourite poem;'* it was long-winded, entitled 'The Lady of Shalott'. Clearly someone had given Danny this book, and she longed to ask him about it but decided he would feel it an invasion of his privacy. *He'll tell me in his own time I suppose,* she sighed to herself, replacing the book carefully where she had found it.

As his eighteenth birthday loomed she had more to think about than what present to buy him. She already knew what she was going to buy him – driving lessons. Kate had suggested it when he was seventeen and offered to insure her car for him so that he could practice, but Mariana was afraid.

"No Kate; he's too young, and his head's all over the place. He needs to show that he's fit to be in charge of a lethal weapon first." Kate understood and said nothing further, but just after Christmas she raised the subject again.

"Look M, you have to let go sometime. He's so much better nowadays, and you need to show him that you trust him."

"I'm not so sure I do trust him," replied Mariana wryly.

"Oh come on, you know he's making an effort. Give him a chance. Once he's passed his test we can club together and buy him a car. Jeff has some contacts, and he'd find him a nice little runner for a few hundred pounds, and get it looked over for him properly. He'll be leaving school in a few months, and whatever he's going to do, he'll do it easier if he has a car."

Kate had organized the driving lessons and his first was booked for the Saturday following his birthday. They had decided not to tell him until his birthday so that it would be a proper surprise, and would perhaps go some way to compensating for the other thing that he needed to be told – the true circumstances of his birth. Mariana was terrified. How would he react? Kate however, was adamant.

"I'm sorry M, the time has come; and if you don't tell him, then I'm going to have to. You can't keep it from him all his life. I don't know what you're so worried about. You acted out of love, and you've never done anything that wasn't in his best interests – except not telling him the truth. He will understand. After all, it's not you he has to forgive; it's the heartless cow who abandoned him in the first place!"

"I don't think she was heartless Kate, just desperate. Do you think he'll want to try and find her?"

"Well that's a possibility, but we'll have to cross that bridge when and if we come to it. He's going to have his work cut out if he does; we don't really have a single clue to her identity. I don't think you need to worry that he's going to abandon you and go back to live with her, even if she wanted him to."

"Alright. I'll tell him on Sunday; but not until the end of the day, I don't want to spoil it for him." They had decided to hold his birthday celebration a day early since his actual birthday fell on a Monday.

January 29th was cold and wet, but Danny was up and out as usual to walk Paddy by the river. Mariana watched from the bedroom window until they disappeared from sight where the ground rose sharply hiding the path along the riverbank. With a sigh, she went downstairs and set his cards and gifts out on the table along with the cake she had baked him. Kate was coming over later with the first hundred pounds towards his car, and a key ring. Mariana had bought him some leather driving gloves, a set of L-plates, and *The Highway Code*. They were going out for lunch to a trendy Italian place Kate knew of in Chester.

"Are you sure there's no one you want to bring along Danny?" Mariana had asked him the previous week.

"No Mum; there's no one, I told you. Get off my case will you?" but he smiled, and gave her a hug. "Stop worrying about me. I'm ok; never been better."

"Driving lessons – wow! Are you sure Mum? I know how you worry. Still, with gloves like these I'm sure to be a good driver." He put them on, flexing the soft leather admiringly. "You can test me on this; I hope I do better than I do in exams," he observed ruefully, flicking through the *Highway Code*. "Thanks Mum. I won't let you down; I know how hard this is for you to do." He hugged her. How grown up he seemed – was, she thought. He had been taller than her since he reached sixteen, but somehow she hadn't noticed it until recently. There was a card from Lorna too, containing a cheque for fifty pounds because Mariana had told her of the plan to buy a car.

Kate dropped them back off after their meal, refusing Mariana's offer of coffee.

"I'd better get back," she said. "Jeff has something planned for this evening, though he won't tell me what. I'll see you next Sunday Danny, and you can show me what you've learned on your first lesson."

"Thanks Auntie Kate; you're the best," said Danny.

"Good luck M," Kate whispered as she embraced her friend. Mariana gave her a wan smile. Danny disappeared to find Paddy.

"I feel sick," said Mariana. "I don't know if I can do it."

"You have to," said Kate. "I meant what I said. Give me a ring later tonight and let me know how it goes."

"I will," said Mariana, and watched her friend drive away with mixed feelings. Kate was an excellent friend, but she couldn't half be bossy sometimes.

Later that evening, Mariana steeled herself for the task ahead. After watching *One Foot in the Grave* with her, Danny said he was going to his room to start learning his highway code.

"Danny, don't go yet. There's something I need to talk to you about," Mariana said, taking a deep breath. It was now or never. Danny looked sharply at her.

"Oh-oh, what now Mum? Is it the girlfriend thing or the driving thing? Can't it wait til tomorrow? I'm a bit bushed."

"No Danny, it can't; because tomorrow I may lose my nerve and then you will have to hear it from Kate, and I'd much rather it came from me." He sat down opposite her, a perplexed frown on his face. What could be so important? And what could make his mother tremble with fear as she was doing now?

"I don't know where to start," she said, and he saw tears welling up in her eyes. "I just want you to know that what I did was out of love Danny. It seemed the right thing to do at the time, and I have never regretted it; but it's time you knew the truth."

"Did what Mum?" He was really worried now. His mother's face had turned pale. She sat upright, twisting her hands in her lap, the tears now flowing freely. A feeling of dread crept through him. *What terrible thing had she done, and to whom?*

"Whatever it is, you can tell me," he said. "I've done some pretty bad things and you've always stuck by me, even when you thought I might have done for that Hayley girl. You're my Mum, and nothing changes that." She sunk her head into her hands and sobbed for a minute, then, pushing her hair back and with a determined set of her mouth she said,

"That's just it; I'm not." Danny stared at her. *What did she mean?* He said nothing, but waited for her to continue. He watched her compose herself and take a deep breath. It seemed to take forever.

"I'm not your mother," she said quietly, looking him in the eye.

"What d'you mean, you're not my mother? Then who the hell is?" His mind whirled; he thought of Kate. *Was it her?* She had always looked after him, and she seemed to have a lot of say in his life. *Had she given him away to her friend or something crazy like that?*

"I don't know Danny; I'm sorry." Mariana watched her son's face register several different emotions within a split second, but mostly bewilderment. She withdrew the note from her pocket; the one that she found in the bag with Danny eighteen years ago, and handed it to him.

"I found you in the park, and I found this with you." Danny took the note from her, his hand shaking, and read it through.

"Oh my God!" he whispered, his voice breaking with emotion.

"Oh Danny, you were so tiny; so helpless, and I loved you from that moment. I couldn't give you up; you were the answer to a prayer. If I had handed you in to the authorities, they would have taken you away from me, and I should never have known what happened to you. Don't you see? I had to keep you; you were sent to me." To her horror he raised his head to look at her, and anger and resentment blazed in his eyes.

"You had no right," he said through clenched teeth. *"No fucking right!"* Mariana flinched; she had never seen him like this.

"Danny I…"

"You had no fucking right," he said again. "If you'd handed me in they might've found my mother. Did you never think of that you selfish bitch?" He rose from his chair and Mariana recoiled involuntarily, suddenly reminded graphically of Terry. *Who was he calling selfish?*

"They wouldn't have found her Danny. She didn't want to be found. She had planned everything, I could tell. I called out to her, told her I would help her, but she must have gone because she never answered. She didn't want you Danny, but I did. Don't tell me about my right; what about yours? You had a right to a home where you were loved and wanted, and that's what I gave you."

"This explains everything," he said now, turning his back on her. "This is why I've never fitted; why I've never been able to love you. I thought I was some kinda freak. I've fought it all my life, that and my so-called dead sister messing with my head. What have you done to me? I'm going out. Come on Paddy!" But Paddy slunk behind the sofa, his tail down, and Danny went without him. Somewhere inside her head, Mariana heard the front door

249

slam behind him. She sank onto the sofa and gave vent to her grief. She had lost him; she had lost her son – yes, he was her son, in every sense of the word but one; but now she had lost him. She wondered where he had gone. It was pitch dark and freezing cold, and he hadn't even taken a coat. She clenched her fist and drove it into the cushion on the back of the sofa. Life was so unfair! Why had Kate made her do this? He need never have known, and where was the harm in that? She punched the cushion again and again, the hot tears cascading down her face, her heart constricting with the sheer agony of knowing that she had destroyed the one thing that really mattered in her life. Paddy lay at the side of the sofa, his head resting on his paws.

The phone rang. She leapt to answer it; it might be Danny.

"Danny I…." but it wasn't him.

"M? You ok? What's the matter?" It was Kate; the last person she wanted to speak to right now.

"Everything's the matter Kate, and it's all your fault!" She slammed the phone down. "It rang again immediately, but she ignored it. She went upstairs to Danny's room and looked out of his window at the meadow below; but beyond the waving ash trees and the gleaming shards of rain caught in the rays from the streetlights, she could see nothing. It was pitch dark.

The front door opened and she ran to look down into the hallway. It was Kate. She climbed the stairs and surveyed the wreckage of her friend in dismay.

"He's gone," Mariana sobbed, and Kate drew her into her arms.

"What happened?" she said, gently stroking back the hair from Mariana's face.

"I told him. He was so angry. He called me a selfish bitch and he's gone; I don't know where. Oh Kate, I shouldn't have told him; you were wrong – this time, you were so wrong!"

"Oh M, I'm sorry. I didn't think he'd take it like that." She gently led her down the stairs and sat her on the sofa.

"What else did he say?"

"He said he's never loved me, and that he thought he was a freak because of that. He said Dani had been messing with his head, but I don't understand what he meant by that." She felt Kate stiffen, and then she said,

"I do I'm afraid. He told me two years ago, after that business with Hayley Price. He made me promise not to tell you. I'm sorry M."

"Oh, I see! It's ok for you to keep secrets, but not me. How could you Kate? I've always trusted you; well, more fool me! What did he tell you?"

"He told me that Dani has been talking to him ever since he started school. All those things he used to do? He reckons it was her controlling him." Mariana stared at her in disbelief. She couldn't take all this in. Her son (she would always think of him as that) had been hearing voices – *didn't crazy people do that? Schizophrenics; wasn't that what they were called?*

"Why couldn't he tell *me*?" she asked.

"He didn't intend telling me M; I wormed it out of him, but only by promising I'd keep it to myself. He thought you would just think he was jealous of Dani and wanted to discredit her. He said you wouldn't believe him; yet clearly he wasn't sure of his own innocence, because she taunted him and told him he was to blame."

"But that's crazy Kate. How can he hear Dani? How would he even know what she sounded like? Besides, she was a sweet little girl and just wouldn't do that sort of thing."

"There you go; that's exactly what he thought you'd say. Ok, Dani's voice is a figment of his imagination M, but there must be a reason he thinks he hears her. I don't pretend to understand it all. He probably needed to see that psychologist the school suggested."

"I didn't want him branded a head case; and anyway, all that seems to have stopped now; he's been so much better since he had Paddy – except for the Hayley business, and he seems to have completely got over that now. He's been so different the past few months. I think he may have a girlfriend; but he won't admit to it. Huh! Perhaps you should ask him, since he seems able to confide in you. What else did he say?"

"Only that you wouldn't talk about Terry to him, and he was having an identity crisis. Still, all that's irrelevant now that he knows Terry's not his real dad."

"Oh God, what have I done? If he was having an identity crisis before, I have just made it twice as bad. Where can he be Kate? It's freezing out there, and I wouldn't know where to begin looking for him."

"He'll be ok; you know what youngsters are like, they go all sorts of places we don't know about. He'll be somewhere sheltering and cooling off, literally. When he's thought things over he'll be back, but you'll probably have a heap more questions to answer, so you'd better be prepared. Whatever he asks you M, try and answer truthfully. I think there's been enough secrets, don't you?"

"You're right. Perhaps I should have told him in the first place, but I saw no harm in him not knowing, and quite honestly I still don't. He would probably never have found out. By the way, what did Jeff have planned?"

"Oh that. He asked me to marry him," said Kate, showing Mariana the sparkling diamond on her left hand. "I said yes."

TWENTY-TWO: FORGIVENESS.

Danny ran from the house. He had no clear idea of where he was going; only that he needed to get away and think about the things he had just heard. Suddenly everything fell into place, and he knew why he was the way he was. Somewhere in his deep subconscious, he had known all along that Mariana wasn't his real mother.

He headed for the main road and crossed over into Crow Lane. Mickey's house was right down at the far end. He had been there a few times. He would wait for her in the tack room when it was too wet to walk by the river, and they would sit there and talk. There had been some pretty severe flooding since December and they had met in this way several times. They had a signal; Danny would tie a piece of rope to the gate of the stable yard so that Mickey would know he was there. It was dark now however, so that wouldn't work. He looked at the luminous hands of his watch; it was just after ten, so she might already be in bed.

Her room, he knew, was at the back of the house; she had shown him once which was her window. She had also shown him where the key of the tack room was kept, and he used it now to let himself in. He searched around, fumbling in the dark, and found a torch. Climbing over the low wall, he made his way through the shrubbery at the back of the house to where he could see her bedroom window. The curtains were drawn across; she must be in bed. He bent down and selected several small pebbles from the path. Moving stealthily across the grass he stood beneath her window and hurled the first one. It hit the wall near the window and bounced off. The next one hit the window, making a much louder noise than he had anticipated. He ducked down behind a bush nervously and waited. Nothing. He tried again, this time striking the window frame. A moment later the curtain twitched then drew aside, and Mickey was looking down at him. Slowly and carefully she raised the sash window a few inches. It squeaked alarmingly and he saw her glance over her shoulder, then she leaned down and hissed through the small space.

"Danny, what are you doing?"

"I have to talk to you," he hissed back. "Can you get out?"

"I'll try," she replied. "Wait for me in the tack room; I may be a while."

She blew him a kiss and withdrew from the window, closing it down silently. He returned to the tack room and sat on a saddle-horse to wait for her.

"Danny, what's going on?" She slipped inside, closing the door behind her. "You look terrible; what's happened?"

He took her in his arms and kissed her. She was wearing her waxed jacket and boots over her pyjamas.

"My Dad'll kill me if he catches me," she said. "I've put clothes in the bed like they do in the movies. I'll just have to hope they think I'm asleep."

Danny related what Mariana had told him and showed her the note.

255

"No wonder I've never felt right," he said. "She had no right to do it Mickey. Why did she do it?"

They were sitting on some bales of straw. He slid down and laid his head in her lap, and she ran her fingers through his hair and stroked his brow gently.

"I think she did it because she loved you," she said softly. "What should she have done? Handed you over to strangers and walked away? The note says *Please look after him and love him*, and that's what she did Danny, isn't it?"

"What if my real mum was looking for me? She might have changed her mind. I should have had that chance, she had no right to deprive me of it."

"Oh come on Danny, get real! Your mother dumped you. She says she loved you, but she couldn't keep you. If that was the truth, she would have been happy with the way things turned out. What makes you think you'd have been better off with someone else – even your real mother? I mean; if anyone was a selfish cow it was her I'd say."

"She shouldn't have fuckin' lied to me," he insisted sullenly. He had thought Mickey at least would see it his way.

"She didn't exactly lie did she? She just didn't tell you the whole truth. All mums do that when they think they're protecting you. You're not the only one whose mum has kept things from you Danny." She was indignant now.

"What d'you mean? I bet your mum never kept any secrets from you."

"Well as a matter of fact, she did. When I was thirteen she told me about my twin brother."

"Twin brother?" echoed Danny, sitting up suddenly. "What twin brother?"

256

"The one that died when we were born," replied Mickey in a small voice. "She didn't want to tell me until I was old enough to understand, and then she said there was never a right time. My dad gave her an ultimatum – you tell her or I will, something like that. They took me to see his grave, and I go there every now and again. I'll show you if you like. Ok, my mum should've told me like when I was five; but she didn't, because she didn't want to make me sad. I love her for that, even if she was wrong."

"I don't know what to say," said Danny. He felt humbled and ashamed by this extraordinary girl. He should have had more compassion. "I love you Mickey Fenton. I'll always love you, you know that don't you?"

"I love you too Danny, but always is a long time. We can't be sure what will happen to us in the future?"

"Oh no, you're off again with your fatalist crap! You read too many of those romantic poems where everyone dies and stuff!"

"Huh! You can't talk, I've seen the stuff you read remember – no wonder you're such a misery sometimes!"

"I am, am I? Well little Miss Sunshine, let's see if I can't make you laugh." He began to tickle her, pushing his cold hands inside her pyjama top so that she shrieked and struggled to escape, giggling all the while. Danny stopped tickling, and ran his hands over her small breasts, kissing her and murmuring endearments. She lay back on the straw bales and they made love, their bodies entwined in absolute harmony, banishing all other thoughts from their minds. Afterwards, they brushed the straw from their clothes, and held each other tight in the darkness, warmed by their overwhelming love.

"Promise me you'll go easy on your mum Danny; I'm sure she meant well, and you might not even like your real mum if you met her – after all, she was the one who abandoned you."

"Alright, oh wise one; I promise."

He made his way home. The rain had stopped; the clouds had rolled away and a full moon rode the sky with phalanxes of glittering stars in its wake. The trees were beginning to pale with frost, but Danny wasn't cold. Mickey's words echoed in his head, and he marveled at the wisdom of one so young. He hoped she had managed to sneak back to her room without getting caught. She had an explanation ready; she would say she had heard Sparky kicking his stable door and had gone to check on him not wanting to disturb her parents over nothing. *Women are so much more devious that us*, he thought to himself.

Kate's car was on the drive. He opened the front door slowly. His mother and Kate were in the lounge. He could hear their voices, but not what they were saying. He closed the door; it clicked loudly into place despite his caution, and the murmur of voices stopped. The lounge door opened and his mother and Kate came out into the hallway.

"Danny!" she cried, "Thank God you're alright!"

"I'm ok Mum, but like I said before, I'm bushed. Goodnight. Goodnight Auntie Kate, come on Paddy." With that, he climbed the stairs with Paddy at his heels. He undressed and climbed into bed. Within minutes he was asleep.

He dreamed of Mickey. She was floating down the river on a raft of flotsam. She was naked except for a white robe, and her chestnut hair flowed over the reeds and floated on the water behind her as the current bore her slowly along. Her eyes were wide open, unblinking. He called to her, but she didn't answer. Then he heard another

258

voice – Danielle's, whispering in low sibilant tones, *"Leave her Danny, let her go, she's not for you, she belongs to the river."*

He woke with a start and knew he had cried out loud. Paddy crawled from his place at the foot of the bed and began licking Danny's face anxiously.

"It's alright Paddy, it was only a dream," said Danny, patting him reassuringly. The sweat stood on his brow and Paddy licked again, relishing the salty taste. Danny sat up and pushed him gently away. He listened, straining his ears into the shadows cast around the room through the curtains by the full moon and the flickering streetlights that lined the lane below his window. He heard nothing, either inside or outside his head. He sank back down onto his pillow and cuddling up to Paddy for comfort, fell back into a deep and this time dreamless sleep.

TWENTY-THREE: WEDDING PLANS.

Kate was excited.

"We've fixed the date," she told Mariana. "We're getting married on my birthday, August 19th. That doesn't give us much time; there's a lot to sort out."

"Are you having a big do then?" asked Mariana.

"Of course! My Mum's been looking forward to this. She was gutted when I married Scott in a registry office. Yep, it's going to be the real deal this time – big white dress and lots of bridesmaids. Thing is, I'll have to have two chief bridesmaids; you, and Rachel. You're about the same height and build so you'll go together well, but you really need to meet her now M, if you're to work together at my wedding."

"I s'pose so. She must be ok if you think so highly of her. Who else are you having?"

"Well, there's Rachel's daughter Mickey; she's fifteen in April; Michael's Molly; and Jeff's little niece Jessica, who's only four. I thought I'd ask Danny to be one of my ushers along with Rachel's brothers Johnny and Jimmy."

"Blimey! You are pushing the boat out, aren't you? You'd better ask Danny when he's in a good mood – you know what he's like; he'll either love the idea or refuse point blank."

"Well I'm bringing Rachel to meet you one day very soon, so I'll ask him then," said Kate. Mariana smiled; Kate, she was sure, would brook no refusal.

When Danny found out the truth about his birth, it was as though a great burden had lifted from Mariana's shoulders, and she realised how wrong she had been to keep it from him. All the lying, all the pretending had been so unnecessary and had in the end only served to make them both miserable. She realised that it was she who had alienated her son, because of Danny's fear that he would always be second best to his sister. Now his resentment was directed at his real mother, and he had forgiven Mariana at last. A few days later he had asked about Danielle again; it was as though he no longer had to fear her and no longer saw her as a rival. Mariana dug the box out from the attic and they went through it together one evening. She retold the sad story of Dani's death, and Terry's part in it.

"If only he'd come home that night," she said sadly. "We would have taken Dani to hospital, and she might have been saved."

"You don't know that Mum," said Danny. "You didn't know what was wrong with her, and by the sounds of him, Terry wouldn't have cared enough to put himself out. I'm so glad he wasn't my dad; I've been worried sick all my life in case I'd turn out like him."

"Oh Danny! I never realised it would affect you like that; I've been so stupid," and she began to cry.

"Hey, it doesn't matter now. You got confused I guess. It was other people you had to lie to not me; I would have understood."

"You're a good boy Danny, and no one is more glad than me that you're nothing to do with that man. We may never know who your real parents are, but I'm sure there must have been some tragic story behind what your mother did. You mustn't judge her you know."

Together they replaced everything in the box, but Mariana decided to keep it behind the sofa instead of returning it to the attic. Danielle would have been twenty-three in a few months' time. She wondered what her daughter would have looked like, what course her life would have taken. Then she reminded herself that had Danielle not died, she would never have found Danny.

With a sickening jolt, she realised that now he knew he wasn't her son, she herself felt less of a connection between them. She had always believed him to be a Godsend; a healing entity whose very existence was for the sole purpose of compensating for her grievous loss. Now she knew that he had never really replaced Dani, and he never could, and she began to wonder where he came from; it began to matter more than she would ever have believed it could. For the first time since she found him she admitted to herself that, given the choice, she would choose Danielle without a doubt.

On the morning she met Rachel for the first time she had been going through Dani's box yet again. It was Sunday morning, and Danny had gone out with Paddy as usual before she was up. She decided to indulge herself as she often did these days in a little nostalgia, a cup of coffee, and a chocolate biscuit. She had bought a photograph album, and she began sorting through the many pictures of Dani and carefully placing them in order between the leaves of the album. There were some of Terry and Dani together (she had long since destroyed the ones of Terry and herself together) and she placed them on the coffee table, uncertain what to do with them. Should she now destroy them too? Obliterate him from her life completely at long last? She had kept them mainly for Danny's sake, so that she could show him what his 'father' looked like – there was no denying he had been a handsome man; but now that Danny knew the truth there was no longer any need to sully her daughter's memory with the photographic duets.

In the midst of her musings the doorbell rang. It was Kate, accompanied by a woman who Mariana judged to be in her thirties. She was a little taller than Mariana but shorter than Kate, with shoulder length chestnut hair.

"Where's your key?" she asked Kate.

"Well, I didn't like to just invade you since I've brought Rachel to meet you," Kate replied. "Rachel, this is my friend Mariana." Rachel smiled a little shyly,

"Hi Mariana," she said, "I've heard so much about you that I feel I know you."

She raised her eyes to Mariana's and suddenly her face changed, and Mariana saw first puzzlement, and then something else – recognition. There was an awkward moment, then Kate brushed past Mariana into the house. Mariana indicated to Rachel to step inside, and closed the door behind her. Kate was in the kitchen.

"Where's Danny?" she asked.

"Out as usual," replied Mariana. "I hardly see him on Sundays; I think he's with that girlfriend he denies having. I don't know why he's being so cagey about it; it worries me – I hope he's not seeing some married woman or anything."

"Oh my God, you don't really think that do you M?" Kate looked horrified.

263

"Don't be daft, I was joking. It's probably some goth girl he thinks I won't approve of; he's always liked all that dark stuff, but I suppose it's harmless really."

"I shouldn't worry; it won't be serious at his age anyway. He probably just doesn't want you fussing over her like an old mother hen," laughed Kate, and turned to Rachel,

"Danny is the apple of Mariana's eye, and when you get to meet him you'll easily see why; he's stunningly beautiful! I doubt whether any girl will ever be good enough for him in M's eyes. Are you ok Rach? You look a bit pale."

Rachel had indeed gone a little pale and silent. She was looking around the house distractedly as though searching for something. She jumped visibly when Kate spoke to her and quickly smiled, but the smile didn't reach her eyes.

"Have you any photos of him?" she asked Mariana.

"Only when he was little," replied Mariana ruefully. "He's always hated having his photo taken and runs a mile if he sees a camera. He's not even on any school photos; he always manages to dodge them somehow. He'll have to overcome his phobia at Kate's wedding I'm afraid." Rachel looked disproportionately disappointed, and Mariana thought, *she's a strange one!*

They took their coffee into the living room. Mariana shoved the photos she had been sorting through to one side to make room for their cups.

"What on earth are you doing?" Kate asked.

"Sorting through Dani's box and putting her photos somewhere better. Should have done it years ago."

"Dani was Mariana's little girl. Remember, I told you she died when she was only four?"

Rachel nodded. She looked as though she was about to throw up. She was staring at the photographs that Mariana had brushed aside, the ones of Terry and Danielle. Kate leaned over and grabbed them.

"That's her; that's little Danielle. Mariana named Danny after her," she said, thrusting them into Rachel's hands. "Isn't she the sweetest thing?"

Rachel said nothing. She was leafing through the photographs studying them intently, a deep frown furrowing her brow. Mariana felt for her; she must be very sensitive to be so upset by the thought of Dani's tragic demise. After several minutes of awkward silence she looked up.

"Who's the man in these pictures?" she asked, her voice sounding small and broken. She looked close to tears, and Mariana sought to lighten the moment.

"Oh, that's Terry, the bastard I married when I was sixteen. The only good thing I ever got from him was my babies. He died in a car accident a few months before Danny was born. But don't waste your sympathy; I was definitely better off without him!"

"He died?" Rachel whispered, her face aghast. "When exactly did he die?"

Mariana thought, *blimey, this is all a bit OTT. She is definitely strange!*

"Friday August 20th 1976," replied Mariana, and heard Rachel's barely perceptible sharp intake of breath. *What was it with this woman?*

"Don't get me wrong; it was a shock," continued Mariana, seeking to disperse the awkwardness of the moment, not understanding why Rachel was so badly affected by the tragic occurrences in the life of someone she had only just met. Then she remembered the public shows of emotion when some celebrity dies that no one has ever actually met, and thought *this is what people do these days I suppose.*

Kate downed the last of her coffee and said,

"We'll have to get off M; Michael's taking us all out for lunch. I'll ring you in the week. I've sent for some brochures, and we should be able to pick our outfits next weekend. Perhaps you could ask Danny about being an usher; you can tell him I would've asked him myself if he'd been here."

"Ok, I'll do that. Goodbye Rachel, it was very nice meeting you." She smiled brightly at Kate's friend – *I suppose it takes all sorts*, she thought, *perhaps she's just having a bad day.*

Rachel mumbled a reply and followed Kate to the car without a backward glance.

TWENTY-FOUR: DOPPELGANGER?

Rachel sat in Kate's car, her stomach churning and Mariana's words screaming in her mind. *He died in a car crash, on Friday 20th August 1976!*

"Are you sure you're ok Rach?" Kate's voice was full of consternation. Her friend looked as though she had been struck by lightning; her face was ashen and there was the glint of tears in her brown eyes.

"I don't feel so good," replied Rachel. "I think I'm going to have to pass on lunch, but the rest of you must go. I'll be ok when I've had a lie down."

"Did it upset you, all that talk of people dying? I never knew Dani, it all happened before I met M; but I shouldn't waste your sympathy on Terry; he was pretty much a waste of space, and I can say that with authority because I knew him."

"He can't have been all bad," Rachel insisted, "can he?"

"Well, probably not, but he kept his good side well hidden, lets put it that way. I know you're not supposed to speak ill of the dead, but honestly Rach, he was such an arrogant bully, and M was no match for him. He even cheated on her with her best friend before they were married – she was pregnant with Danielle at the time. No, he had very few redeeming qualities, and probably loads of affairs."

Rachel fell silent for the rest of the way home. She immediately went to her room to lie down, leaving Kate to explain to Michael that she'd taken a funny turn. He went and sat on the bed beside her and took her hand.

"What is it darling?" he asked her gently.

"It's nothing Michael; I'll be alright soon; I just came over all queasy. You go ahead and take the others to lunch; if you don't mind I'll just stay here quietly for an hour or two. Is Mickey back yet?"

"She is; she got home just before you. I can't really disappoint her; she was looking forward to going out. You get well my love, and I'll see you later. Can I get you anything?"

"No thanks, I just need to sleep," she answered, and turned away from him as he left the room. Minutes later she heard the car move off down the graveled drive.

As soon as she saw the photographs, the pieces of the jigsaw had slipped inexorably into place. Terry was, unmistakably, her Dan. His face leaped out of the photographs at her like a physical blow; his languid blue eyes with their heavy lids and long lashes; his long hair, darker than when she knew him, but otherwise not much different; the dazzling smile that could turn her legs to jelly; and to seal the deal, the tattoos on his forearms. She stared at the pictures, feeling a numbness spread over her body. She had recognised Mariana immediately as the woman whom she saw with Daniel on that day in the park so many years ago. She was just gathering her wits after the shock of recognition and the realisation that after eighteen years, she had finally found her son again. There's only so much a person can handle, and the realisation that her Dan and

Mariana's Terry were one and the same, and that he hadn't dumped her but had died, was more than she could bear. As the car rolled away down the drive she began to weep violently, her body wracked with sobs and a sharp physical pain in her chest so that she could scarcely breathe. She railed against a God that, once again, had proved himself terrible in his injustice. Why did these things keep happening to her? What more could the Almighty throw at her in his determination to destroy her; and what could she possibly have done to deserve it all? After some time she stopped her weeping and went to the window. The window overlooked the garden at the front of the house; the gracious sweep of the tree-lined gravel drive, and the winter jasmine that was in full bloom because she liked to make sure that something was, all the year round. Daffodils had pushed their green blades through the cold, hard earth and stood three or four inches high. Clumps of snowdrops lit the ground beneath the trees that in spring would be bright and fragrant with apple and cherry blossom. Michael maintained that trees should have some function other than mere decoration, so the apples and cherries would be gathered and consumed in due course. That was typical of Michael, she thought. Everything he did had a considered and valid purpose. He wasn't given to reckless impulse, and he rarely if ever put a foot wrong. She had never understood where he had gone wrong with Susannah, but she was more than happy to step into her shoes. She remembered the early days of their relationship. It was several weeks before they slept together, but when it happened it was like coming home and discovering that some wonderful transformation had taken place in one's absence. Their love soared to another level, and when she walked down the aisle in the pretty village church to stand beside him, all her past sorrows were banished from her

269

mind and she had finally freed herself of her lost son and his errant father.

It was eighteen months before she fell pregnant, although they were both eager for a child. She was beginning to wonder if Daniel's ignominious birth had in some way damaged her ability to conceive, and it was a huge relief when she realised that their dream of a family was about to come true. Michael insisted she went private, and booked her in at the Nuffield hospital for her antenatal care. The obstetrician examined her thoroughly.

"Your husband said this is your first child," he observed, eyeing her sharply through his spectacles. "However, my examination tells me it may not be. Can you enlighten me?"

She admitted she had had a child before she met Michael, but didn't elaborate.

"He doesn't know; he can't know," she pleaded.

"Don't worry, Mrs. Fenton," he reassured her. "Everything that transpires between you and this hospital is completely confidential; you have my word and the Hippocratic oath to thank for that." He smiled indulgently.

"We all do things when we are young that we later regret; it's not my place or anyone else's to judge. I'm sure you have your reasons for not divulging your past to your husband." For some reason she interpreted his words in the exact opposite way from which they sounded. She was consumed with guilt and embarrassment. His next words, however, drove all that from her mind.

"Are there twins in your family?" he asked.

"Yes," she answered, "I have twin brothers, and Michael has twins from his first marriage – why?"

"Because I believe you are expecting not one baby, but two. I shall be able to make a more accurate assessment further down the line, but it seems highly likely in view of your family history."

Rachel was thrilled; she couldn't wait to tell Michael. She had to admit to herself that part of the reason she was so excited was because she had previously felt that Susannah, by presenting him with twins, had trumped in advance any contribution she might make to his future family. Now they were quits!

The day of the birth drew near, and Rachel could barely contain her excitement. The diagnosis of twins had been confirmed, and the pregnancy had progressed smoothly, except that towards the end she found her enormous proportions difficult to cope with.

It was late April and Spring was well under way when she felt the first pangs of labour. She remembered the last time; her fear and her determination, and her despair at having to go through with it alone. How different things were this time, she thought. It was a beautiful sunny day and Michael drove her to the hospital where she was quickly ensconced in her private room for the early stages. Her window looked out over the hospital shrubbery, and was decorated in pretty pastel colours and supplied with a television and the latest glossy magazines, as well as a pile of leaflets on baby care. At home, the nursery was prepared with two matching cots and American style décor. Michael had spared no expense, and in one corner of the room stood a large hand-crafted rocking horse; dappled grey like Mr. Pickles, with leather harness and a real mane and tail. It would be a long time before the twins were old enough to play with it, but Rachel would often perch sideways on it and rock herself gently whilst she dreamed of her impending family.

Suddenly, the monitors began to beep ominously, and the room became a hive of activity. One of the babies was in distress, and they would have to be born quickly. Rachel had dearly wanted a natural birth, but now she was wheeled into theatre to have an emergency caesarean instead. Michael walked beside her, holding her hand and reassuring her gently.

"Don't worry," he said, "When you wake up I'll be here, holding our babies. I love you Rachel, and our babies. I can't wait to meet them." He bent and kissed her as the doors to the theatre anteroom swallowed her up.

When she woke she was back in her room. The curtains were drawn and there was a hushed atmosphere that seemed at odds with the excitement that had pervaded before she went down. Michael was sitting in the chair beside her bed. *Where were her babies?* Panic flooded over her.

"Hello Darling," whispered Michael softly, leaning over to kiss her gently. "How are you feeling?" He seemed subdued, his eyes full of concern.

"Where are my babies?" she asked, feeling a growing lump of fear in her throat. Michael squeezed her hand and to her horror, tears began to well in his eyes.

"I'm so sorry darling," he said, as the lump rose, threatening to overwhelm her and stop her breathing. "The little girl is fine, but the little boy didn't make it."

"No, that can't be," she cried. "They were both fine when I came in. What happened?"

"They don't know. He stopped breathing, and by the time they got you to theatre and delivered him it was too late. That's all I know. I don't think they know why it happened themselves. We've got a beautiful baby daughter though Rachel; and she's absolutely fine."

"A daughter," Rachel repeated. "We have a daughter, and our son is dead."

In her mind she knew she was to blame. She had abandoned her firstborn son, and now God had punished her by taking her new son away from her. She didn't even really believe in God, but somehow when either really good or really bad things happened, she had always held him responsible.

They named him John after Rachel's father. He looked perfect; there was nothing visibly wrong with him, and it broke her heart that he had to undergo a post mortem to determine the cause of death. The post mortem was inconclusive and simply showed that he had died from lack of oxygen. They buried him in a corner of the little churchyard where they were married; near to the grave of Michael's grandparents, rather than in the vast cemetery in town where Rachel's father lay.

They named the little girl Michaela after her father. She was a placid baby and slept through the night after the first three months. Rachel took her regularly to visit her brother's grave, but stopped these visits before she was three years old, deciding that it might frighten her to be told at such a tender age about his death. Children worry about these things she knew; so Mickey knew nothing of her sibling until her thirteenth birthday.

"We can have another son," Michael told her. "We've plenty of time."

"I don't want any more children," she insisted, "I don't want to run the risk of losing another child." Michael couldn't understand why one tragedy should put her off in this way – anyone would think she had lost more than one baby. He decided to say nothing more for the present; he was sure she would come round to the idea, given time. But the years passed and she remained adamant, and in the end he gave up. He lavished all his attention on Mickey and denied her nothing. She was a bright girl and in spite of being the centre of attention, she was also caring and kind, and Rachel could not have wished for a better daughter. Mickey's grandmother adored her, as did her uncles Johnny and Jimmy, and her half brother and sister. After Rachel told her about her brother she began visiting his grave. She decorated it with small toys she bought him, or shells and pebbles that she brought back from trips to the seaside, and she would talk to him and tell him what she had been doing since her last visit. Rachel came across her once when she herself was visiting and stood listening for a few minutes before creeping silently away. She was quite touched by her devotion to the brother she never knew, and didn't want to embarrass her or spoil her moment.

Now Rachel reflected on all this, and searched her heart. Was she glad that she gave Danny away and had ended up with this enviable life? Would she have been equally happy if Dan had stayed around and they had been a family, the three of them? But it had all been built on a lie anyway; Dan couldn't be with her; he already had a wife. She reflected on what both Mariana and Kate had said about Terry, and tried to reconcile it with her memories of Dan. Yes, he could certainly be moody and unpredictable, and sometimes he had the ability to seriously undermine her self-esteem; but he had his tender side too, and he was good fun. No, she couldn't equate the Dan she remembered with the vision of Terry that the other two women had implanted in her mind; *but there again,* she thought, *I didn't really know him that well or that long, perhaps the rot would have set in later.*

She wondered what she should do. She so wanted to know more about Danny. He was to be an usher at Kate's wedding so she would get the chance to talk to him then, but she needed to know more; she needed to fill in the gaps and feel a part of his life. She made up her mind to visit Mariana again and tell her who she was.

I'll go tomorrow, she told herself. *There's no time like the present.*

TWENTY-FIVE: RACHEL'S STORY.

Mariana watched Kate's car move slowly down the road and out of sight and then returned to the living room. She gathered up the coffee cups and washed them absently, her mind on other things. Rachel had behaved very strangely, and somewhere in the back of her mind she believed it had something to do with Terry. Suddenly the dreams that had plagued her after he died came flooding back. Had he really been unfaithful to her throughout their marriage? Had she dredged the dreams up from her subconscious mind because in her heart of hearts, she had known this to be the case? Was Rachel one of his other women, and if so, was she seeing him when he died? She knew that Rachel was younger than Kate by four years, and that would have made her only eighteen when he died. It was quite possible that Terry might have had an affair with a young girl – after all, she was only fifteen when they met, and he didn't seem to have a problem with that.

She wiped her soapy hands on a tea towel and returned to the living room. The photographs were lying where Rachel had left them. Terry smiled up at her mockingly and she hastily pushed them back into the box.

If Rachel had been seeing Terry when he died then she wouldn't have known about the accident, since no one would have told her. Perhaps she was unaware that he was married. Mariana trawled up the vision of Rachel's face when she saw the photographs and tried to remember the questions she had asked. Drat! She wished now that she had paid more attention instead of just thinking how weird the woman was. She had certainly asked about the exact date of his death, because Mariana had wondered why; most people would only ask what year it was. *Oh well,* she thought as she replaced the box behind the sofa. *When I see her at Kate's wedding, I might just ask her outright.*

The back door slammed and Danny came in.

"I'm starving!" he said. "Are we having Sunday dinner?" Mariana jerked herself back to the present. She had forgotten all about lunch.

"Oh, I'm sorry Danny," she said. "I forgot about lunch, I've had visitors."

"What sort of visitors?" he asked; visitors were a rarity, apart from Kate, and she was more like family.

"Well, Kate brought her friend Rachel to see me; she's going to be one of her bridesmaids – oh, and she wants to know if you'll be an usher."

"Oh God, do I have to?" Danny said with a groan. "I hate bloody weddings!"

"Oh, come on Danny, don't be a grouch; it might even be fun. I believe Rachel has a daughter, Michaela. She must be at your school but she's quite a bit younger than you so you probably won't know her. Anyway, I've told Kate you'll do it now, and you can't let her down."

A slow smile spread over Danny's face.

"Ok Mum," he said. "Tell Auntie Kate I'll do it. Will I have to wear a penguin suit?" He laughed to himself at the thought of what Mickey would make of that!

"Oh, I should think so, it's going to be quite a posh do you know; She's having five bridesmaids – including me."

277

"Blimey Mum, aren't you a bit old for that?"

"You cheeky beggar! I'll have you know I still scrub up ok Danny Harding, and I'm not *that* much older than Kate."

"Only kidding Mum," he said, and gave her a quick hug. "Who are the other four then?"

"Well, there's Rachel, who'll be walking with me; then there's Rachel's step-daughter Molly, who's twenty-something; then behind her Michaela; and Jeff's little neice will be at the back, she's only four."

Mickey in a bridesmaid's dress, Danny thought, *that would be interesting!* Mickey was an irrefutable tomboy, and she wouldn't take kindly to frills and flounces.

Mariana found some sausages in the fridge, and they had bangers 'n mash for their Sunday lunch. Danny was cheerful and to Mariana's relief seemed to have forgotten the crisis of a few days earlier. Mariana also forgot about Rachel's strange behaviour, and also her less than loyal thoughts regarding Daniel and his sister and the choices that thankfully she would never have to make.

The next day after Danny had left for school she dragged the box out one more time from behind the sofa. Delving into it she withdrew the photographs of Terry and tearing them into tiny pieces, deposited them firmly in the bin in the kitchen. *Let that be an end to it once and for all,* she told herself.

The doorbell rang – who could that be? She glanced through the kitchen window. A bright metallic blue Mazda sports car was parked on the concrete apron in front of the garage. She knew no one with a car like that.

She hurried to the front door and opened it to see Rachel standing there.

"Can I come in?" she asked. "We need to talk."

Mariana stood back to let her in. She looked pale and drawn, except for a slight flush on her neck and two bright red spots on her cheeks. Mariana showed her into the living room.

"Can I get you a coffee or anything?" she asked politely.

"No thanks," replied Rachel with an attempt at a smile that appeared more of a grimace.

"I won't beat about the bush," she said, looking Mariana directly in the eye, the flush on her neck and face increasing rapidly. "I'm Danny's mother."

Mariana was dumbstruck; but some small part of her knew she wasn't completely surprised. Her suspicions that Rachel had a connection with Terry had led her to the inkling that in that case she might be Danny's mother, but she hadn't wanted to admit it even to herself, and had pushed the thought resolutely into the bin with the photographs. She stared at this woman whose existence she had known of for years without realising that she would one day impact so devastatingly on her own life. She looked small and almost frail, and it must have taken a great deal of courage to make this visit. Mariana clutched at a slender straw of doubt.

"Are you sure?" she asked, "I mean, can you prove it?"

"I can tell you that he was born sometime around midnight on Saturday 29th January, 1977. I can't tell you the exact time, because I wasn't wearing a watch. It was a cold and frosty night; I dressed him and wrapped him in a blanket, and placed him in a holdall for safety. I wrote a note asking whoever became his new mother to love him and look after him. In the morning I hid in some bushes, and I saw you take him away – you had a black dog with you. You called out to me, and believe me it was the hardest thing I have ever done to remain hidden as I watched you take my son away."

"Then why?" asked Mariana.

"Because I thought his father had abandoned me; and my own father was at risk of a fatal heart attack if he got upset. He would have been devastated if he'd known I was expecting an illegitimate child, so I had to give Daniel away; I couldn't risk being responsible for my father's death. I had searched for Dan for months to no avail, and now I know why. Dan was Terry; and Terry was dead. Less than two days after Daniel was born my father died anyway, and everything I had been through had been in vain."

Mariana was silent. She tried and failed to imagine what this poor woman must have been through in those few months. Rachel continued.

"I thought you would take him to the hospital. I looked out in the papers for a report of a foundling baby, but there was none. I thought if I could find him I would be able to have him back. My mother would be upset, but she would have coped, and it may even have helped her to get over losing my dad. It was four months later that I eventually saw you and Danny in the park. I recognised you immediately, and I came over and spoke to you."

With absolute clarity, Mariana remembered the incident, and she also remembered thinking that there was something about the girl in the park that troubled her.

"You told me about Danielle and I knew I couldn't take Danny from you. It was the end of my dream of having him back. I couldn't put you through the pain of losing another child, and clearly he had fallen on his feet."

Mariana moved to her side.

"Oh you poor thing," she whispered, and put her arms around her. Rachel leaned against her and they both wept together.

"What do we do now?" Mariana asked after some minutes. "We have to tell Danny; he has a right to know."

"We can't tell him," Rachel replied. "Does he know you're not his real mother?"

"He does, but he's only just found out. He took it badly at first but he seems ok with it now, although he was understandably angry with you for abandoning him, and with me for not telling him the truth. I'm sure once he knows the whole story he'll forgive you Rachel. You can be part of his life; isn't that what you want?"

"Of course it is, but it's not that simple. I never told Michael about him. I have a good marriage and a beautiful daughter, and this could blow the whole thing apart when Michael finds out I've been deceiving him all these years. Mickey's twin brother died at birth, and I have refused to have any more children because I seem to have a knack of losing them. Michael didn't understand; he thought I was over-reacting to losing John. I should have told him then; he might have forgiven me, but now…."

"What a mess," said Mariana. "What a total and utter mess! We are both as bad as each other. Why didn't we have the courage to tell the truth? We have lied to so many people between us, and now we're entangled in our web of lies with no easy way to escape."

"Like the Lady of Shalott," said Rachel, unexpectedly. "Oh, don't mind me. It's Mickey; she loves poetry and The Lady of Shallot is one of her favourites. I know it's got something about a web in it, and the poor woman is cursed and can't escape it without dying. Your saying that just reminded me of it."

Something niggled at the back of Mariana's mind, but slipped away again before she could grasp its significance.

They decided to do nothing until they had slept on it and thought things through properly.

"We don't want to make the same mistakes again," said Mariana. "We must decide when and where to tell them, and then we must tell them everything. No more lies and deception. That way we have the best chance of coming out of this without destroying our families in the process."

"You're right," said Rachel. "Somehow we have to find a way to tell them that will provide some damage limitation. I have the biggest problem, so please don't tell Danny until I've thought things through. I'll be in touch when I'm ready." She took Mariana's hand. "Thank you," she said, "for being so understanding, and also for everything you have done for Danny."

Mariana looked into her brown eyes and a chill ran through her. What had she done for Danny other than screw him up? Rachel didn't know about the voices, and the difficulties her son had suffered all his life. She didn't know he was known as The Freak at school, and had been suspected of murder at the tender age of sixteen. She didn't even know he was a loner, an eighteen year old boy who had never had a girlfriend like normal boys. No, she hadn't done such a great job and she dreaded Rachel finding out. Yes, Rachel had a difficult task ahead of her, but Mariana was standing at the top of a slippery slope and she could feel her feet sliding out from under her.

TWENTY-SIX: NO MORE SECRETS.

"I don't understand," said Kate. 'How can we have been so close to the truth all these years and not realise? How did Rachel not realise who you were? – God knows I've talked about you enough, and sometimes Danny too."

"I don't know," said Mariana. "I suppose she just didn't make the link. She didn't know my name after all, or that my child was a foundling. Danny is a pretty common name; there are three others in Danny's class at school, and you didn't even know she had a child, so I suppose that was all it took. She wouldn't have expected her child to be living here in Farnley, just down the road from her. Look, I'm glad it took this long – this was the thing I dreaded, Danny's real mother finding him; but it doesn't matter now; he's grown up. If Rachel and I had met when I first moved here as you wanted us to, I should have lost him. Now, he can see her if he wishes, but he will still be my son."

"My God M," Kate said, "Look what keeping secrets does. Rachel had a secret that she shared with no one; you had a secret that you shared with me. I'm as much to blame for this mess as either of you, I should've made you see sense."

"If you had, I would have lost Danny. There's no way they would have let me keep him, a single woman with no real prospects."

"That's true; but if you had handed him over there would have been publicity about the abandoned baby boy, and when her father died Rachel would have been able to claim him. Wouldn't that have been the most just and natural outcome? I'm sure she would then have wanted to meet you and thank you for what you did, and the truth about Terry and Dan would also have come to light. You would have had to get over it and move on, and in time you might have met someone decent and had more children of you own. No M; no good came of this, and in my heart I knew it wouldn't. I should never have encouraged you; it was just that I had never seen you look so happy as that day when you found him."

"I had never been so happy, except when Danielle was born. I was free of Terry, and I had my Dani back – that's what I thought. But I was wrong Kate, wasn't I." Tears began to well in her eyes and course down her cheeks silently. "He wasn't Dani, and it wasn't long before I realised. I think I knew I had made a mistake when he started school and everything started to go wrong. I was scared Kate. He was out of control, and I didn't know who he was. I thought I could make him mine, but somehow he always knew he wasn't. Somewhere deep inside he always knew, and it ate away at him and almost drove him crazy. Oh Kate, what have I done to that beautiful boy?"

Kate put her arms around her friend and tried to comfort her, but she was inconsolable.

"I'm a bad, wicked woman," sobbed Mariana. "Terry was right all along. I'm stupid and selfish and worthless. I've destroyed Danny, and I've destroyed Rachel, all through my own selfishness. Right now, I wish I were dead."

"Come on M; pull yourself together. Things will work out, they always do. Rachel will tell Michael, and because he loves her he'll forgive her. Danny will forgive her too once he knows her story; he's already forgiven you. Danny will gain a sister, and Mickey will have a brother to replace the one she lost. Everything will be ok, I promise you; it's never too late for the truth M. Now, dry your eyes and try to think positively. Trust me; by the time I get married all will be forgiven and forgotten, because at the end of the day we all only did what we felt we had to do."

It was several weeks before Mariana heard from Rachel again. At first she jumped each time the doorbell went, thinking it would be her; but gradually life returned to normal as it is wont to do, and sometimes she almost convinced herself that nothing had changed.

Kate was in a state of mounting excitement with her wedding now only four months away, and could talk of little else, and Danny seemed none the worse for finally knowing that he was a foundling. Mariana began to put it all out of her mind. Perhaps Rachel had decided not to divulge the truth after all and life would continue as normal – after all, she had made a good life for herself and she would now be able to see Danny – he didn't have to know she was his mother.

Now Mariana could see how much like Terry he was in appearance – the eyes, the prominent cheekbones and the square jaw. He appeared to have taken little from his mother except perhaps his interest in literature and the arts – he certainly hadn't got that from Terry, she thought. After a while she stopped making comparisons and searching for similarities, and just accepted that he was Danny; unique, and in her eyes incomparable. She had got him through the difficult years and now she could enjoy the young man he had become and feel proud.

The visit therefore, when it came at the beginning of April, was a shock. There stood Rachel on the doorstep, a look of determination on her face.

"It's time Mariana," she said. "It's Mickey's fifteenth birthday next week. She needs to know she has a brother; they are both missing out on so much. I'm going to tell her the night before her birthday, and I want Danny to come to her party the following weekend." Her brown eyes regarded Mariana steadily, challenging her to disagree.

"What do you want me to do?" she asked.

"Sometime on Tuesday evening I want you to tell Danny. He'll have a few days to get used to the idea before he meets her and that should make it less awkward at the party. Danny will be Mickey's guest of honour, since now everyone will have to know – I want no more secrets in our lives. I hope Michael will understand – if he doesn't, he'll keep up appearances for Mickey's sake, I think I can safely assume that."

"You've really got it all worked out haven't you!" Mariana said bitterly. "At the end of the day, I'm the one who's come out of this worst. What I did is probably a criminal offence!"

"I don't think you can be brought to book now after all these years, and I'm sure everyone will realise that you acted with the best motives. After all, once it's all out in the open, no great harm will have been done to Danny, and isn't that all that really matters?"

"Of course," agreed Mariana. *You don't know the half of it yet.*

She watched Rachel drive away. *I suppose I should have invited her in,* she thought.

Tuesday evening came around all too quickly. Mariana waited for Danny to come back from his walk with Paddy. With the advent of spring he had been staying out later in the evenings, and it was almost nine when she heard the front door closing behind him.

"*Danny,*" she called out to him. He was inclined to go straight to his room and if she didn't do this thing immediately, she knew she would lose her nerve.

"What is it?" he asked, poking his head round the door. "What's up Mum? You look a bit worried."

"Danny sit down, there's something I need to tell you," she said wearily.

"Oh-oh, what now?" he said, slouching onto a chair, his long legs dangling over the arm. "Let me guess – you've found out my real dad was the Yorkshire Ripper!"

"Danny stop it, this isn't something to joke about. As a matter of fact I do know who your father is now, and you're not going to like it, not one little bit." Danny sat upright and leaned towards her. He watched her struggling with what she was about to tell him, and his heart lurched sickeningly. He had an overwhelming feeling of foreboding.

"Come on Mum," he said quietly, "spit it out!"

"It's Terry; your father is Terry." Mariana watched his jaw drop, and he stared at her in disbelief.

"It can't be – how can it be? Mum, I don't understand. You've only just told me he isn't. I just come to terms with that, and you go and change your fuckin' mind. What the hell are you playing at, have you completely lost the plot?"

"Terry was having an affair when he died, and you are the result. By some twist of Fate it was me who found you. I don't know why these things happen Danny, but that's the truth and there's nothing I can do to change it."

"Why are you telling me this now? When did you find out, and how?"

287

"I found out just over two months ago, and I'm telling you now because I have promised your mother." His eyes widened and the colour drained from his face.

"My *mother* – you know who she is? Who is she?" He was kneeling down beside her now, eagerly searching her face. "Please Mum, I need to know."

"It's Rachel, Kate's friend," she said, her voice rasping through her dry lips.

Danny thought for a moment then recoiled in horror, his ashen face distorted with emotions she couldn't fathom.

"No," he whispered. "She can't be! You're lying. *Rachel can't be my mother!*" his voice rose to a crescendo as he stood and strode across the room, slamming his fist into the wall. Mariana leapt to her feet in terror – what was wrong with him? His fist slammed into the wall again and again; his knuckles were broken and bleeding. With each blow he shouted "NO!" again and again. Then he was gone, running from the house as though the very Devil were after him. Mariana ran after him calling out to him, but he had vanished into the night.

TWENTY-SEVEN: THE AFTERMATH.

'Out flew the web and floated wide;
The mirror crack'd from side to side;
'The curse is come upon me,' cried
The Lady of Shalott.'

Danny ran towards Crow Lane End nursing his injured hand, his heart pounding wildly. There must be some mistake; his mother wasn't right in the head, and if he was going to find out the truth, he must ask Rachel himself. He turned into Crow Lane and as he approached the lane where he and Mickey would meet, he could see the lights of her house at the bottom of the road and he could just make out two people standing at the top of the drive near the doorway. He could hear voices, someone was shouting, and as he drew nearer he heard Mickey's name. He reached the lane and heard a noise in the bushes; a shrill whimpering sound that cut him to the quick. He turned into the lane straining his eyes through the darkness. The moon sailed from behind a cloud and there she was; his Mickey, crouched against the hedgerow, her face buried in her arms, whimpering and keening like an injured animal.

"Mickey," he whispered, as he crouched down and gathered her into his arms. She leaned against him and held him tightly, then suddenly she pushed him away.

"No Danny, we can't – we can't!" She looked up at him, her eyes wild and staring in her white face. She was wearing a white cotton robe and slippers.

"It's true then," he said, a great well of sadness overwhelming him. He pulled her to her feet and they began to walk slowly down the lane towards the river, hand in hand.

"Danny what are we going to do?" she asked. Her tears had stopped and she regarded him with her brown eyes. She looked even younger than her bare fifteen years, like a frightened child. He wanted to hold her and protect her. How could this be happening to them?

"We'll run away," he said, the idea coming to him suddenly. "We'll run away where nobody knows us."

"Where though Danny? We've got no money."

"You can get money can't you? I bet you've got some money of your own."

"I have, but it wouldn't be easy to get it, and when they find out about us they're not going to let me out of their sight."

"You mean they don't know? I thought you must've told them."

"No, I didn't tell them, I thought you'd told yours," she answered. I just ran out because I didn't want to hear what they were saying. My Dad's in shock; she told him about you last night, and then they told me together. Danny, I can't get my head round this. You're my *brother,* for God's sake!" She stopped, and stared at him as though she were seeing him for the first time.

"I can't be with you any more Danny," she said hesitantly. "Not now, it would be wrong."

"But Mickey, we love each other; nothing's changed."

"Everything's changed," she replied woodenly. "I can't love you; I don't love you; I feel sick at the thought of what we've been doing. Go away Danny; I don't want to see you any more." She pushed him aside and began to run down the path towards the sandbanks.

"Mickey, don't go!" he shouted. She paused and turned to look at him. "Please don't push me away. We can work something out; I love you Mickey; *I love you!*"

"Danny, leave me alone!" she shouted back, and started running again. He stood and watched her go; a ghostly figure, the white robe flowing behind her. He felt helpless and powerless. Perhaps if he just left her alone she would change her mind. He turned and trudged up the rising ground towards home.

Mariana was in the kitchen, sitting at the table with her head in her hands. She looked up at him as he came through the back door. Paddy leapt up and ran to his master, burying his nose against his legs.

"You'd better tell me the whole story," said Danny resignedly. He surveyed the wreckage of the woman who had ruined his life, and felt nothing but pity. She hadn't meant for all this to happen, and as yet she had no idea of the extent of the damage her secret had caused. He wondered if Mickey had gone home. He hoped so; he hadn't liked leaving her on her own like that. She was a sensible girl though, and she knew that riverbank like the back of her hand. Tomorrow at school he would find her, and they would work out what to do. He wasn't going to give up on her; he couldn't. She was probably home now, sitting in the kitchen drinking hot chocolate as she had told him she did each night before going to bed.

His mother bathed and bound his hand as he listened to the whole sorry tale of his birth. It was the strangest feeling to suddenly have a whole new identity. He had a grandmother and two uncles he had never seen, as well as his step brother and sister, and the half sister he didn't want to admit to right now. He couldn't think of Mickey as his sister, and he doubted he ever would. They would just have to be extra careful to keep their relationship a secret, and when he left school and got a job they could go away somewhere nobody knew them and start a new life. He knew he'd be able to talk her round once she'd calmed down. No one at school knew they were an item, not as far as he knew anyway. The only possible weak link was Mickey's friend Sophie, but he knew they had fallen out because she had called him Danny the Freak, so probably Mickey had kept her in the dark aswell.

When Mariana had finished talking he went to bed. He was weary, but not sleepy; there was too much going on in his head. Tomorrow was Mickey's fifteenth birthday. He opened his bedside cabinet, and took out the present he had bought her the previous weekend. It was a silver pendant; a heart broken in two halves, each one suspended on a silver chain; with *Danny* inscribed on one half, and *Mickey* on the other. He held it up to the light and twirled it so that it gleamed. He imagined her face when he gave it to her; she would love it, he was sure. He replaced it in its velvet-lined box and tucked it under his pillow. He lay on his bed with Paddy across his feet and thought about where he and Mickey might go next year. They could even go abroad – no one would find them there. He could get bar work or a labouring job and he would come home to her at the end of the day, and at night they would sleep in each other's arms. *Hell no*, they couldn't go abroad because of Paddy. Paddy would have to go with them, so it would have to be here in the UK, or possibly somewhere like the Isle of Man he thought. Paddy's tail thumped against the bed as though he had read his thoughts.

He heard the doorbell and wondered who it could be at this time of night. He opened his bedroom door and stuck his head out. He could hear voices in the hallway but he didn't recognize them. Then he heard the word Mickey and shot to the top of the stairs to listen.

These must be Mickey's parents – this must be his mother! Oh no! Mickey must have told them about him! He leaned over the banisters. The woman whom he now knew to be his mother had long chestnut hair and a wide mouth like Mickey's. She was agitated, distraught.

"We thought she might have come here," she was saying. "We thought she might have wanted to see who Danny was. Are you sure you haven't seen her?"

"I'm quite sure," Mariana answered. Danny went out for a while earlier, but I've been here all evening and no one came here. Besides, she wouldn't have known where we lived."

"Yes I know, but she could have asked somebody." Rachel pointed out. "Will you ask Danny?" We don't know what she was wearing. She was terribly upset when I told her about Danny – completely over-reacted. She ran out in her nightclothes, but she may have had something in the tack room to put on; she often goes and sits in there when she wants to be alone. We left her to cool off a bit. We were talking, and she must have been gone over half an hour before we started to get worried. Then Michael went to fetch her and she wasn't there. We've searched the house and the grounds but there's no sign of her. I can't think of anywhere she'd go."

"*Danny,*" Mariana was calling him. A cold fear had crept over him. *Mickey was still out there somewhere! Why did he leave her, and where on earth could she be?*

"Danny, *come down here now will you?*" His mother sounded angry now. Danny made his way slowly down the stairs.

"Have you seen Michaela, Danny?" Rachel addressed him, looking searchingly at him as though she expected Mickey might be hiding behind him.

"Danny doesn't know her," his mother interjected. "How would he know if he'd seen her?"

"No one's been here," said Danny truthfully. "Perhaps she's gone to a friend's house." He hoped fervently that this was indeed what had happened, but his hopes were soon dashed.

"We've called her friends; none of them have seen her," said Michael. "We're just clutching at straws, Rachel darling; we need to phone the police," he said. "We've wasted enough time already."

Danny's blood curdled – phone the police! It sounded as though they really thought something must have happened to her.

"We'd better go home first, just in case she's back. I'm sorry to have troubled you Mariana," said Rachel. Then she added, "Did you tell Danny?"

"Yes, I did," replied Mariana, and Rachel turned to Danny.

"I'm sorry Danny," she said, "for everything. I hope you can forgive me." With that, she turned and followed her husband out of the door.

TWENTY-EIGHT: ACTS OF CRUELTY.

Colin was sick to death of listening to his wife whining on at him. What was it this time? He'd left his boots in the kitchen – what the fuck!

"Don't you ever tidy up after yourself you bloody waste of space. It's not like you've got anything else to do after all," she railed him. She banged the mud off the boots outside the kitchen door and placed them neatly on the rack in the little glass porch on the back of the house; the porch that Colin had built to house the outdoor clothes and the tumble dryer when they first came there to live. 'Sandra's Palace', he had dubbed the house back then, teasing her gently as she fussed and primped with matching curtains and chair covers from Plumbs, and brightly coloured kitchen appliances that cost an arm and a leg but it didn't matter, because Colin was working and earning good money. It was his pleasure to do little jobs around the house and garden for her, and in bed at night she would reward him generously with the best sex he had ever had. It seemed a long time ago now, and everything had changed since his accident.

He was sick to death of the weekly trips to the job centre and Sandra nagging him ceaselessly to take some job, any job, it didn't matter to her. Well, it bloody well mattered to him.

He was sick to death of her constant carping on about her sister Julie's husband who worked in some factory or other on the industrial estate and had just taken her on holiday to Spain, as he did every year. Bloody Spain! He shuddered at the thought. The only good thing about it was the cheap booze and the chance to eye up some decent flesh — young, tanned flesh, not too much, not too little, just nicely rounded and soft to the touch. Now without Sandra tagging along, Spain would be a whole different ball game he thought, and licked his lips as he savoured the fantasy.

"I'm a fucking joiner, not a charlady," he retorted now, turning the television on and lighting a cigarette.

"Well why don't you join something then?" The heavy sarcasm grated on his nerves. "The bloody Foreign Legion might be good."

"Oh, you're funny aren't you? It's not my fault I ended up a bloody cripple is it?"

"It's your fault you never went for any compo, you cretin. What did you think we were going to live on all those months you couldn't work? You should have known where your loyalties lay and we wouldn't be in this mess."

"Oh shut up woman for fuck's sake. I've told you till I'm blue in the face — it was my own fault. I couldn't make Geoff pay for my own bloody stupidity, and it wouldn't have held water if I'd tried you stupid cow! So what if you have to go out and work? It won't kill you. Christ, I brought you a rabbit for the pot again today didn't I? Not to mention that salmon last week — cost you a fortune in Sainsbury's that would!" Sandra was unimpressed.

"It's a pity you can't put your good arm to better use than fishing. I haven't seen you doing your exercises today; you know what the physio said, you need to do them regular."

"It's alright for you to talk. It bloody hurts doing them exercises. I have been doing them anyway, my arm's a whole lot better than it was last year – I'll be strong enough to strangle you soon, so you'd better watch out!" In fact, Colin's arm was a lot stronger than he let on. He knew he wasn't up to the precision work he used to do, and in the absence of that, he was quite happy living on benefits and Sandra's part time job that paid her cash in hand. It meant he had the house to himself every weekday morning and there was enough spare cash for Sandra's catalogue and an occasional night out for him with the lads.

At night, Colin would go down the lane at Crow End and set his snares in the hedgerow at the base of the rising ground. Two or three times a week, he would find a rabbit or sometimes a hedgehog in the snare in the morning. It was a pity about the hedgehogs; they were wasted for they would have made a poor meal indeed, and Sandra wouldn't relish the thought of cooking them, but for all her faults, she could make a feast of a mangy old rabbit any day. By the time she came home from work the rabbit would be skinned and quartered, and he was careful that she never saw its agonized twisted features from its slow strangulation in the snare.

As Spring progressed, Colin looked forward to the warm balmy evenings when the young lovers that frequented the riverside would provide some entertainment as he lurked in the confines of a dry ditch edged with reeds or sapling thicket and watched their amorous antics. He was stealthy and patient – sometimes a week could pass and he would see nothing.

He had seen Danny and Mickey on several occasions, but he couldn't get close because of the damn dog. Once it had come bounding over when he was fishing near the boardwalk. He aimed a swipe at it with his rod, and the boy scowled at him from beneath the black hair that hung down over his face. *Skinny little bastard; looked like a puff of wind would blow him away.* That was some time ago, not long after his accident, when fishing was about the limit of his capabilities. Since then his arm had improved, but Sandra didn't need to know that, and neither did the social. He knew Danny lived in the same row of houses as he and Sandra, but he didn't know his name.

When Mickey appeared hand-in-hand with Danny one day, he recognized her immediately as the girl he had seen on her pony a few times. He was retrieving a rabbit from a snare once when she trotted by, the pony shying at the sight of the animal dangling from his hand dripping blood onto the footpath. The girl glared at him with disgust written all over her stuck-up little face. He didn't suppose she ever had to eat rabbit pie, the spoilt little cow. Quite tidy though, with nice little tits that showed through her blouse and lovely long silky hair – he wouldn't mind twisting that in his hands and having a bit of a feel around. Show her what a real man can do, he thought, instead of that half-starved article she was shagging.

He and Sandra rarely had sex these days. She would go to bed early with a book and leave him to his beer and telly, and she was always asleep when he came to bed. Occasionally he chanced his arm, but was met with a stony back or even a swipe across the head, and in the end he gave up.

"Get a job, and your luck might be in," she told him. He looked at his wife objectively – some four stone heavier than when he married her. They had three grown up kids, and motherhood had taken its inevitable toll – the sagging breasts in spite of the bra that she steadfastly refused to take off, the belly that hung in folds, the loosely flapping bingo wings and the neck like a prize turkey. No, Sandra really didn't float his boat any more, he thought. He had kept himself in pretty good shape, and he knew how to use what he'd been given. Given half a chance, he could show any girl a good time.

Tuesday evening was the last straw. Sandra was in the bath, and Colin was watching the porn movie he kept hidden under the sideboard. She would lie in the bath for an hour or more, and he would have plenty of warning when she got out and pulled the plug. His excitement mounted as the film progressed, and he was so absorbed that he missed the sound of the water rushing down the pipes. He used his good arm to best effect, and was just about to climax when Sandra entered the room and saw what he was doing.

"You dirty little pervert!" she cried, and slapped him soundly across the head. "Is this what you get up to when I'm not around you sad, pathetic little git." Colin bridled "Who the fuck are you calling a little git? Just because you're built like a brick shithouse you cow. He lunged and made a grab for her. In his extreme state of arousal, even his wife looked tempting. She slapped him again, and tried to pull away but he had twisted the towel around his good arm and she was trapped. He forced her back onto the sofa as he unzipped his trousers and tried to enter her. She screamed, and this time punched him full in the face. He let go, feeling his lip swell and tasting blood.

"You bitch!" he yelled. She pulled the towel around her again and made for the door.

"Get out Colin; get out NOW!" She opened the door to the porch and threw his coat and boots at him, as she turned and fled up the stairs. He heard her barricading the bedroom door with a chair. Wearily, he fastened his trousers, pulled on his boots and coat and set off down to the river, snares in hand. The moon sailed in and out of the clouds lighting his way as he trudged down the hill. As he approached the thicket at the bottom of the hill where the gate led into the lane, he saw something white coming along the riverbank. The moon sailed out into a clear patch of sky and he recognized the pony girl. She was hurrying along the riverbank, pale and anxious looking. She was dressed in what looked like a nightdress, with a white robe that flew out behind her as she ran. She turned in under the trees just as the moon disappeared again, plunging the landscape into darkness.

Now was his chance. He slipped silently from his hiding place and stole past her in the darkness to stand by the gate that led to the lane. She called out as he passed – calling out to her puny boyfriend. Danny; that was his name! Colin felt his anger growing – he'd show the little bitch; he'd had enough of bloody women and their teasing ways. The moon emerged again and illuminated her pale face as she saw him standing before her barring her escape. She screamed, and turned to run up the hill whence he had come. He caught her easily, and put his hand over her mouth cutting off the sound. She bit him – the little bitch bit him! He threw her to the ground and heard the crack of her head on the stony ground. She lay there, groaning softly. Her nightdress had risen almost to her waist, exposing her smooth white thighs. Boy, oh boy! Was she something! He seized the nightdress in both hands and ripped it apart. He leaned over her as he unzipped his trousers. Her eyes opened, and for a split second gazed into his own, and he saw fear, but more than that he saw contempt, then they closed again, and her lips moved in a silent appeal – Danny, they said. Then he was inside her, pounding at her flesh in a frenzy of anger and lust. He put

300

his hands around her throat and squeezed as he reached his climax, but she had lost consciousness already and denied him the pleasure of watching her struggle for breath.

Afterwards, he brushed himself down, and with a quick glance along the moonlit riverbank to make sure he wasn't observed, he flung her slight body over his shoulder and carried her down to the water's edge, where he placed her on a raft of flotsam. Only now he noticed with a touch of remorse her still beauty – the white robe and her chestnut hair floating on the water around her. He launched her into the middle of the cold, slow waters. No one would suspect him; after all, you can't strangle someone with just one arm.

TWENTY-NINE: THE MIRROR CRACK'D.

Mickey stopped running. She turned and saw Danny climbing the rising ground towards his house. Suddenly, she longed to run after him and let him hold her in his arms and tell her everything was going to be alright. Perhaps there was some mistake; or perhaps this was a bad dream from which she would wake shortly to find herself tucked up in her bed. She looked down at her nightclothes and suddenly realised that she was cold. She shivered and drew her robe around her, fastening it with its attached tie belt. She had gone further than she had intended, and she could see the shimmering sandbank in the moonlight. The moon was high in the sky now, casting an eerie light over the meadow and the dark, silent, slow-moving river. She was out of breath from running and decided to sit for a minute or two before making her way back home.

She sat on the edge of the sandbank. The village on the other side of the river was silhouetted by the golden light of its street lamps, the church tower looked dark and brooding, the light glinting on the flagpole with its bright dragon flag hanging listlessly in the still night air. Camelot, she thought ironically. Danny was her Lancelot, and she had left her loom for love of him, and now the spell was broken forever, and she felt the cold shadow of doom falling over her as the moon slid behind a dark cloud.

Yesterday she had been so happy; anticipating her birthday, and wondering what gift Danny had got her. She knew he'd bought her something special; he had hinted as much. Tomorrow she would be fifteen – *only another year til we're legal,* he had said. Now they would never be legal, but she knew she couldn't stop loving him. Perhaps he was right, and they could run away together and hide from everyone. She pictured his face in her mind, and her heart ached for what might have been. She would talk to him; she owed him that. He was right, she thought angrily, they hadn't harmed anyone; it was their mothers who were guilty of lying and deceiving, and not her and Danny.

A slight rustle in the reeds behind her made her whip round suddenly, but there was nothing there. Perhaps it was a water rat or a hedgehog, she thought. Somewhere across the river a tawny owl yelped, answered by a second as they hunted in the moonlight along the meadow. The moon sailed free again and she decided to head for home by its light. She was uneasy now; she had never been down by the river alone at night. The adrenalin rush had carried her here without fear – nothing could be worse than what was happening to her and Danny; but now she shivered again, but not from cold so much as a sudden feeling of foreboding. She hurried along the path until she reached the belt of trees that marked the end of the lane and the moon slid out of view once again. *Not far now,* she thought as she turned right past the rising ground where she had last seen Danny. Suddenly she sensed someone behind her, stepping out from the shadow of the trees – Danny!

She called out to him, "Danny, is that you?" and strained her eyes into the darkness as something moved past her silently and stealthily. Then the moon emerged again lighting up the landscape, and she saw him – but it wasn't Danny.

He was standing now between her and the lane that led to safety, his eyes gleaming lasciviously as he wiped beads of perspiration from his brow. Mickey screamed and started to run towards the rising ground and Danny's house, since the man was blocking the lane. In two strides he had reached her and caught her. She felt his hand over her mouth. It was rough and calloused; it tasted foul, and smelt of metal. She bit down hard on the palm and tried to scream again. He threw her to the ground and her head struck a rock with a sickening thud. A shaft of pain shot through her head, and in that fleeting moment she knew for certain that she was going to die.

She tried to call for Danny; his face was vivid in her mind; his beautiful eyes, his gentle lips, the sight, the sound, the smell and the feel of him. She tried desperately to hold onto these things, but she felt herself slipping down into hell as the vile man climbed on top of her.

Mercifully, oblivion came swiftly.

THIRTY: HELTER-SKELTER.

"I'm going out to look for her," Danny told his mother. "Come on Paddy."

"Danny wait, where are you going? She could be anywhere. *Danny!*" He paid no heed but left through the back door, slamming it shut behind him. Paddy loped beside him keeping close to his heels, sliding under the stile as Danny clambered over it at the end of the path. He scrambled down the hill to where he last saw Mickey running away along the riverbank in her ghostly white robe. He stood at the bottom of the lane. Had she gone home now he wondered, or was she still down by the river somewhere? She would be cold and alone, and probably frightened. He turned to face the river. If she'd gone home he didn't need to worry; but if not he really needed to find her and persuade her to do so. Something white caught his eye at the side of the path where the ground began to rise in the direction of his house. He bent and picked it up. It was a fragment of fabric; torn and frayed – soft cotton fabric like the robe that Mickey had been wearing.

A cold hand clutched at his heart. He searched around the area but found nothing more. Paddy was sniffing at the ground intently, casting to and fro over a small area. He paused and looked up at Danny, whining softly.

"What is it Boy?" Danny put a hand on his dog's head. "Where's Mickey? d'you know where she is Boy?" Paddy whined again and licked his hand, then set off down towards the riverbank. Danny followed as the dog cast along the path, heading towards the sandbanks. Halfway there, Paddy stopped suddenly and ran into the reeds that fringed the riverbank barking loudly. Danny rushed to see what he was barking at just as a startled mallard flew up from the reeds between Paddy's front paws, and clattered away over the river.

"It's only a duck Paddy, yer daft bugger," said Danny and continued on his way to the sandbanks. When he reached there Paddy was nowhere to be seen. He found his whistle in his pocket and blew it once, twice, and Paddy bounded into view. "Don't do that Paddy," Danny told him sternly. "I don't want you getting lost aswell." He sat on the edge of the sandbank on the exact same spot where Mickey had sat earlier had he but known it. He stared across the river at the village on the other side. Mickey had told him she liked to imagine it was Camelot, and that one day the Lady of Shalott would come floating gracefully down the river on her shallow boat. He smiled into the darkness. Mickey was an incurable romantic – Camelot indeed; only Mickey could possibly see it that way! He repressed a sudden shiver – why were romance and death so inextricably linked in all Mickey's favourite poems?

The church clock across the way struck midnight, the chimes seeming endless. He remembered Mickey saying once that she would count the chimes when she heard them from her bed and hold her breath lest there should be thirteen instead of twelve. He found himself doing it now.

306

He had asked her what would happen if thirteen chimes were heard.

"It would be the last thing you ever heard," she said. The chimes echoed across the river and he realised that he had lost count.

"Come on Paddy; we'll go home past Crow Lane End," he said. When they reached the bottom of the lane he took the fragment of fabric out of his pocket and examined it again. Perhaps her robe had caught on the hawthorn hedge at the entrance to the lane as she passed and had been carried on the breeze to the rising ground. It seemed a logical explanation, and he felt relieved as he made his way up the lane. He turned left at the top and clipped Paddy's lead on as he made his way to Mickey's house. There were lights on still, quite a number of them.

"Stay here Boy," he told Paddy and dropped his lead by the gate that led into the paddock. Paddy sat obediently, watching his master as he made his way stealthily along the side of the paddock to the stable yard. He fumbled for the tack room key in its hiding place in the rain gutter, opened the door and stepped inside. The familiar smells of leather and straw, saddle soap and linseed oil assaulted his nostrils, but the tack room was empty. He sat on a straw bale and stared into the darkness. "Please God, let her be alright," he whispered softly. He felt close to her in here, he could almost feel her presence. After a few minutes he went back outside, locked the door and replaced the key. He climbed over the low wall and made his way round to stand beneath her bedroom window. The light was on and the curtains were drawn. He heaved a sigh of relief and bent to pick up a pebble. As he did so, the light went on in the adjoining room and he saw Mickey's father approach the window. He ducked down quickly behind a shrub and crawled away; he would have to wait until tomorrow to talk to her. As he slipped over the wall back into the yard he glanced back. Michael was still standing there staring out into the darkness.

Mariana was asleep on the sofa when he arrived home.

"Come on Mum," he said. "Get to bed."

"I can't stop thinking about that girl," she said. "If anything's happened to her I shall be partly to blame."

"I'm sure she's fine," said Danny reassuringly. He wanted to tell her that he knew she was at home in her bedroom right now, but he couldn't. They must keep their secret now at all costs.

The next day at school an announcement was made in assembly. Michaela Fenton, who was in form 4A, was missing from home. There was absolute silence at first, and then whispered comments throughout the assembly hall. Mickey was the girl who had everything, and now she was missing. Everyone thought of Hayley Price.

"We must all pray for her safe return," said the headmaster. "In the meantime, if anyone can throw any light on where she might have gone please come to my office where your information can be given in the strictest confidence."

Danny stood in stunned silence ignoring the whispers around him, a sick feeling in the pit of his stomach. She hadn't come home; he had been mistaken. She was out there somewhere still, and it didn't look good. Mickey. Lovely Mickey, the most exquisite being on the planet, had met some terrible fate alone in the cold and dark; he knew it now with cold certainty. His head rang with the sound of her voice; her laughter echoed through his brain, and visions of her face floated in and out of his consciousness. He felt faint; there was a loud ringing in his ears, and he wished he could wake from this nightmare.

"Danny," someone was speaking to him. It was Sophie, Mickey's friend.

"*Danny!*" she grasped his arm and shook him. "Where is she?" she asked vehemently, thrusting her face into his. "I know you've been seeing each other."

Danny started, and stared at her uncomprehendingly. What business was it of hers? He gathered his wits. Did Mickey tell her then, or was she just guessing?

"I don't know where she is," he said quietly. "I wish I did." He pushed her away. "Leave me alone," he said and walked quickly away.

He went to the library, to the study booth where he and Mickey would sit twice a week with their books and talk about the things that interested them. She would tease him about his gothic tastes in literature and try to influence him with romantic verse. He had learned her favourite poem off by heart, and one day had he surprised her by reciting it in full. She listened entranced, with tears glistening in her eyes as he recited in hushed tones the seemingly prophetic words of Christina Rossetti:

Remember me when I am gone away,
Gone far away into the silent land;
When you can no more hold me by the hand,
Nor I half turn to go yet turning stay.
Remember me when no more day by day
You tell me of our future that you plann'd:
Only remember me; you understand
It will be late to counsel then or pray.
Yet if you should forget me for a while
And afterwards remember, do not grieve:
For if the darkness and corruption leave
A vestige of the thoughts that once I had,

*Better by far you should forget and smile
Than that you should remember and be sad.'*

He laid his head on his arms and began to sob silently and relentlessly. He would never forget; he would never smile again. Mickey had gone, and taken his soul with her.

'Danny Harding to the headmaster's office please.' The disembodied voice of the tannoy system brought him back to himself. He wiped his eyes and made his way there slowly as the announcement was repeated. *What now?*

He knocked on the door. It opened and the school secretary stood aside to allow him entrance. The headmaster was seated behind his desk and two men whom he had never seen before were also seated side-by-side on the left. The secretary indicated the chair on the right, and Danny sat down.

"Danny," said the headmaster, his tone clearly meant to be reassuring, but managing to be patronising instead. "These gentlemen are police officers and they would like to ask you a few questions." Danny stared blindly at the two plain-clothes men, one of whom cleared his throat.

"Would you prefer to wait until your mother arrives Danny? We have sent a car for her, and she should be here at any minute."

"Which one?" asked Danny. "I have two actually." He wondered what on earth had possessed him to say such a thing – they must think he'd lost the plot.

"You are the son of Mariana Harding are you not?" the other policeman said tersely. *We've got a right one here,* he thought, *facetious little bastard!*

"We'll ignore that remark Danny," said the headmaster. "Please refrain from any more jokes, this is a serious matter."

310

"Sorry," said Danny sullenly. "But it wasn't a joke." At that moment there was a knock on the door and without waiting for an answer his mother swept in, looking drawn and anxious.

"What's going on?" she asked, looking from one to another of the three men.

"Mrs. Harding I presume," said the first policeman. "You are Danny's mother? He seems to be slightly confused on that score."

"I'm sorry," Mariana said as she took the one remaining chair by Danny's side, the heat spreading rapidly up her neck and face. "We've been having a bit of a family crisis. Danny was adopted, and he has just met his natural mother for the first time – it's been a bit of a shock to him."

"A shock," reiterated the second policeman. "Why's that then?" Mariana looked uncomfortable.

"I'm afraid I neglected to tell him the truth about his birth until recently," she said. "It came as a shock to him to learn I wasn't his natural mother. Michaela is his half sister, so he's had two shocks in a short space of time. Has Michaela been found?" The policemen glanced at one another and then the second one spoke, watching Danny's face intently.

"I'm afraid so, Mrs. Harding. She was found by the bridge in Farnley at ten o'clock this morning by a man walking his dog. I'm afraid she is dead."

They heard Danny's gasp of horror, and watched the colour drain from his face. He sunk his head into his hands. The first policeman spoke again.

"What happened to your hand Danny?"

"He punched the wall," said Mariana defensively. "I was there, I saw him do it. It was when he found out who his real mother was. It was nothing to do with Michaela if that's what you're getting at!" She glared at the policemen. "Why are you picking on Danny? He was at home with me last night. He only found out yesterday that he had a sister, and now he has lost her.

311

I think your questioning him is inappropriate. Now perhaps you would like to arrange for us to be taken home. Come on Danny." She took Danny's arm and hauled him to his feet. He stumbled after her out of the room and they sat on the chairs in the corridor and waited for the police driver to arrive.

"Hmmmm!" said the first policeman. "Methinks the lady protesteth too much. Let me know when the PM comes back and we'll get him in for questioning again. He's eighteen isn't he? We don't have to have his mother present if we get him down the station.

Danny and his mother climbed into the back of the police car and it moved slowly – far too slowly, out of the school gates. Faces appeared at the windows of the school, and whispered comments circulated. The shock waves of Mickey's demise had ricocheted around the school. Danny the Freak had been at it again.

"He was shagging her, I know he was," Sophie told her classmates. "I warned her not to go near him, but she wouldn't listen, and now look what he's done." She wept dramatically, whilst reveling in the attention.

At home Mariana drew the curtains closed although not really knowing why – it seemed the right thing to do. Danny threw himself face down on the sofa.

"Danny, it's alright," Mariana knelt beside him stroking the hair back from his forehead. Her heart went out to him; this was all too much for him to take. She hated Rachel for what she had done. Because she had wanted everything her way, Danny's newfound sister was dead and it looked as though he was being blamed, though she couldn't for the life of her imagine why.

The door opened, and Kate came in. She took in the scene before her; Danny prone on the sofa, his mother kneeling beside him.

"My God M, I heard what happened," she said. "I got to work this morning and the factory was closed. There was a notice up on the door saying that it will be closed until further notice. I went round to Michael's and he told me what happened. Whilst I was there the police came and said they'd found a body. I can't believe it – poor Michaela! Michael said that she ran out of the house after Rachel told her Danny was her brother. She must have fallen into the river in the dark."

"Kate, shut up," said Mariana. "Can't you see how upset he is? He never got the chance to get to know her, and now they're trying to say he had something to do with her death. Its like Hayley Price all over again – why can't they leave us alone?"

"Oh I'm sorry, I didn't mean to be insensitive. Perhaps it's just as well he didn't get to know her; she was such a lovely girl, and this would have been terribly upsetting for him."

Danny couldn't take any more. Pushing his mother aside he hauled himself off the sofa and ran upstairs, slamming his bedroom door and locking it.

She was waiting there – Danielle. *Where were you last night Danny?* Her voice was soft, persuasive, inviting him to confide in her. *Where were you when your sister died? You should've been there Danny – or maybe you were.*

"He's taken this really badly Kate," said Mariana sadly. "Coming on top of everything else it's really screwed him up. I don't know what to do for the best."

"It's awful. Rachel's in bits, it's the second child she's lost remember. Michael had called the doctor; he was there when I left. The police came back and wanted to talk to Michael in private, so I left. Shall I make some coffee?"

"Ok, thanks. I think it's best to just leave Danny alone for a while. Perhaps he'll be able to talk about it later and get it off his chest."

They sat down with their coffees, and Kate turned on the television:

The body recovered from the river Dee near Chester this morning has been confirmed as that of Michaela Fenton, who would have been fifteen today. Police revealed that she had been strangled and sexually assaulted. She was found floating on a raft of flotsam by the bridge at Farnley, wearing a white cotton bathrobe. The case has been dubbed 'The Lady of Shalott murder' by Cheshire police.'

Mariana and Kate sat in silence, watching the rest of the news report recounted by a journalist standing by the bridge where Mickey's body had been found. A small crowd of ghoulish onlookers had gathered, and he interviewed one or two of them. They confirmed that Mickey was a lovely girl and her family well respected in the area. *Strangled and sexually assaulted!* It was incomprehensible. Mickey hadn't fallen into the river; she had been thrown in, or maybe even placed on her raft of flotsam and launched into the current.

"Oh my God!" Mariana whispered. "How are we going to tell Danny? What will this do to him? It was bad enough when we thought it had been an accident; it seemed to affect him deeply. Heaven knows how he's going to react to this dreadful news. I'm afraid for him Kate, he's teetering on the brink; I can feel it. He even went out to look for her last night, I've no idea where, but he was gone for over an hour. He seemed fine when he came home, so he must have thought she was ok I suppose. I didn't ask him anything, he might have taken it the wrong way."

Upstairs, Danny lay on his bed clinging to his mind by a thread, his eyes wide open, because when he closed them the vision of Mickey appeared as she had in his dream. She was lying on her raft of flotsam, deathly still and white, her arms crossed over her naked breasts. The white robe and her chestnut hair floated around her and her eyes were open but unseeing.

314

Danielle was singing softly, the tune unknown, the words familiar:

'Under tower and balcony
By garden wall and gallery.
A pale, pale corpse she floated by
Deadcold between the houses high.
Dead into tower'd Camelot'

Kate stayed with Mariana for most of the afternoon.

"What about your wedding Kate?" Mariana asked her.

"I don't know; it somehow doesn't seem important now. We'll probably cancel the church and settle for the registry office; I can hardly go ahead with a big celebration now.

"Why don't you just set it back a bit until the autumn? Life goes on Kate, and perhaps by then it will be good for everyone to have something to celebrate."

"Yes, I suppose you're right. I'll have a word with Jeff in a day or two. The dresses are all ordered now, but we won't be needing Mickey's will we." With that, she began to cry. Mariana wasn't sure she had ever seen Kate cry before, and for once it was her turn to offer a comforting arm.

After Kate left that afternoon, Danny came down from his room and called Paddy to his side.

"Danny, where are you going?" Mariana asked anxiously. She didn't want him going near the bridge and all the activity going on down there.

"I have to walk Paddy," he replied, and left.

He and Paddy retraced their steps of the previous night. At the bottom of the rising ground where he had found the fabric he could now see clearly a flattened patch of grass and scuff marks in the turf. He walked along the path by the riverbank until he reached the place where Paddy had put up the mallard. The reeds were flattened in a path to the water's edge, and the ground trampled by something much larger than Paddy.

315

Further up river towards the sandbanks, he could see uniformed policemen combing the reeds, casting to and fro for evidence. With a chill, he realised that this was now a crime scene, and Mickey's death was therefore no accident. He called Paddy to heel and headed back the way they came; he didn't want to run into the searchers. There were more people in the lane leading to Crow Lane and he turned quickly when he reached the bottom and scrambled up the rising ground and over the stile.

When he reached home, there was a police car outside. He opened the back door silently and crept into the kitchen. He could hear voices in the living room. The door was open, and there was no way he could manage to sneak past and go to his room without being seen. He gestured to Paddy to lie down, and went to the doorway to listen. His mother was speaking, her voice high and verging on hysteria.

"That simply can't be!" she was saying. "Danny didn't even know her; she's over three years younger than him; I'm sure they have never knowingly met. They were to meet for the first time at Mickey's birthday party on Saturday. I won't listen to this. Who is the girl who is spreading this poison?" Danny's heart went into his mouth as he realised that Sophie must have known after all.

"If you don't mind Mrs. Harding, we'd like to take a look in Danny's room."

"Why? What for? What are you accusing him of? Danny wouldn't hurt a fly!"

"That's not what we've heard. We understand he has quite a record of bullying in the past Mrs. Harding. Is that not why you moved here in the first place?"

"In the past; exactly. In primary school to be precise. I'm sick of this! Why aren't you out there looking for the real killer instead of persecuting my son! One minute you tell me they have been sleeping together, and the next you accuse him of raping and strangling her! Why would he do that if they were already sleeping together? – it doesn't make any sense!" Danny recoiled in horror at her words. Mickey had been raped and strangled! He felt the bile rising in his throat and struggled to control it, leaning over the sink and retching violently. Somewhere inside his head he heard the policemen climb the stairs, his mother following anxiously, pleading with them to leave her son alone.

Danny pictured them going through his room systematically; examining his CD collection critically, and his collection of books with their strange haunting illustrations of death and violence. They would leaf through the short stories of Edgar Allen Poe and H.P. Lovecraft, and the Manson Family story entitled Helter Skelter that he had read from cover to cover with morbid curiosity.

They would find the pendant in its velvet-lined box with their names engraved on it. They would find the book of poetry Mickey gave him, in which over the months she had underlined stanzas and scribbled little love notes in the margins during her visits to his room. They would find also, the scrap of white cotton fabric from her robe that Danny had hidden under his pillow. His mother would follow them around the room as the damning evidence was revealed piece by piece, wringing her hands and pleading his case – *I know he's a bit strange, but it's not his fault; he hears voices. He's a good boy my Danny; he wouldn't hurt a fly!* But in her heart she would be wondering, as she had when Hayley died; she would remember that he went out in the dark the night before, and she would wonder, as indeed he did himself.

He was damned! He closed the kitchen door carefully and called Paddy to him. He knelt and hugged him tightly. "I love you Paddy," he whispered. "Be a good boy, and look after Mum." Tears flowed down his face and Paddy gently licked them away. "You knew, didn't you Boy. You knew where it happened, and you tried to tell me. Oh God! I can't bear it; I can't bear what happened to her. Oh Mickey! My beautiful,

beautiful Mickey! I have to go now Paddy, I have to go to Mickey; she'll be waiting for me. He stood, and Paddy leapt up eagerly to follow him.

"No Boy, you stay here," he whispered, and holding him back with one hand he silently opened the door and slipped outside. He hurried along the path to the stile and climbed over, looking over his shoulder to check that he wasn't being followed. No, they would be too busy going through his stuff; it would take them some time.

He ran down the hill for the last time, stopping when he reached the flattened patch on the grass. He lay down and touched the ground where Mickey drew her last breath, trying not to imagine what she had gone through, but just to connect with her lingering spirit. The sky had clouded over and rain threatened. The searchers had moved on down river and he was alone. He walked slowly down to the sandbanks, drinking in the familiar sights and sounds that over the past few years had been his solace. The river was calm and sluggish, but the ripples in the centre were strong and fast, bearing with them everything that crossed their path. Whoever had murdered Mickey must have known that, and pushed her lifeless body out into the water so that the current would carry it away from the scene. Perhaps one day something would come to light that would clear Danny's name. He hoped so for his mothers' sake, both of them.

He glanced across at 'Camelot'. The bright red dragon on the flagpole dangled at half-mast against the leaden sky – news travels fast, he thought. Below the far bank, a heron stood motionless, leaning forward slightly on his stilt-like legs, poised to strike and spear himself a meal. As Danny entered the shallows the heron took off, his neck bent like the u-bend on a washbasin, his massive wings bearing him in slow motion to the tall trees at the foot of the sandstone cliffs.

Suddenly, Danny felt a hand in his; small and soft. He glanced downward. A little girl not more than four years old was clutching his hand, her dark curls and limpid blue eyes reflecting his own. Danielle! She smiled at him.

"Don't be afraid Danny, I'm coming with you," she said.

The water was cold; much colder than Danny had anticipated; it took his breath away as he waded in past his waist, holding tightly to his sister's hand, the sticky river mud and trailing weed dragging at his legs. Past his chest now, as he fought the instinctive urge to free himself from the cloying mud and clinging weed and swim. Ever deeper, ever colder, his mind and body turning numb, until he reached the centre where the water filled his lungs as he plunged beneath the surface and let his beloved river carry him swiftly on its silky cold depths to find his love.

In the distance, alone in the kitchen, Paddy raised his muzzle to the ceiling and howled a long, mournful howl.

THE END.

Thank you for purchasing
The Foundling.
I hope you have enjoyed it,
and welcome your feedback.

annie27965@gmail.com

Printed in Great Britain
by Amazon

86201742R00185